AF355480

Frederik Pohl, Cyril M. Kornbluth

Two Dooms: Two Dystopian Novels
(Illustrated)

e-artnow 2020

Frederik Pohl, Cyril M. Kornbluth

Two Dooms: Two Dystopian Novels
(Illustrated)

The Syndic, Wolfbane

Illustrator: Nigel Sussman, Wood

e-artnow, 2020
Contact: info@e-artnow.org

ISBN 978-80-273-0930-6

Contents

The Syndic

There have been a thousand tales of future Utopias and possible civilizations. They have been ruled by benevolent dictatorships and pure democracies, every form of government from extreme right to absolute left. Unique among these is the easy-going semi-anarchistic society ruled by The Syndic.

"It was not until February 14th that the Government declared a state of unlimited emergency. The precipitating incident was the aerial bombardment and destruction of B Company, 27th Armored Regiment, on Fort George Hill in New York City. Local Syndic leaders had occupied and fortified George Washington High School, with the enthusiastic co-operation of students, faculty and neighborhood. Chief among them was Thomas 'Numbers' Cleveland, displaying the same coolness and organizational genius which had brought him to pre-eminence in the metropolitan policy-wheel organization by his thirty-fifth year.

"At 5:15 A.M. the first battalion of the 27th Armored took up positions in the area as follows: A Company at 190th Street and St. Nicholas Avenue, with the mission of preventing reinforcement of the school from the I.R.T. subway station there; Companies B, C, and D hill down from the school on the slope of Fort George Hill poised for an attack. At 5:25 the sixteen Patton tanks of B Company revved up and moved on the school, C and D Companies remaining in reserve. The plan was for the tanks of B Company to surround the school on three sides-the fourth is a precipice-and open fire if a telephone parley with Cleveland did not result in an unconditional surrender. There was no surrender and the tanks attacked.

"Cleveland's observation post was in the tower room of the school. Seeing the radio mast of the lead tank top the rise of the hill, he snapped out a telephone order to contact pilots waiting for the word at a Syndic field floating outside the seven mile limit. The pilots, trained to split-second precision in their years of public service, were airborn by 5:26, but this time their cargo was not liquor, cigarettes or luggage. In three minutes, they were whipping rocket bombs into the tanks of Company B; Cleveland's runners charged the company command post; the trial by fire had begun.

"Before it ended North America was to see deeds as gallant and strategy as inspired as any in the history of war: Cleveland's historic announcement —'It's a great day for the race!' —his death at the head of his runners in a charge on the Fort Totten garrison, the firm hand of Amadeo Falcaro taking up the scattered reins of leadership, parley, peace, betrayal and execution of hostages, the Treaty of Las Vegas and a united Mob-Syndic front against Government, O'Toole's betrayal of the Continental Press wire room and the bloody battle to recapture that crucial nerve center, the decisive march on Baltimore...."

B. Arrowsmith Hynde,

The Syndic —a Short History.

* * * * *

"No accurate history of the future has ever been written —a fact which I think disposes of history's claim to rank as a science. Astronomers quail at the three-body problem and throw up their hands in surrender before the four-body problem. Any given moment in history is a problem of at least two billion bodies. Attempts at orderly abstraction of manipulable symbols from the realities of history seem to me doomed from the start. I can juggle mean rain-falls, car-loading curves, birth-rates and patent applications, but I cannot for the life of me fit the recurring facial carbuncles of Karl Marx into my manipulations-not even, though we know, well after the fact, that agonizing staphylococcus aureus infections behind that famous beard helped shape twentieth-century totalitarianism. In pathology alone the list could be prolonged indefinitely: Julius Caesar's epilepsy, Napoleon's gastritis, Wilson's paralysis, Grant's alcoholism, Wilhelm II's withered arm, Catherine's nymphomania, George III's paresis, Edison's deafness, Euler's blindness, Burke's stammer, and so on. Is there anybody silly enough to maintain that the world today would be what it is if Marx, Caesar, Napoleon, Wilson, Grant, Wilhelm, Catherine, George, Edison, Euler and Burke-to take only these eleven-were anything but what they were? Yet that is the assumption behind theories of history which exclude the carbuncles of Marx from their referents-that is to say, every theory of history with which I am familiar....

"Am I then saying that history, past and future, is unknowable; that we must blunder ahead in the dark without planning because no plan can possibly be accurate in prediction and useful in application? I am not. I am expressing my distaste for holders of extreme positions, for possessors of eternal truths, for keepers of the flame. Keepers of the flame have no trouble with the questions of ends and means which plague the rest of us. They are quite certain that their ends are good and that therefore choice of means is a trivial matter. The rest of us, far from certain that we have a general solution of the two-billion body problem that is history, are much more likely to ponder on our means...."

F. W. Taylor,

Organization, Symbolism and Morale

PART I.

CHAPTER I.

Charles Orsino was learning the business from the ground up-even though "up" would never be very high. He had in his veins only a drop or two of Falcaro blood: enough so that room had to be made for him; not enough for it to be a great dearth of room. Counting heavily on the good will of F. W. Taylor, who had taken a fancy to him when he lost his parents in the Brookhaven Reactor explosion of '83, he might rise to a rather responsible position in Alky, Horsewire, Callgirl, recruitment and Retirement or whatever line he showed an aptitude for. But at 22 one spring day, he was merely serving a tour of duty as bagman attached to the 101st New York Police Precinct. A junior member of the Syndic customarily handled that job; you couldn't trust the cops not to squeeze their customers and pocket the difference.

He walked absently through the not-unpleasant routine of the shakedown. His mind was on his early-morning practice session of polo, in which he had almost disgraced himself.

"Good afternoon, Mr. Orsino; a pleasure to see you again. Would you like a cold glass of beer while I get the loot?"

"No, but thanks very much, Mr. Lefko —I'm in training, you know. Wish I could take you up on it. Seven phones, isn't it, at ten dollars a phone?"

"That's right, Mr. Orsino, and I'll be with you as soon as I lay off the seventh at Hialeah; all the ladies went for a plater named Hearthmouse because they thought the name was cute and left me with a dutch book. I won't be a minute."

Lefko scuttled to a phone and dickered with another bookie somewhere while Charles absently studied the crowd of chattering, laughing horseplayers. ("Mister Orsino, did you come out to make a monkey of yourself and waste my time? Confound it, sir, you have just fifty round to a chukker and you must make them count!" He grinned unhappily. Old Gilby, the pro, could be abrasive when a bone-head play disfigured the game he loved. Charles had been sure Benny Grashkin's jeep would conk out in a minute-it had been sputtering badly enough-and that he would have had a dirt-cheap scoring shot while Benny changed mounts. But Gilby blew the whistle and wasn't interested in your fine-spun logic. "Confound it, sir, when will you young rufflers learn that you must crawl before you walk? Now let me see a team rush for the goal-and I mean *team*, Mr. Orsino!")

"*Here* we are, Mr. Orsino, and just in time. There goes the seventh."

Charles shook hands and left amid screams of "Hearthmouse! Hearthmouse!" from the lady bettors watching the screen.

High up in the Syndic Building, F. W. Taylor-Uncle Frank to Charles-was giving a terrific tongue-lashing to a big, stooped old man. Thornberry, president of the Chase National Bank, had pulled a butch and F. W. Taylor was blazing mad about it.

He snarled: "One more like this, Thornberry, and you are out on your padded can. When a respectable member of the Syndic chooses to come to you for a line of credit, you will in the future give it without any tom-fool quibbling about security. You bankers seem to think this is the middle ages and that your bits of paper still have their old black magic.

"Disabuse yourself of the notion. Nobody except you believes in it. The Inexorable Laws of Economics are as dead as Dagon and Ishtar, and for the same reason. No more worshippers. You bankers can't shove anybody around any more. You're just a convenience, like the non-playing banker in a card game.

"What's real now is the Syndic. What's real about the Syndic is its own morale and the public's faith in it. Is that *clear?*"

Thornberry brokenly mumbled something about supply and demand.

Taylor sneered. "Supply and demand. Urim and Thummim. Show me a supply, Thornberry, show me a —oh, hell. I haven't time to waste re-educating you. Remember what I told you and don't argue. Unlimited credit to Syndic members. If they overdo it, *we'll* rectify the situation. Now, get out." And Thornberry did, with senile tears in his eyes.

At Mother Maginnis' Ould Sod Pub, Mother Maginnis pulled a long face when Charles Orsino came in. "It's always a pleasure to see you, Mr. Orsino, but I'm afraid this week it'll be no pleasure for you to see me."

She was always roundabout. "Why, what do you mean, Mrs. M.? I'm always happy to say hello to a customer."

"It's the business, Mr. Orsino. It's the business. You'll pardon me if I say that I can't see how to spare twenty-five dollars from the till, not if my life depended on it. I can go to fifteen, but so help me —"

Charles looked grave-graver than he felt. It happened every day. "You realize, Mrs. Maginnis, that you're letting the Syndic down. What would the people in Syndic Territory do for protection if everybody took your attitude?"

She looked sly. "I was thinking, Mr. Orsino, that a young man like you must have a way with the girls —" By a mighty unsubtle maneuver, Mrs. Maginnis' daughter emerged from the back room at that point and began demurely mopping the bar. "And," she continued, "sure, any young lady would consider it an honor to spend the evening with a young gentleman from the Syndic —"

"Perhaps," Charles said, rapidly thinking it over. He would infinitely rather spend the evening with a girl than at a Shakespeare revival as he had planned, but there were drawbacks. In the first place, it would be bribery. In the second place, he might fall for the girl and wake up with Mrs. Maginnis for his mother-in-law —a fate too nauseating to contemplate for more than a moment. In the third place, he had already bought the tickets for himself and bodyguard.

"About the shakedown," he said decisively. "Call it fifteen this week. If you're still doing badly next week, I'll have to ask for a look at your books-to see whether a regular reduction is in order."

She got the hint, and colored. Putting down fifteen dollars, she said: "Sure, that won't be necessary. I'm expecting business to take a turn for the better. It's sure to pick up."

"Good, then." To show there were no hard feelings, he stayed for a moment to ask: "How are your husbands?"

"So-so. Alfie's on the road this week and Dinnie's got the rheumatism again but he can tend bar late, when it's slow."

"Tell him to drop around to the Medical Center and mention my name, Mrs. Maginnis. Maybe they can do something for him."

She glowed with thanks and he left.

It was pleasant to be able to do things for nice people; it was pleasant to stroll along the sunny street acknowledging tipped hats and friendly words. (That team rush for the goal had been a sorry mess, but not his fault-quite. Vladek had loosed a premature burst from his fifty caliber at the ball, and sent it hurling off to the right; they had braked and backed with much grinding of gears to form V again behind it, when Gilby blew the whistle again.)

* * * * *

A nervous youngster in the National Press Service New York drop was facing his first crisis on the job. Trouble lights had flashed simultaneously on the Kansas City-New York, Hialeah-New York and Boston-New York trunks. He stood, paralyzed.

His supervisor took it in in a flash and banged open the circuit to Service. To the genial face that appeared on the screen, he snapped: "Trace Hialeah, Boston and Kansas City-in that order, Micky."

Micky said: "Okay, pal," and vanished.

The supervisor turned to the youngster. "Didn't know what to do?" he asked genially. "Don't let it worry you. Next time you'll know. You noticed the order of priority?"

"Yes," the boy gulped.

"It wasn't an accident that I gave it to him that way. First, Hialeah because it was the most important. We get the bulk of our revenue from serving the horse rooms-in fact, I understand we started as a horse wire exclusively. Naturally the horse-room customers pay for it in the long run, but they pay without pain. Nobody's forcing them to improve the breed, right?

"Second, Boston-New York trunk. That's common-carrier while the Fair Grounds isn't running up there. We don't make any profit on common-carrier service, the rates are too low, but we owe it to the public that supports us.

"Third, Kansas City-New York. That's common carrier too, but with one terminal in Mob Territory. No reason why we should knock ourselves out for Regan and his boys, but after the other two are traced and closed, we'll get around to them. Think you got it straight now?"

"Yes," the youngster said.

"Good. Just take it easy."

* * * * *

The supervisor moved away to do a job of billing that didn't need immediate doing; he wanted to avoid the very appearance of nagging the boy. He wondered too, if he'd really put it over, and decided he hadn't. Who could, after all. It took years on the wires to get the feel. Slowly your motivation changed. You started by wanting to make a place for yourself and earn some dough. After years you realized, not with a blinding flash, but gradually, that you were working for quite another reason. Nice gang here that treats you right. Don't let the Syndic down. The customers pay for their fun and by God, you see that they get it or bust a gut trying.

* * * * *

On his way to the 101st Precinct station house, the ears of Charles Orsino burned as he thought of the withering lecture that had followed the blast on Gilby's whistle. "*Mister* Orsino, is it or is it not your responsibility as team captain to demand that a dangerous ball be taken out of play? And did or did not that last burst from Mister Vladek beat the ball out of round, thus giving rise to a distinct possibility of dangerous ricochets?" The old man was right of course, but it had been a pocked and battered practice ball to start with; in practice sessions, you couldn't afford to be fussy-not with regulation 18 inch armor steel balls selling for thirty dollars each at the pro shop.

He walked between the two green lamps of the precinct station and dumped his bag on the sergeant's desk. Immediately the sergeant started a tale of woe: "Mr. Orsino, I don't like to bother you with the men's personal troubles, but I wonder if you could come through with a hundred dollar present for a very deserving young fellow here. It's Patrolman Gibney, seven years in the old 101st and not a black mark against him. One citation for shooting it out with a burglar and another for nabbing a past-post crook at Lefko's horse room. Gibney's been married for five years and has two of the cutest kids you ever saw, and you know that takes money. Now he wants to get married again, he's crazy in love with the girl and his first wife don't mind, she says she can use a helping hand around the house, and he wants to do it right with a big wedding.

"If he can do it on a hundred, he's welcome to it," Charles said, grinning. "Give him my best wishes." He divided the pile of bills into two orderly stacks, transferred a hundred dollars to one and pocketed the other.

He dropped it off at the Syndic Building, had an uninteresting dinner in one of its cafeterias and went to his furnished room downtown. He read a chapter in F. W. Taylor's —Uncle Frank's —latest book, *Organization, Symbolism and Morale,* couldn't understand a word he read, bathed and got out his evening clothes.

* * * * *

A thin and attractive girl entered a preposterously-furnished room in the Syndic Building, arguing bitterly with a white-bearded, hawk-nosed old man.

"My dear ancestor," she began, with exaggerated patience.

20

"God-damn it, Lee, don't call me an ancestor! Makes me feel as if I was dead already."

"You might as well be for all the sense you're talking."

"All right, Lee." He looked wounded and brave.

"Oh, I didn't mean to hurt your feelings, Edward —" She studied his face with suddenly-narrowed eyes and her tone changed. "Listen, you old devil, you're not fooling me for a minute. I couldn't hurt your feelings with the blunt edge of an axe. You're not talking me into anything. It'd just be sending somebody to his death. Besides, they were both accidents." She turned and began to fiddle with a semi-circular screen whose focus was a large and complicated chair. Three synchronized projectors bore on the screen.

The old man said very softly: "And what if they weren't? Tom McGurn and Bob were good men. None better. If the damn Government's knocking us off one by one, something ought to be done. And you seem to be the only person in a position to do it."

"Start a war," she said bitterly. "Sweep them from the seas. Wasn't Dick Reiner chanting that when I was in diapers?"

"Yes," the old man brooded. "And he's still chanting it now that you're in-whatever young ladies wear nowadays. Promise me something, Lee. If there's another try, will you help us out?"

"I am so sure there won't be," she said, "that I'll promise. And God help you, Edward, if you try to fake one. I've told you before and I tell you now that it's almost certain death."

* * * * *

Charles Orsino studied himself in a three-way mirror.

The evening suit was new; he wished the gunbelt was. The holster rode awkwardly on his hip; he hadn't got a new outfit since his eighteenth birthday and his chest had filled out to the last hole of the cross-strap's buckle since then. Well, it would have to wait; the evening would cost him enough as it was. Five bodyguards! He winced at the thought. But you had to be seen at these things and you had to do it right or it didn't count.

He fell into a brief reverie of meeting a beautiful, beautiful girl at the theater, a girl who would think he was interesting and handsome and a wonderful polo player, a girl who would happily turn out to be in the direct Falcaro line with all sorts of powerful relations to speak up for him....

Someone said on his room annunciator: "The limousine is here, Mr. Orsino. I'm Halloran, your chief bodyguard."

"Very well, Halloran," he said casually, just as he'd practiced it in the bathroom that morning and rode down.

The limousine was a beauty and the guards were faultlessly turned out. One was democratic with one's chief guard and a little less so with the others. As Halloran drove, Charles chatted with him about the play, which was Julius Caesar in modern dress. Halloran said he'd heard it was very good.

* * * * *

Their arrival in the lobby of the Costello created no sensation. Five bodyguards wasn't a lot of bodyguards, even though there seemed to be no other Syndic people there. So much for the beautiful Falcaro girl. Charles chatted with a television director he knew slightly. The director explained to him that the theater was sick, very sick, that Harry Tremaine, —he played Brutus-made a magnificent stage picture but couldn't read lines.

By then Halloran was whispering in his ear that it was time to take their seats. Halloran was sweating like a pig and Charles didn't get around to asking him why. Charles took an aisle seat, Halloran was across the aisle and the others sat to his side, front and rear.

The curtain rose on "New York —A Street."

The first scene, a timekiller designed to let fidgeters subside and coughers finish their coughing, was a 3-D projection of Times Square, with a stylized suggestion of a public relations consultant's office "down in one" on the apron.

When Caesar entered Orsino started, and there was a gratified murmur around the auditorium. He was made up as French Letour, one of the Mobsters from the old days-technically a hero, but one who had sailed mighty close to the wind. This promised to be interesting.

"Peace, ho! Caesar speaks."

And so to the apron where the soothsayer-public relations consultant-delivered the warning contemptuously ignored by Letour-Caesar, and the spotlight shifted to Cassius and Brutus for their long, foreboding dialogue. Brutus' back was to the audience when it started; he gradually turned —

"What means this shouting? I do fear the people will choose Caesar for their king!"

And you saw that Brutus was Falcaro-old Amadeo Falcaro himself, with the beard and hawk nose and eyebrows.

Well, let's see now. It must be some kind of tortured analogy with the Treaty of Las Vegas when Letour made a strong bid to unite Mob and Syndic and Falcaro had fought against anything but a short-term, strictly military alliance. Charles felt kind of sore about Falcaro not getting the title role, but he had to admit that Tremaine played Falcaro as the gutsy magnifico he had been. When Caesar re-entered, the contrast became clear; Caesar-Letour was a fidgety, fear-ridden man. The rest of the conspirators brought on through Act One turned out to be good fellows all, fresh and hearty; Charles guessed everything was all right and he wished he could grab a nap. But Cassius was saying:

"Him and his worth and our great need of him —"

All very loyal, Charles thought, smothering a yawn. A life for the Syndic and all that, but a high-brow version. Polite and dignified, like a pavanne at Roseland. Sometimes-after, say, a near miss on the polo field-he would wonder how polite and dignified the great old days actually had been. Amadeo Falcaro's Third Year Purge must have been an affair of blood and guts. Two thousand shot in three days, the history books said, adding hastily that the purged were unreconstructed, unreconstructable thugs whose usefulness was past, who couldn't realize that the job ahead was construction and organization.

* * * * *

And Halloran was touching Charles on the shoulder. "Intermission in a second, sir."

They marched up the aisle as the curtain fell to applause and the rest of the audience began to rise. Then the impossible happened.

Halloran had gone first; Charles was behind him, with the four other guards hemming him in. As Halloran reached the door to the lobby at the top of the aisle, he turned to face Charles and performed an inexplicable pantomime. It was quite one second before Charles realized that Halloran was tugging at his gun, stuck in the holster.

The guard to the left of Charles softly said: "Jesus!" and threw himself at Halloran as the chief guard's gun came loose. There was a .45 caliber roar, muffled. There was another that crashed, unmuffled, a yard from Charles' right ear. The two figures at the head of the aisle collapsed limply and the audience began to shriek. Somebody with a very loud voice roared: "Keep calm! It's all part of the play! Don't get panicky! It's part of the play!"

The man who was roaring moved up to the aisle door, fell silent, saw and smelled the blood and fainted.

A woman began to pound the guard on Charles' right with her fists, yelling: "What did you do to my husband? You shot my husband!" She meant the man who had fainted; Charles peeled her off the bodyguard.

Somehow they got into the lobby, followed by most of the audience. The three bodyguards held them at bay. Charles found he was deaf in his right ear and supposed it was temporary. Least of his worries. Halloran had taken a shot at him. The guard named Weltfisch had intercepted it. The guard named Donnel had shot Halloran down.

He said to Donnel: "You know Halloran long?"

Donnel, not taking his eyes from the crowd, said: "Couple of years, sir. He was just a guy in the bodyguard pool."

"Get me out of here," Orsino said. "To the Syndic Building."

In the big black car, he could almost forget the horror; he could hope that time would erase it completely. It wasn't like polo. That shot had been *aimed.*

The limousine purred to a halt before the titanic bulk of the Syndic Building, was checked and rolled on into the Unrestricted Entrance. An elevator silently lifted the car and passengers past floors devoted to Alcohol Clerical, Alcohol Research, and Testing, Transport, Collections Audit and Control, Cleaning and Dying, Female Recruitment and Retirement, up, up, up, past sections and sub-sections Charles had never entered, Syndic member though he was, to an automatic stop at a floor whose indicator said: *enforcement and public relations.*

It was only 9:45 P.M.; F. W. Taylor would be in and working. Charles said: "Wait here, boys," and muttered the code phrase to the door. It sprang open.

F. W. Taylor was dictating, machine-gun fashion, to a mike. He looked dog-tired. His face turned up with a frown as Charles entered and then the frown became a beam of pleasure.

"Charles, my boy! Sit down!" He snapped off the machine.

"Uncle —" Charles began.

"It was so kind of you to drop in. I thought you'd be at the theater."

"I was, Uncle, but —"

"I'm working on a revision for the next edition of *Organization, Symbolism and Morale*. You'd never guess who inspired it."

"I'm sure I wouldn't, Uncle. Uncle —"

"Old Thornberry, President of the Chase National. He had the infernal gall to refuse a line of credit to young McGurn. *Bankers!* You won't believe it, but people used to *beg* them to take over their property, tie up their incomes, virtually enslave them. People *demanded* it. The same way they demanded inexpensive liquor, tobacco and consumer goods, clean women and a chance to win a fortune and our ancestors obliged them. Our ancestors were sneered at in their day, you know. They were called criminals when they distributed goods and services at a price people could afford to pay."

"Uncle!"

"Hush, boy, I know what you're going to say. You can't fool the people forever! When they'd had enough hounding and restriction, they rose in their might.

"The people demanded freedom of choice, Falcaro and the rest rose to lead them in the Syndic and the Mob and they drove the Government into the sea."

"Uncle Frank —"

"From which it still occasionally ventures to annoy our coastal cities," F. W. Taylor commented. He warmed to his subject. "You should have seen the old boy blubber. The last of the old-time bankers, and they deserved everything they got. They brought it on themselves. They had what they called laissez-faire, and it worked for awhile until they got to tinkering with it. They demanded things called protective tariffs, tax remissions, subsidies-regulation, regulation, regulation, always of the other fellow. But there were enough bankers on all sides for everybody to be somebody else's other fellow. Coercion snowballed and the Government lost public acceptance. They had a thing called the public debt which I can't begin to explain to you except to say that it was something written on paper and that it raised the cost of everything tremendously. Well, believe me or not, they *didn't* just throw away the piece of paper or scratch out the writing on it. They let it ride until ordinary people couldn't afford the pleasant things in life."

"Uncle —"

* * * * *

A cautious periscope broke the choppy water off Sea Island, Georgia. At the other end of the periscope were Captain Van Dellen of the North American Navy, lean as a hound, and fat little Commander Grinnel.

"You might take her in a little closer, Van," said Grinnel mildly.

"The exercise won't do you any lasting damage," Van Dellen said. Grinnel was very, very, near to a couple of admirals and normally Van Dellen gave him the kid-glove treatment in spite of ranking him. But this was *his* ship and no cloak and dagger artist from an O.N.I. desk was telling him how to con it.

Grinnel smiled genially at the little joke. "I could call it a disguise," he said patting his paunch, "but you know me too well."

"You'll have no trouble with a sea like this," Van Dellen said, strictly business. He tried to think of some appropriate phrase to recognize the danger Grinnel was plunging into with no resources except quick wits, a trick ring and a pair of guns. But all that bubbled up to the top of his head was; thank God I'm getting rid of this bastardly little Sociocrat. He'll kill me some day if he gets a clean shot and the chance of detection is zero. Thank God I'm a Constitutionist. We don't go in for things like that-or do we? Nobody ever tells me anything. A hack of a pigboat driver. And this little bastard's going to be an admiral some day. But that boy of mine'll be an admiral. He's brainy, like his mother.

Grinnel smiled and said: "Well, this would be it, wouldn't it?"

"Eh?" Van Dellen asked. "Oh. I see what you mean. Chuck!" he called a sailor. "Break out the Commander's capsules. Pass the word to stand by for ejection."

The Commander was fitted, puffing, into the capsule. He growled at the storekeeper: "You sure this was just unsealed? It feels sticky already."

A brash jayee said: "I saw it unsealed myself three minutes ago, Commander. It'll get stickier if we spend any more time talking. You have" —he glanced at his chronometer —"seventeen minutes now. Let me snap you in."

The Commander huddled down after a searching glance at the jayee's face which photographed it forever in his memory. The top snapped down. Some day-some happy day-that squirt would very much regret telling him off. He gave an okay sign to Van Dellen who waved back meagerly and managed a smile. Three crewmen fitted the capsule into its lock.

Foomf!

It was through the hatch and bobbing on the surface. Its color matched the water's automatically. Grinnel waggled the lever that aimed it inshore and began to turn the propellor crank. He turned fast; the capsule-rudders, crank, flywheel, shaft and all-would dissolve in approximately fifteen minutes. It was his job to be ashore when that happened.

And ashore he'd be practically a free agent with the loosest sort of roving commission, until January 15th. Then his orders became most specific.

CHAPTER III.

Charles Orsino squirmed in the chair. "Uncle —" he pleaded.

"Yes," F. W. Taylor chuckled, "Old Amadeo and his colleagues were called criminals. They were called bootleggers when they got liquor to people without worrying about the public debt or excise taxes. They were called smugglers when they sold cheap butter in the south and cheap margerine in the north. They were called counterfeiters when they sold cheap cigarettes and transportation tickets. They were called high-jackers when they wrested goods from the normal inflation-ridden chain of middlemen and delivered them at a reasonable price to the consumers.

"They were criminals. Bankers were pillars of society.

"Yet these bankers who dominated society, who were considered the voice of eternal truth when they spoke, who thought it was insanity to challenge their beliefs, started somewhere and perhaps they were the best thing for their day and age that could be worked out...."

* * * * *

Father Ambrosius gnawed at a bit of salt herring, wiped his hands, dug through the litter in his chest and found a goose quill and a page of parchment. He scrubbed vigorously with a vinegar-soaked sponge, at the writing on the parchment and was pleased to see that it came off nicely, leaving him a clean surface to scribble his sermon notes on. He cut the quill and slit it while waiting for the parchment to dry, wondering idly what he had erased. (It happened to be the last surviving copy of Tacitus' *Annals*, VII. i-v.)

To work then. The sermon was to be preached on Sexagesima Sunday, a prelude to the solemn season of Lent. Father Ambrosius' mind wandered in search of a text. Lent ... salt herring ... penitence ... the capital sins ... avarice ... usury ... delinquent pew rent ... fat-headed young Sir Baldwin in his tumbledown castle on the hill ... salt herring now and *per saeculae saeculorum* unless Sir Baldwin paid up his delinquent pew rent.

At the moment, Sir Baldwin came swaggering into the cell. Father Ambrosius rose courteously and said, with some insincerity: "*Pax vobiscum.*"

"Eh?" asked Sir Baldwin, his silly blue eyes popping as he looked over his shoulder. "Oh, you meant me, padre. It don't do a bit of good to chatter at me in Latin, you know. The king's Norman is what I speak. I mean to say, if it's good enough for his majesty Richard, it's good enough for me, what? Now, what can I do for you, padre?"

Father Ambrosius reminded him faintly: "You came to see me, Sir Baldwin."

"Eh? Oh. So I did. I was huntin' stag, padre, and I lost him after chasin' the whole morning, and what I want to know is, who's the right saint chap to ask for help in a pickle like that? I mean to say, I wanted to show the chaps some good sport and we started this beast and he got clean away. Don't misunderstand me, padre, they were good chaps and they didn't rot me about it, but that kind of talk gets about and doesn't do one a bit of good, what? So you tell me like a good fellow who's the right saint chap to put the matter in the best light for me?"

Father Ambrosius repressed an urge to grind his teeth, took thought and said: "St. Hubert, I believe, is interested in the stag hunt."

"Right-oh, padre! St. Hubert it is. Hubert, Hubert. I shan't forget it because I've a cousin named Hubert. Haven't seen him for years, poor old chap. He had the fistula-lived on slops and couldn't sit his horse for a day's huntin'. Poor old chap. Well, I'm off-no, there's another thing I wanted. Suppose this Sunday you preach a howlin' strong sermon against usury, what? That chap in the village, the goldsmith fellow, has the infernal gall to tell me I've got to give him Fallowfield! Forty acres, and he has the infernal gall to tell me they aren't mine any more. Be a good chap, padre, and sort of glare at him from the pulpit a few times to show him who you mean, what?"

"Usury *is* a sin," Father Ambrosius said cautiously, "but how does Fallowfield enter into it?"

Sir Baldwin twiddled the drooping ends of his limp, blond mustache with a trace of embarrassment. "Fact is, I told the chap when I borrowed the twenty marks that Fallowfield would stand as security. I ask you, padre, is it my fault that my tenants are a pack of lazy, thieving Saxon swine and I couldn't raise the money?"

The parish priest bristled unnoticeably. He was pure Saxon himself. "I shall do what I can," he said. "And Sir Baldwin, before you go —"

The young man stopped in the doorway and turned.

"Before you go, may I ask when we'll see your pew rent, to say nothing of the tithe?"

Sir Baldwin dismissed it with an airish wave of the hand. "I thought I just told you, padre. I haven't a farthing to my name and here's this chap in the village telling me to clear out of Fallowfield that I got from my father and his father before him. So how the devil-excuse me-can I pay rent and tithes and Peters pence and all the other things you priest chaps expect from a man, what?" He held up his gauntleted hand as Father Ambrosius started to speak. "No, padre, not another word about it. I know you'd love to tell me I won't go to heaven if I act this way. I don't doubt you're learned and all that, but I can still tell you a thing or two, what? The fact is, I *will* go to Heaven. You see, padre, God's a gentleman and he wouldn't bar another gentleman over a trifle of money trouble that could happen to any gentleman, now would he?"

The fatuous beam was more than Father Ambrosius could bear; his eyes fell.

"Right-oh," Sir Baldwin chirped. "And that saint chap's name was St. Hubert. I didn't forget, see? Not quite the fool some people think I am." And he was gone, whistling a recheat.

Father Ambrosius sat down again and glared at the parchment. Preach a sermon on usury for that popinjay. Well, usury *was* a sin. Christians were supposed to lend to one another in need and not count the cost or the days. But who had ever heard of Sir Baldwin ever lending anything? Of course, he was lord of the manor and protected you against invasion, but there didn't seem to be any invasions anymore....

Wearily, the parish priest dipped his pen and scratched on the parchment: RON. XIII ii, viii, XV i. "Whosoever resisteth the power resisteth the ordinance of God ... owe no man any thing ... we that are strong ought to bear the infirmities of the weak...." A triple-plated text, which, reinforced by a brow of thunder from the pulpit should make the village goldsmith think twice before pressing his demand on Sir Baldwin. Usury *was* a sin.

There was a different knock on the door frame.

The goldsmith, a leather-aproned fellow named John, stood there twisting his cap in his big, burn scarred hands.

"Yes, my son? Come in." But he scowled at the fellow involuntarily. He should know better than to succumb to the capital sin of avarice. "Well, what is it?"

"Father," the fellow said, "I've come to give you this." He passed a soft leather purse to the priest. It clinked.

Father Ambrosius emptied it on his desk and stirred the broad silver coins wonderingly with his finger. Five marks and eleven silver pennies. No more salt herring until Lent! Silver forwarded to his bishop in an amount that would do credit to the parish! A gilding job for the image of the Blessed Virgin! Perhaps glass panes in one or two of the church windows!

And then he stiffened and swept the money back into the purse. "You got this by sin," he said flatly. "The sin of avarice worked in your heart and you practiced the sin of usury on your fellow Christians. Don't give this money to the Church; give it back to your victims."

"Father," the fellow said, nearly blubbering, "excuse me but you don't understand! They come to me and come to me. They say it's all right with them, that they're hiring the money the way you'd hire a horse. Doesn't that make sense? Do you think I *wanted* to become a moneylender? No! I was an honest goldsmith and an honest goldsmith can't help himself. All the money in the village drifts somehow into his hands. One leaves a mark with you for safekeeping and pays you a penny the year to guard it. Another brings you silver coins to make into a basin, and you get to keep whatever coins are left over. And then others come to you and say 'Let me have soandso's mark to use for a year and then I'll pay it back and with it another mark'. Father, they beg me! They say they'll be ruined if I don't lend to them, their old parents will die if they can't fee the leech, or their dead will roast forever unless they can pay for masses and what's a man to *do*?"

"Sin no more," the priest answered simply. It was no problem.

The fellow was getting angry. "Very well for you to sit there and say so, father. But what do you think paid for the masses you said for the repose of Goodie Howat's soul? And how did Tom the Thatcher buy his wagon so he could sell his beer in Glastonbury at a better price? And how did Farmer Major hire the men from Wealing to get in his hay before the great storm could ruin it? And a hundred things more. I tell you, this parish would be a worse place without John Goldsmith and he doesn't propose to be pointed at any longer as a black sinner! I didn't want to fall into usury but I did, and *when* I did, I found out that those who hoist their noses highest at the moneylender when they pass him in the road are the same ones who beg the hardest when they come to his shop for a loan!"

The priest was stunned by the outburst. John seemed honest, the facts were the facts-can good come out of evil? And there were stories that His Holiness the Pope himself had certain dealings with the Longobards-benchers, or bankers or whatever they called themselves....

"I must think on this, my son," he said. "Perhaps I was over hasty. Perhaps in the days of St. Paul usury was another thing entirely. Perhaps what you practice is not *really* usury but merely something that resembles it. You may leave this silver with me."

When John left, Father Ambrosius squeezed his eyes tight shut and pressed the knuckles of both hands to his forehead. Things *did* change. Under the dispensation of the Old Testament, men had more wives than one. That was sinful now, but surely Abraham, Isaac and Jacob were in heaven? Paul wrote his epistles to little islands of Christians surrounded by seas of pagans. Surely in those days it was necessary for Christians to be bound closely together against the common enemy, whereas in these modern times, the ties could be safely relaxed a trifle? How could sinning have paid for the repose of Goodie Howat's soul, got a better price for brewer Thatcher's ale and saved the village hay crop? The Devil was tricky, but not *that* tricky, surely. A few more such tricks and the parish would resemble the paradise terrestrial!

Father Ambrosius dashed from his study to the altar of the little stone church and began furiously to turn the pages of the huge metal-bound lectern Bible.

"For the love of money is the root of all evil —"

It burst on Father Ambrosius with a great light that the words of Paul were in reference not to *John Goldsmith's* love of money but to *Sir Baldwin's* love of money.

He dashed back to his study and his pen began to squeak over the parchment, obliterating the last dim trace of Tacitus' *Annals*, VIII i.v. The sermon would be a scorcher, all right, but it wouldn't scorch John Goldsmith. It would scorch Sir Baldwin for ruthlessly and against the laws of God and man refusing to turn Fallowfield over to the moneylender. There would be growls of approval in the church that Sunday, and many black looks directed against Sir Baldwin for his attempt to bilk the parish's friend and benefactor, the moneylender.

* * * * *

"And that," F. W. Taylor concluded, chuckling, "is how power passes from one pair of hands to another, and how public acceptance of the change follows on its heels. A strange thing-people always think that each exchange of power is the last that will ever take place."

He seemed to be finished.

"Uncle," Orsino said, "somebody tried to kill me."

Taylor stared at him for a long minute, speechless. "What happened?" he finally asked.

"I went formal to the theater, with five bodyguards. The chief guard, name of Halloran, took a shot at me. One of my boys got in the way. He was killed."

Taylor's fingers began to play a tattoo on his annunciator board. Faces leaped into existence on its various screens as he fired orders. "Charles Orsino's chief bodyguard for tonight-Halloran. Trace him. The works. He tried to kill Orsino."

He clicked off the board switches and turned grimly to Orsino. "Now you," he said. "What have *you* been up to?"

"Just doing my job, uncle," Orsino said uneasily.

"Still bagman at the 101st?"

"Yes."

"Fooling with any women?"

"Nothing special, uncle. Nothing intense."

"Disciplined or downgraded anybody lately?"

"Certainly not. The precinct runs like a watch. I'll match their morale against any outfit east of the Mississippi. Why are you taking this so heavy?"

"Because you're the third. The other two-your cousin Thomas McGurn and your uncle Robert Orsino-didn't have guards to get in the way. One other question."

"Yes, uncle."

"My boy, *why* didn't you tell me about this when you first came in?"

CHAPTER IV.

A family council was called the next day. Orsino, very much a junior, had never been admitted to one before. He knew why the exception was being made, and didn't like the reason.

Edward Falcaro wagged his formidable white beard at the thirty-odd Syndic chiefs around the table and growled: "I think we'll dispense with reviewing production and so on. I want to talk about this damn gunplay. Dick, bring us up to date."

He lit a vile cigar and leaned back.

Richard W. Reiner rose.

"Thomas McGurn," he said, "killed April 15th by a burst of eight machine gun bullets in his private dining room at the Astor. Elsie Warshofsky, his waitress, must be considered the principal suspect, but —"

Edward Falcaro snapped: "Suspect, hell! She killed him, didn't she?"

"*I was about to say*, but the evidence so far is merely cumulative. Mrs. Warshofsky jumped-fell-or was pushed-from the dining room window. The machine gun was found beside the window.

"There are no known witnesses. Mrs. Warshofsky's history presents no unusual features. An acquaintance submitted a statement-based, she frankly admitted, on nothing definite-that Mrs. Warshofsky sometimes talked in a way that led her to wonder if she might not be a member of the secret terrorist organization known as the D.A.R. In this connection, it should be noted that Mrs. Warshofsky's maiden name was Adams.

"Robert Orsino, killed April 21st by a thermite bomb concealed in his pillow and fuzed with a pressure-sensitive switch. His valet, Edward Blythe, disappeared from view. He was picked up April 23rd by a posse on the beach of Montauk Point, but died before he could be questioned. Examination of his stomach contents showed a lethal quantity of sodium fluoride. It is presumed that the poison was self-administered."

"Presumed!" the old man snorted, and puffed out a lethal quantity of cigar smoke.

"Blythe's history," Reiner went on blandly, "presents no unusual features. It should be noted that a commerce-raider of the so-called United States Government Navy was reported off Montauk Point during the night of April 23rd-24th by local residents.

"Charles Orsino, attacked April 30th by his bodyguard James Halloran in the lobby of the Costello Memorial Theater. Halloran fired one shot which killed another bodyguard and was then himself killed. Halloran's history presents no unusual features except that he had a considerable interest in-uh-history. He collected and presumably read obsolete books dealing with pre-Syndic Pre-Mob America. Investigators found by his bedside the first volume of a work published in 1942 called *The Growth of The American Republic* by Morison and Commager. It was opened to Chapter Ten, The War of Independence!"

Reiner took his seat.

F. W. Taylor said dryly: "Dick, did you forget to mention that Warshofsky, Blythe and Halloran are known officers of the U. S. Navy?"

Reiner said: "You are being facetious. Are you implying that I have omitted pertinent facts?"

"I'm implying that you artistically stacked the deck. With a rumor, a dubious commerce-raider report and a note on a man's hobby, you want us to sweep the bastards from the sea, don't you-just the way you always have?"

"I am not ashamed of my expressed attitude on the question of the so-called United States Government and will defend it at any proper time and place."

"Shut the hell up, you two," Edward Falcaro growled. "I'm trying to think." He thought for perhaps half a minute and then looked up, baffled. "Has anybody got any ideas?"

Charles Orsino cleared his throat, amazed at his own temerity. The old man's eyebrows shot up, but he grudgingly said: "I guess you can say something, since they thought you were important enough to shoot."

Orsino said: "Maybe it's some outfit over in Europe or Asia?"

Edward Falcaro asked: "Anybody know anything about Europe or Asia? Jimmy, you flew over once, didn't you? To see about Anatolian poppies when the Mob had trouble with Mex labor?"

Jimmy Falcaro said creakily: "Yeah. It was a waste of time. They have these little dirt farmers scratching out just enough food for the family and maybe raising a quarter-acre of poppy. That's *all* there is from the China Sea to the Mediterranean. In England-Frank, you tell 'em. You explained it to me once."

Taylor rose. "The forest's come back to England. When finance there lost its morale and couldn't hack its way out of the paradoxes that was the end. When that happens you've got to have a large, virile criminal class ready to take over and do the work of distribution and production. Maybe some of you know how the English were. The poor beggars had civilized all the illegality out of the stock. They couldn't do anything that wasn't respectable. From sketchy reports, I gather that England is now forest and a few hundred starving people. One fellow says the men still wear derbies and stagger to their offices in the city.

"France is peasants, drunk three-quarters of the time.

"Russia is peasants, drunk *all* the time.

"Germany-well, there the criminal class was *too* big and *too* virile. The place is a cemetery."

He shrugged: "Say it, somebody. The Mob's gunning for us."

Reiner jumped to his feet. "I will *never* support such a hypothesis!" he shrilled. "It is *mischievous* to imply that a century of peace has been ended, that our three-thousand-mile border with our friend to the West —"

Taylor intoned satirically: "*Un*-blemished, my friends, by a *single* for-ti-fi-*ca*-tion —"

Edward Falcaro yelled: "Stop your damn foolishness, Frank Taylor! This is no laughing matter."

Taylor snapped: "Have you been in Mob Territory lately?"

"I have," the old man said. He scowled.

"How'd you like it?"

Edward Falcaro shrugged irritably. "They have their ways, we have ours. The Regan line is running thin, but we're not going to forget that Jimmy Regan stood shoulder to shoulder with Amadeo Falcaro in the old days. There's such a thing as loyalty."

F. W. Taylor said: "There's such a thing as blindness."

He had gone too far. Edward Falcaro rose from his chair and leaned forward, bracing himself on the table. He said flatly: "This is a statement, gentlemen. I won't pretend I'm happy about the way things are in Mob Territory. I won't pretend I think old man Regan is a balanced, dependable person. I won't pretend I think the Mob clients are enjoying anywhere near the service that Syndic clients enjoy. I'm perfectly aware that on our visits of state to Mob Territory we see pretty much what our hosts want us to see. But I cannot believe that any group which is rooted on the principles of freedom and service can have gone very wrong.

"Maybe I'm mistaken, gentlemen. But I cannot believe that a descendant of Jimmy Regan would order a descendant of Amadeo Falcaro murdered. We will consider every other possibility first. Frank, is that clear?"

"Yes," Taylor said.

"All right," Edward Falcaro grunted. "Now let's go about this thing systematically. Dick, you go right down the line with the charge that the Government's responsible for these atrocities. I hate to think that myself. If they are, we're going to have to spend a lot of time and trouble hunting them down and doing something about it. As long as they stick to a little commerce-raiding and a few coastal attacks, I can't say I'm really unhappy about them. They don't do much harm, and they keep us on our toes and-maybe this one is most important-they keep our client's memories of the bad old days that we delivered them from alive. That's a great deal to surrender for the doubtful pleasures of a long, expensive campaign. If assassination's in the picture I suppose we'll have to knock them off-but we've got to be *sure*."

"May I speak?" Reiner asked icily.

The old man nodded and re-lit his cigar.

"I have been called-behind my back, naturally —a fanatic," Reiner said. He pointedly did not look anywhere near F. W. Taylor as he spoke the word. "Perhaps this is correct and perhaps fanaticism is what's needed at a time like this. Let me point out what the so-called Government stands for: brutal 'taxation,' extirpation of gambling, denial of life's simple pleasures to the poor and severe limitation of them to all but the wealthy, sexual prudery viciously enforced by penal laws of appalling barbarity, endless regulation and coercion governing every waking minute of the day. That was its record during the days of its power and that would be its record if it returned to power. I fail to see how this menace to our liberty can be condoned by certain marginal benefits which are claimed to accrue from its continued existence." He faltered for a moment as his face twisted with an unpleasant memory. In a lower, unhappier voice, he went on: "I —I was alarmed the other day by something I overheard. Two small children were laying bets at the Kiddy Counter of the horse room I frequent, and I stopped on my way to the hundred-dollar window for a moment to hear their childish prattle. They were doping the forms for the sixth at Hialeah, I believe, when one of them digressed to say: 'My Mommy doesn't play the horses. She thinks all the horse rooms should be closed.'

"It wrung my heart, gentlemen, to hear that. I wanted to take that little boy aside and tell him: 'Son, your Mommy doesn't have to play the horses. Nobody has to play the horses unless he wants to. But as long as one single person wants to lay a bet on a horse and another person is willing to take it, nobody has the right to say the horse rooms should be closed.' Naturally I did not take the little boy aside and tell him that. It would have been an impractical approach to the problem. The *practical* approach is the one I have always advocated and still do. Strike at the heart of the infection! Destroy the remnants of Government and cauterize the wound so that it will never re-infect again. Nor is my language too strong. When I realize that the mind of an innocent child has been corrupted so that he will prattle that the liberties of his brothers must be infringed on, that their harmless pleasures must be curtailed, my blood runs cold and I call it what it is: *treason*."

Orsino had listened raptly to the words and joined in a burst of spontaneous applause that swept around the table. He had never had a brush with Government himself and he hardly believed in the existence of the shadowy, terrorist D.A.R., but Reiner had made it sound so near and menacing!

But Uncle Frank was on his feet. "We seem to have strayed from the point," he said dryly. "For anybody who needs his memory refreshed, I'll state that the point is two assassinations and one near miss. I fail to see the connection, if any with Dick Reiner's paranoid delusions of persecution. I especially fail to see the relevance of the word 'treason.' Treason to what-us? The Syndic is not a government. It must not become enmeshed in the symbols and folklore of a government or it will be first chained and then strangled by them. The Syndic is an organization of high morale and easy-going, hedonistic personality. The fact that it succeeded the Government occurred because the Government had become an organization of low morale and inflexible, puritanic, sado-masochistic personality. I have no illusions about the Syndic lasting forever, and I hope nobody else here has. Naturally I want it to last our lifetime, my children's lifetime, and as long after that as I can visualize my descendants, but don't think I have any burning affection for my unborn great-great grandchildren. Now, if there is anybody here who doesn't want it to last that long, I suggest to him that the quickest way to demoralize the Syndic is to adopt Dick Reiner's proposal of a holy war for a starter. From there we can proceed to an internal heresy hunt, a census, excise taxes, income taxes and wars of aggression. Now, what about getting back to the assassinations?"

Orsino shook his head, thoroughly confused by now. But the confusion vanished as a girl entered the room, whispered something in the ear of Edward Falcaro and sat down calmly by his side. He wasn't the only one who noticed her. Most of the faces there registered surprise and some indignation. The Syndic had a very strong tradition of masculinity.

Edward Falcaro ignored the surprise and indignation. He said placidly: "That was very interesting, Frank, what I understood of it. But it's always interesting when I go ahead and do something because it's the smart thing to do, and then listen to you explain my reasons-including fifty or sixty that I'm more than positive never crossed my mind."

There was a laugh around the table that Charles Orsino thought was unfair. He knew, Edward Falcaro knew, and everybody knew that Taylor credited Falcaro with sound intuitive judgment rather than analytic power. He supposed the old man-intuitively-had decided a laugh was needed to clear the air of the quarrel and irrelevance.

Falcaro went on: "The way things stand now, gentlemen, we don't know very much, do we?" He bit a fresh cigar and lighted it meditatively. From a cloud of rank smoke he said: "So the thing to do is find out more, isn't it?" In spite of the beard and the cigar, there was something of a sly, teasing child about him. "So what do you say to slipping one of our own people into the Government to find out whether they're dealing in assassination or not?"

Charles Orsino alone was naive enough to speak; the rest knew that the old man had something up his sleeve. Charles said: "You can't do it, sir! They have lie-detectors and drugs and all sorts of things —" His voice died down miserably under Falcaro's too-benign smile and the looks of irritation verging on disgust from the rest. The enigmatic girl scowled. *Goddam them all!* Charles thought, sinking into his chair and wishing he could sink into the earth.

"The young man," Falcaro said blandly, "speaks the truth-no less true for being somewhat familiar to us all. But what if we have a way to get around the drugs and lie-detectors, gentlemen? Which of you bold fellows would march into the jaws of death by joining the Government, spying on them and trying to report back?"

Charles stood up, prudence and timidity washed away by a burning need to make up for his embarrassment with a grandstand play. "I'll go, sir," he said very calmly. *And if I get killed that'll show 'em; then they'll be sorry.*

"Good boy," Edward Falcaro said briskly, with a well-that's that air. "The young lady here will take care of you."

Charles steadily walked down the long room to the head of the table, thinking that he must be cutting a rather fine figure. Uncle Frank ruined his exit by catching his sleeve and halting him as he passed his seat. "Good luck, Charles," Uncle Frank whispered. "And for Heaven's sake, keep a better guard up. Can't you see the old devil planned it this way from the beginning?"

"Good-bye, Uncle Frank," Charles said, suddenly feeling quite sick as he walked on. The young lady rose and opened the door for him. She was graceful as a cat, and a conviction overcame Charles Orsino that he was the canary.

CHAPTER V.

Max Wyman shoved his way through such a roar of voices and such a crush of bodies as he had never known before. Scratch Sheet Square was bright as day-brighter. Atomic lamps, mounted on hundred-story buildings hosed and squirted the happy mob with blue-white glare. The Scratch Sheet's moving sign was saying in fiery letters seventy-five feet tall: *"11:58 PM EST ... December 31st ... Cops say two million jam NYC streets to greet New Year ... 11:59 PM EST ... December 31st ... Falcaro jokes on TV 'Never thought we'd make it' ... 12:00 midnight January 1st ... Happy New Year..."*

The roar of voices had become insane. Max Wyman held his head, hating it, hating them all, trying to shut them out. Half a dozen young men against whom he was jammed were tearing the clothes off a girl. They were laughing and she was too, making only a pretense of defending herself. It was one of New York's mild winter nights. Wyman looked at the white skin not knowing that his eyes gloated. He yelled curses at her, and the young men. But nobody heard his whiskey-hoarsened young voice.

Somebody thrust a bottle at him and made mouths, trying to yell: "Happy New Year!" He grabbed feverishly at the bottle and held it to his mouth, letting the liquor gurgle once, twice, three times. Then the bottle was snatched away, not by the man who had passed it to him. A hilarious fat woman plastered herself against Wyman and kissed him clingingly on the mouth, to his horror and disgust. She was torn away from him by a laughing, white-haired man and turned willingly to kissing him instead.

Two strapping girls jockeyed Wyman between them and began to tear *his* clothes off, laughing at their switcheroo on the year's big gag. He clawed out at them hysterically and they stopped, the laughter dying on their lips as they saw his look of terrified rage. A sudden current in the crowd parted Wyman from them; another bottle bobbed on the sea of humanity. He clutched at it and this time did not drink. He stuffed it hurriedly under the waistband of his shorts and kept a hand on it as the eddy of humanity bore him on to the fringes of the roaring mob.

"Syndic leaders hail New Year ... Taylor praises Century of Freedom ... 12:05 AM EST January 1st..."

Wyman was mashed up against a girl who first smiled at his young face invitingly ... and then looked again. "Get away from me!" she shrieked, pounding on his chest with her small fists. You could hear individual voices now, but the crowd was still dense. She kept screaming at him and hitting him until suddenly Scratch Sheet Square Upramp loomed and the crowd fizzed onto it like uncorked champagne, Wyman and the screaming girl carried along the moving plates underfoot. The crowd boiled onto the northbound strip, relieving the crush; the girl vanished, whimpering, into the mob.

Wyman, rubbing his ear mechanically, shuffled with downcast eyes to the Eastbound ramp and collapsed onto a bench gliding by at five miles per hour. He looked stupidly at the ten-mile and fifteen-mile strips, but did not dare step onto them. He had been drinking steadily for a month. He would fall and the bottle would break.

He lurched off the five-mile strip at Riverside Downramp. Nobody got off with him. Riverside was a tangle of freightways over, under and on the surface. He worked there.

Wyman picked his way past throbbing conveyors roofed against pilferage, under gurgling fuel and water and waste pipes, around vast metal warehouses and storage tanks. It was not dark or idle in Riverside. Twenty-four hours was little enough time to bring Manhattan its daily needs and carry off its daily waste and manufactures. Under daylight atomics the transport engineers in their glass perches read the dials and turned the switches. Breakdown crews scurried out from emergency stations as bells clanged to replace a sagging plate, remag a failing ehrenhafter, unplug a jam of nylon bales at a too-sharp corner.

He found Breakdown Station 26, hitched his jacket over the bottle and swayed in, drunk enough to think he could pretend he was sober. "Hi," he said hoarsely to the shift foreman. "Got jammed up in the celebration."

"We heard it clear over here," the foreman said, looking at him closely. "Are you all right, Max?"

The question enraged him. "'Smatter?" he yelled. "Had a couple, sure. Think 'm drunk? Tha' wha' ya think?"

"Gee," the foreman said wearily. "Look, Max, I can't send you out tonight. You might get killed. I'm trying to be reasonable and I wish you'd do as much for me. What's biting you, boy? Nobody has anything against a few drinks and a few laughs. I went on a bender last month myself. But you get so Goddammed *mean* I can't stand you and neither can anybody else."

Wyman spewed obscenity at him and tried to swing on him. He was surprised and filled with self-pity when somebody caught his arm and somebody else caught his other arm. It was Dooley and Weintraub, his shift-mates, looking unhappy and concerned.

"Lousy rats!" Wyman choked out. "Leas' a man's buddies c'd do is back'm up...." He began to cry, hating them, and then fell asleep on his feet. Dooley and Weintraub eased him down onto the floor.

The foreman mopped his head and appealed to Dooley: "He always like this?" He had been transferred to Station 26 only two weeks before.

Dooley shrugged. "You might say so. He showed up about three months ago. Said he used to be a breakdown man in Buffalo, on the yards. He knew the work all right. But I never saw such a mean kid. Never a good word for anybody. Never any fun. Booze, booze, booze. This time he really let go."

Weintraub said unexpectedly: "I think he's what they used to call an alcoholic."

"What the hell's that?" the foreman demanded.

"I read about it. It's something they used to have before the Syndic. I read about it. Things were a lot different then. People picking on you all the time, everybody mad all the time. The girls were scared to give it away and the boys were scared to take it-but they did anyway and it was kind of like fighting with yourself *inside* yourself. The fighting wore some people out so much they just couldn't take it any more. Instead of going on benders for a change of pace like sensible people, they boozed *all* the time-and they had a fight inside themselves about *that* so they boozed harder." He looked defensive at their skeptical faces. "I *read* it," he insisted.

"Well," the foreman said inconclusively, "I heard things used to be pretty bad. Did these alcoholers get over it?"

"I don't know," Weintraub admitted. "I didn't read that far."

"Hm. I think I'd better can him." The foreman was studying their faces covertly, hoping to read a reaction. He did. Both the men looked relieved. "Yeh. I think I'd better can him. He can go to the Syndic for relief if he has to. He doesn't do us much good here. Put some soup on and get it down him when he wakes up." The foreman, an average kindly man, hoped the soup would help.

But at about three-thirty, after two trouble calls in succession, they noticed that Wyman had left leaving no word.

* * * * *

The fat little man struggled out of the New Year's eve throng; he had been caught by accident. Commander Grinnel did not go in for celebrations. When he realized that January fifteenth was now fifteen days away, he doubted that he would ever celebrate again. It was a two-man job he had to do on the fifteenth, and so far he had not found the other man.

He rode the slidewalk to Columbus Square. He had been supplied with a minimum list of contacts. One had moved, and in the crazily undisciplined Syndic Territory it was impossible to trace anybody. Another had died-of too much morphine. Another had beaten her husband almost to death with a chair leg and was in custody awaiting trial. The Commander wondered briefly and querulously: why do we always have such unstable people here? Or does that louse Emory deliberately saddle me with them when I'm on a mission? Wouldn't put it past him.

The final contact on the list was a woman. She'd be worthless for the business of January fifteenth; that called for some physical strength, some technical knowledge, and a residual usefulness to the Government. Professor Speiser had done some good work here on industrial sabotage, but taken away from the scene of possible operations, she'd just be a millstone. He had his record to think of.

Sabotage —

If a giggling threesome hadn't been looking his way from a bench across the slidewalk, he would have ground his teeth. In recent weeks, he had done what he estimated as an easy three million dollars worth of damage to Mob Territory industry. And the stupid fools hadn't *noticed* it! Repair crews had rebuilt the fallen walls, mechanics had tut-tutted over the wrecked engines and replaced them, troubleshooters had troubleshot the scores of severed communications lines and fuel mains.

He had hung around.

"Sam, you see this? Melted through, like with a little thermite bomb. How in the hell did a thing like that happen?"

"I don't know. I wasn't here. Let's get it fixed kid."

"Okay ...you think we ought to report this to somebody?"

"If you want to. I'll mention it to Larry. But I don't see what he can do about it. Must've been some kids. You gotta put it down as fair wear and tear. But boys will be boys."

Remembering, he did grind his teeth. But they were at Columbus Square.

* * * * *

Professor Speiser lived in one of the old plastic brick faculty houses. Her horsy face, under a curling net, looked out of the annunciator plate. "Yes? What is it?"

"Professor Speiser, I believe you know my daughter, Miss *Freeman*. She asked me to look you up while I was in New York. Have I come much too late?"

"Oh, dear. Why, no. I suppose not. Come in, Mr. —Mr. Freeman."

In her parlor, she faced him apprehensively. When she spoke she rolled out her sentences like the lecturer she was. "Mr. Freeman-as I suppose you'd prefer me to call you-you asked a moment ago whether you'd come too late. I realize that the question was window-dressing, but my answer is quite serious. You have come too late. I have decided to dissociate myself from-let us say, from your daughter, Miss Freeman."

The Commander asked only: "Is that irrevocable?"

"Quite. It wouldn't be fair of me to ask you to leave without an explanation. I am perfectly willing to give one. I realize now that my friendship with Miss Freeman and the work I did for her stemmed from, let us say a certain vacancy in my life."

He looked at a picture on her desk of a bald, pleasant-faced fellow with a pipe.

She followed his eyes and said with a sort of shy pride: "That is Dr. Mordecai, of the University's Faculty of Dentistry. Like myself, a long-time celibate. We plan to marry."

The Commander said: "Do you feel that Dr. Mordecai might like to meet my daughter?"

"No. I do not. We expect to have very little time for outside activities, between our professional careers and our personal lives. Please don't misunderstand, Mr. Freeman. I am still your daughter's friend. I always shall be. But somehow I no longer find in myself an urgency to express the friendship. It seems like a beautiful dream-and a quite futile one. I have come to realize that one can live a full life without Miss Freeman. Now, it's getting quite late —"

He smiled ruefully and rose. "May I wish you every happiness, Professor Speiser?" he said, extending his hand.

She beamed with relief. "I was so afraid you'd —"

Her face went limp and she stood swaying drunkenly as the needle in the ring popped her skin.

The Commander, his face as dead as hers, disconnected his hand and sheathed the needle carefully again. He drew one of his guns, shot her through the heart and walked out of the apartment.

Old fool! She should have known better.

* * * * *

Max Wyman stumbled through the tangle of Riveredge, his head a pot of molten lead and his legs twitching under him as he fled from his shame.

Dimly, as if with new eyes, he saw that he was not alone. Riveredge was technically uninhabited. Then what voices called guardedly to him from the shadows: "Buddy-buddy-wait up a minute, buddy-did you score? Did you score?"

He lurched on and the voices became bolder. The snaking conveyors and ramps sliced out sectors of space. Storage tanks merged with inflow mains to form sheltered spots where they met. No spot was without its whining, appealing voice. He stood at last, quivering, leaning against a gigantic I-beam that supported a heavy-casting freightway. A scrap sheet of corrugated iron rested against the bay of the I-beam, and the sheet quivered and fell outward. An old man's voice said: "You're beat, son. Come on in."

He staggered a step forward and collapsed on a pallet of rags as somebody carefully leaned the sheet back into place again.

CHAPTER VI.

Max Wyman woke raving with the chuck horrors. There was somebody there to hand him candy bars, sweet lemonade, lump sugar. There was somebody to shove him easily back into the pallet of rags when he tried to stumble forth in a hunt for booze. On the second day he realized that it was an old man whose face looked gray and paralyzed. His name was T. G. Pendelton, he said.

After a week, he let Max Wyman take little walks about their part of Riverside-but not by night. "We've got some savage people here," he said. "They'd murder you for a pint. The women are worse. If one calls to you, don't go. You'll wind up dumped through a manhole into the Hudson. Poor folk."

"You're *sorry* for them?" Wyman asked, startled. It was a new idea to him. Since Buffalo, he had never been sorry for anybody. Something awful had happened there, some terrible betrayal ... he passed his bony hand across his forehead. He didn't want to think about it.

"Would I live here if I weren't?" T. G. asked him. "Sometimes I can help them. There's nobody else to help them. They're old and sick and they don't fit anywhere. That's why they're savage. You're young-the only young man I've ever seen in Riveredge. There's so much outside for the young. But when you get old it sometimes throws you."

"The Goddammed Syndic," Wyman snarled, full of hate.

T. G. shrugged. "Maybe it's too easy for sick old people to get booze. They lose somebody they spent a life with and it throws them. People harden into a pattern. They always had fun, they think they always will. Then half of the pattern's gone and they can't stand it, some of them. You got it early. What was the ringing bell?"

Wyman collapsed into the bay of the I-beam as if he'd been kicked in the stomach. A wave of intolerable memory swept over him. A ringing bell, a wobbling pendulum, a flashing light, the fair face of his betrayer, the hateful one of Hogan, stirred together in a hell brew. "Nothing," he said hoarsely, thinking that he'd give his life for enough booze to black him out. "Nothing."

"You kept talking about it," T. G. said. "Was it real?"

"It couldn't have been," Wyman muttered. "There aren't such things. No. There was her and that Syndic and that louse Hogan. I don't want to talk about it."

"Suit yourself."

He did talk about it later, curiously clouded though it was. The years in Buffalo. The violent love affair with Inge. The catastrophic scene when he found her with Regan, king-pin mobster. The way he felt turned inside-out, the lifetime of faith in the Syndic behind him and the lifetime of a faith in Inge ahead of him, both wrecked, the booze, the flight from Buffalo to Erie, to Pittsburgh, to Tampa, to New York. And somehow, insistently, the ringing bell, the wobbling pendulum and the flashing light that kept intruding between episodes of reality.

T. G. listened patiently, fed him, hid him when infrequent patrols went by. T. G. never told him his own story, but a bloated woman who lived with a yellow-toothed man in an abandoned storage tank did one day, her voice echoing from the curving, windowless walls of corrugated plastic. She said T. G. had been an alky chemist, reasonably prosperous, reasonably happy, reasonably married. His wife was the faithful kind and he was not. With unbelievable slyness she had dulled the pain for years with booze and he had never suspected. They say she had killed herself after one frightful week-long debauche in Riveredge. T. G. came down to Riveredge for the body and returned after giving it burial and drawing his savings from the bank. He had never left Riveredge since.

"Worsh'p the grun' that man walks on," the bloated woman mumbled. "Nev' gets mad, nev' calls you hard names. Give y'a bottle if y' need it. Talk to y' if y' blue. Worsh'p that man."

Max Wyman walked from the storage tank, sickened. T. G.'s charity covered that creature and him.

It was the day he told T. G.: "I'm getting out of here."

The gray, paralyzed-looking face almost smiled. "See a man first?"

"Friend of yours?"

"Somebody who heard about you. Maybe he can do something for you. He feels the way you do about the Syndic."

Wyman clenched his teeth. The pain still came at the thought. Syndic, Hogan, Inge and betrayal. God, to be able to hit back at them!

The red ride ebbed. Suddenly he stared at T. G. and demanded: "Why? Why should you put me in touch? What is this?"

T. G. shrugged. "I don't worry about the Syndic. I worry about people. I've been worrying about you. You're a little insane, Max, like all of us here."

"God damn you!"

"He has...."

Max Wyman paused a long time and said: "Go on, will you?" He realized that anybody else would have apologized. But he couldn't and he knew that T. G. knew he couldn't.

The old man said: "A little insane. Bottled-up hatred. It's better out of you than in. It's better to sock the man you hate and stand a chance of having him sock you back than it is just to hate him and let the hate gnaw you like a grave-worm."

"What've you got against the Syndic?"

"Nothing, Max. Nothing against it and nothing for it. What I'm for is people. The Syndic is people. You're people. Slug 'em if you want and they'll have a chance to slug you back. Maybe you'll pull down the Syndic like Samson in the temple; more likely it'll crush you. But you'll be *doing* something about it. That's the great thing. That's the thing people have to learn-or they wind up in Riveredge."

"You're crazy."

"I told you I was, or I wouldn't be here."

The man came at sunset. He was short and pudgy, with a halo of wispy hair and the coldest, grimmest eyes that Wyman had ever seen. He shook hands with Wyman, and the young man noted simultaneously a sharp pain in his finger and that the stranger wore an elaborate gold ring. Then the world got hazy and confused. He had a sense that he was being asked questions, that he was answering them, that it went on for hours and hours.

When things quite suddenly came into focus again, the pudgy man was saying: "I can introduce myself now. Commander Grinnel, of the North American Navy. My assignment is recruiting. The preliminary examination has satisfied me that you are no plant and would be a desirable citizen of the N. A. Government. I invite you to join us."

"What would I do?" Wyman asked steadily.

"That depends on your aptitudes. What do you think you would like to do?"

Wyman said: "Kill me some Syndics."

The commander stared at him with those cold eyes. He said at last: "It can probably be arranged. Come with me."

* * * * *

They went by train to Cape Cod. At midnight on January 15th, the commander and Wyman left their hotel room and strolled about the streets. The commander taped small packets to the four legs of the microwave relay tower that connected Cape Cod with the Continental Press common carrier circuits and taped other packets to the police station's motor pool gate.

At 1:00 A.M., the tower exploded and the motor pool gate fused into an impassible puddle of blue-hot molten metal. Simultaneously, fifty men in turtle-neck sweaters and caps appeared from nowhere on Center Street. Half of them barricaded the street, firing on citizens and cops who came too close. The others systematically looted every store between the barricade and the beach.

Blinking a flashlight in code, the commander approached the deadline unmolested and was let through with Wyman at his heels. The goods, the raiders, the commander and Wyman were aboard a submarine by 2:35 and under way ten minutes later.

After Commander Grinnel had exchanged congratulations with the sub commander, he presented Wyman.

"A recruit. Normally I wouldn't have bothered, but he had a rather special motivation. He could be very useful."

The sub commander studied Wyman impersonally. "If he's not a plant."

"I've used my ring. If you want to get it over with, we can test him and swear him in now."

They strapped him into a device that recorded pulse, perspiration, respiration, muscle-tension and brainwaves. A sweatered specialist came and mildly asked Wyman matter-of-fact questions about his surroundings while he calibrated the polygraph.

Then came the pay-off. Wyman did not fail to note that the sub commander loosened his gun in his holster when the questioning began.

"Name, age and origin?"

"Max Wyman. Twenty-two. Buffalo Syndic Territory."

"Do you like the Syndic?"

"I hate them."

"What are your feelings toward the North American Government?"

"If it's against the Syndic, I'm for it."

"Would you rob for the North American Government?"

"I would."

"Would you kill for it?"

"I would."

"Have you any reservations yet unstated in your answers?"

"No."

It went on for an hour. The questions were re-phrased continuously; after each of Wyman's firm answers, the sweatered technician gave a satisfied little nod. At last it ended and he was unstrapped from the device.

Max was tired.

The sub commander seemed a little awed as he got a small book and read from it: "Do you, Max Wyman, solemnly renounce all allegiances previously held by you and pledge your allegiance to the North American Government?"

"I do," the young man said fiercely.

In a remote corner of his mind, for the first time in months, the bell ceased to ring, the pendulum to beat and the light to flash.

Charles Orsino knew again who he was and what was his mission.

CHAPTER VII.

It had begun when the girl led him through the conference room door. Naturally one had misgivings; naturally one didn't speak up. But the vault-like door far downstairs was terrifying when it yawned before you and even more so when it closed behind you.

"What is this place?" he demanded at last. "Who are you?"

She said: "Psychology lab."

It produced on him the same effect that "alchemy section" or "Division of astrology" would have on a well-informed young man in 1950. He repeated flatly: "Psychology lab. If you don't want to tell me, very well. I volunteered without strings." Which should remind her that he was a sort of hero and should be treated with a certain amount of dignity and that she could save her corny jokes.

"I meant it," she said, fiddling busily with the locks of yet another vault-like door. "I'm a psychologist. I'm also by the way, Lee Falcaro-since you asked."

"The old man-Edward Falcaro's line?" he asked.

"Simon pure. He's my father's brother. Father's down in Miami, handling the tracks and gaming in general."

The second big door opened on a brain-gray room whose air had a curiously dead feel to it. "Sit down," she said, indicating a very unorthodox chair. He did, and found that the chair was the most comfortable piece of furniture he had ever known. Its contact with his body was so complete that it pressed nowhere, it poked nowhere. The girl studied dials in its back nevertheless and muttered something about adjusting it. He protested.

"Nonsense," she said decisively. She sat down herself in an ordinary seat. Charles shifted uneasily in his chair to find that it moved with him. Still no pressure, still no poking.

"You're wondering," she began, "about the word 'psychology'. It has a bad history and people have given it up as a bad job. It's true that there isn't pressure nowadays to study the human mind. People get along. In general what they want they get, without crippling effort. In your uncle Frank Taylor's language, the Syndic is an appropriately-structured organization of high morale and wide public acceptance. In my language the Syndic is a father-image which does a good job of fathering. In good times, people aren't introspective.

"There is, literally, no reason why my line of the family should have kept up a tradition of experimental psychology. Way, way back, old Amadeo Falcaro often consulted Professor Oscar Sternweiss of the Columbia University psychology faculty-he wasn't as much of a dashing im-provisor as the history books make him out to be. Eventually one of his daughters married one of Sternweiss' sons and inherited the Sternweiss notebooks and library and apparatus. It became an irrational custom to keep it alive. When each academic school of psychology managed to prove that every other school of psychology was dead wrong and psychology collapsed as a science, the family tradition was unaffected; it stood outside the wrangling.

"Now, you're wondering what this has to do with trying to slip you into the Government."

"I am," Charles said fervently. If she'd been a doll outside the Syndic, he would minutes ago have protested that all this was foolish and walked out. Since she was not only in the Syndic, but in the Falcaro line, he had no choice except to hear her babble and *then* walk out. It was all rot, psychology. Id, oversoul, mind-vectors, counseling, psychosomatics-rot from sick-minded old men. Everybody knew —

"The Government, we know, uses deinhibiting drugs as a first screening of its recruits. As an infallible second screening, they use a physiological lie-detector based on the fact that telling a lie causes tensions in the liar's body. We shall get around this by slipping you in as a young man who hates the Syndic for some valid reason —"

"Confound it, you were just telling me that they can't be fooled!"

"We won't fool them. You'll *be* a young man who hates the Syndic. We'll tear down your present personality a gray cell at a time. We'll pump you full of Seconal every day for a quarter of a year.... We'll obliterate your personality under a new one. We'll bury Charles Orsino under a mountain of suggestions, compulsions and obsessions shoveled at you sixteen hours a day while you're too groggy to resist. Naturally the supplanting personality will be neurotic, but that works in with the mission."

He struggled with a metaphysical concept, for the first time in his life. "But-but-how will I know I'm *me*?"

"We think we can put a trigger on it. When you take the Government oath of allegiance, you should bounce back."

He did not fail to note a little twin groove between her brows that appeared when she said *think* and *should*. He knew that in a sense he was nearer death now than when Halloran's bullet had been intercepted.

"Are you staying with it?" she asked simply.

Various factors entered into it. *A life for the Syndic*, as in the children's history books. That one didn't loom very large. But multiply it by *it sounds like more fun than hot-rod polo*, and that by *this is going to raise my stock sky-high with the family* and you had something. Somehow, under Lee Falcaro's interested gaze, he neglected to divide it by *if it works*.

"I'm staying with it," he said.

She grinned. "It won't be too hard," she said. "In the old days there would have been voting record, social security numbers, military service, addresses they could check on-hundreds of things. Now about all we have to fit you with is a name and a subjective life."

It began that spring day and went on into late fall.

The ringing bell.

The flashing light.

The wobbling pendulum.

You are Max Wyman of Buffalo Syndic Territory. You are Max Wyman of Buffalo Syndic Territory. You are Max Wyman of Buffalo Syndic....

Mom fried pork sausages in the morning, you loved the smell of pumpernickel from the bakery in Vesey Street.

Mr. Watsisname the English teacher with the mustache wanted you to go to college —

—but the stockyard job was closer, they needed breakdown men —
You are Max Wyman of Buffalo Syndic Territory. You are —

The ringing bell.

The flashing light.

The wobbling pendulum.

And the pork sausages and the teacher with the mustache and poems you loved and

page 24, paragraph 3, maximum speed on a live-cattle walkway is three miles per hour: older walkways hold this speed with reduction gears coupled to a standard 18-inch ehren-hafter unit. Standard practice in new construction calls for holding speed by direct drive from a specially-wound ehrenhafter. This places a special obligation in breakdown main-tenance men, who must distinguish between the two types, carry two sets of wiring dia-grams and a certain number of mutually-uninterchangeable parts, though good design principles hold these to a minimum. The main difference in the winding of a standard 18-incher and a lowspeed ehrenhafter rotor —

Of course things are better now, Max Wyman, you owe a great debt to Jim Hogan, Father of the Buffalo Syndic, who fought for your freedom in the great old days, and to his descendants who are tirelessly working for your freedom and happiness.

And bow-happiness is a girl named Inge Klohbel now that you're almost a man.

You are Max Wyman of Buffalo Syndic Territory. You are Max Wyman of Buffalo Syndic Territory.

And Inge Klohbel is why you put away the crazy dream of scholarship, for her lips and hair and eyes and legs mean more to you than anything, more than

Later phonologic changes include palatal mutation; i.e., before cht *and* hs *the diphthongs* eo, io, *which resulted from breaking, became* ie (i, y) *as in* cneoht, chieht, *and* seox (x *equalling* hs), siex, six, syx....

the crazy dream of scholarship, what kind of a way is that to repay the Mob and

The ringing bell.

The flashing light.

The wobbling pendulum.

repay the Syndic and young Mike Hogan all over the neighborhood suddenly and Inge says he did stop and say hello but of course he was just being polite.

so you hit the manuals hard and one day you go out on a breakdown call and
none of the older men could figure out why the pump was on the blink; a roaring,
chewing monster of a pump it was, sitting there like a dead husk and the cattlefeed
backed up four miles to a storage tank in the suburbs and the steers in the yards
bawling with hunger, and you traced the dead wire, you out with the spot-welder,
a zip of blue flame and the pump began to chew again and you got the afternoon
off.

* * * * *

And there they were.

    *Lee Falcaro: (Bending over the 'muttering, twitching carcass) Adrenalin. Brighter pic-
ture and louder sound.*

    *Assistant: (Opening a pinch cock in the tube that enters the arm, increasing video con-
trast, increasing audio): He's weakening.*

    Lee Falcaro: (In a whisper) I know. I know. But this is IT.

    Assistant: (Inaudibly) You cold-blooded bitch.

You are Max Wyman, you are Max Wyman, and you don't know what to do about the Syndic
that betrayed you, about the girl who betrayed you with the living representative of the Syndic,
about the dream of scholarship that lies in ruins, the love that lies in ruins after how many
promises and vows, the faith of twenty years that lies in ruins after how many declarations.
The ringing bell.
The flashing light.
The wobbling pendulum.
And a double whiskey with a beer chaser.
*Lee Falcaro: The alcohol. (It drips from a sterile graduate, trickles through the rubber tubing and
into the arm of the mumbling, sweating carcass. The molecules mingle with the molecules of serum: In
seconds they are washed against the cell-walls of the forebrain. The cell-walls their structure as the alcohol molecules bumble against them; the lattices of jelly that wall in the cytoplasm and nuclear jelly become thinner than they were. Streams of electrons that had coursed in familiar paths through chains of
neurones find easier paths through the poison-thinned cell-walls. A "Memory" or an "Idea" or a "Hope"
or a "Value" that was a configuration of neurones linked by electron streams vanishes when the electron
streams find an easier way to flow a New "Memories," "Ideas," "Hopes" and "Values" that are configu-
rations of neurones linked by electron streams are born.)*
Love and loyalty die, but not as if they had never been. Their ghosts remain, Max Wyman
and you are haunted by them. They hound you from Buffalo to Erie, but there is no oblivion
deep enough in the Mex joints, or in Tampa tequila or Pittsburgh zubrovka or New York gin.
You tell incurious people who came to the place on the corner for a shot and some talk that
you're the best breakdown man that ever came out of Erie; you tell them women are no God-
damn good, you tell them the Syndic-here you get sly and look around with drunken caution,
lowering your voice-you tell them the Syndic's no God-damned good, and you drunkenly recite
poetry until they move away, puzzled and annoyed.

    *Lee Falcaro: (Passing a weary hand across her forehead) well, he's had it. Disconnect the
tubes, give him a 48-hour stretch in bed and then get him on the street pointed towards
Riveredge.*

Assistant: Does the apparatus go into dead storage?

Lee Falcaro: (Grimacing uncontrollably) No. Unfortunately, no.

Assistant: (Inaudibly, as she plucks needle-tipped tubes from the carcass' elbows) who's the next sucker?

CHAPTER VIII.

The submarine surfaced at dawn. Orsino had been assigned a bunk and, to his surprise, had fallen asleep almost at once. At eight in the morning, he was shaken awake by one of the men in caps.

"Shift change," the man explained laconically.

Orsino started to say something polite and sleepy. The man grabbed his shoulder and rolled him onto the deck, snarling: "You going to *argue?*"

Orsino's reactions were geared to hot-rod polo-doing the split-second right thing after instinctively evaluating the roll of the ball, the ricochet of bullets, the probable tactics and strategy of the opposing four. They were not geared to a human being who behaved with the blind ferocity of an inanimate object. He just gawked at him from the deck, noting that the man had one hand on a sheath knife.

"All right, buster," the man said contemptuously, apparently deciding that Orsino would stay put. "Just don't mess with the Guard." He rolled into the bunk and gave a good imitation of a man asleep until Orsino worked his way through the crowded compartment and up a ladder to the deck.

There was a heavy, gray over-cast. The submarine seemed to be planing the water; salt spray washed the shining deck. A gun crew was forward, drilling with a five-incher. The rasp of a petty-officer singing out the numbers mingled with the hiss and gurgle of the spray. Orsino leaned against the conning tower and tried to comb his thoughts out clean and straight.

It wasn't easy.

He was Charles Orsino, very junior Syndic member, with all memories pertaining thereto.

He was also, more dimly, Max Wyman with *his* memories. Now, able to stand outside of Wyman, he could recall how those memories had been implanted-down to the last stab of the last needle. He thought some very bitter thoughts about Lee Falcaro-and dropped them, snapping to attention as Commander Grinnel pulled himself through the hatch. "Good morning, sir," he said.

The cold eyes drilled him. "Rest," the commander said. "We don't play it that way on a pigboat. I hear you had some trouble about your bunk."

Orsino shrugged uncomfortably.

"Somebody should have told you," the commander said. "The boat's full of Guardsmen. They have a very high opinion of themselves-which is correct. They carried off the raid in good style. You don't mess with Guards."

"What are they?" Orsino asked.

Grinnel shrugged. "The usual elite," he said. "Loman's gang." He noted Orsino's blank look and smiled coldly. "Loman's President of North America," he said.

"On shore," Orsino hazarded, "we used to hear about somebody named Ben Miller."

"Obsolete information. Miller had the Marines behind him. Loman was Secretary of Defense. He beached the Marines and broke them up into guard detachments. Took away their heavy weapons. Meanwhile, he built up the Guard, very quietly-which, with the Secretary of Information behind him, he could do. About two years ago, he struck. The Marines who didn't join the Guard were massacred. Miller had the sense to kill himself. The Veep and the Secretary of State resigned, but it didn't save their necks. Loman assumed the Presidency automatically, of course, and had them shot. They were corrupt as hell anyway. They were owned body and soul by the southern bloc."

Two seamen appeared with a folding cot, followed by the sub commander. He was red-eyed with lack of sleep. "Set it there," he told them, and sat heavily on the sagging canvas. "Morning, Grinnel," he said with an effort. "Believe I'm getting too old for the pigboats. I want sun and air. Think you can use your influence at court to get me a corvette?" He bared his teeth to show it was a joke.

Grinnel said, with a minimum smile: "If I had any influence, would I catch the cloak-and-dagger crap they sling at me?"

The sub commander rolled back onto the cot and was instantly asleep, a muscle twitching the left side of his face every few seconds.

Grinnel drew Orsino to the lee of the conning tower. "We'll let him sleep," he said. "Go tell that gun crew Commander Grinnel says they should lay below."

Orsino did. The petty officer said something exasperated about the gunnery training bill and Orsino repeated his piece. They secured the gun and went below.

Grinnel said, with apparent irrelevance: "You're a rare bird, Wyman. You're capable-and you're uncommitted. Let's go below. Stick with me."

* * * * *

He followed the fat little commander into the conning tower. Grinnel told an officer of some sort: "I'll take the con, mister. Wyman here will take the radar watch." He gave Orsino a look that choked off his protests. Presumably, Grinnel knew that he was ignorant of radar.

The officer, looking baffled, said: "Yes, Commander." A seaman pulled his head out of a face-fitting box and told Wyman: "It's all yours, stranger." Wyman cautiously put his face into the box and was confronted by meaningless blobs of green, numerals in the dark, and a couple of arrows to make confusion complete.

He heard Grinnel say to the helmsman: "Get me a mug of joe, sailor. I'll take the wheel."

"I'll pass the word, sir."

"Nuts you'll pass the word, sailor. Go get the coffee-and I want it now and not when some steward's mate decides he's ready to bring it."

"Aye, aye, sir." Orsino heard him clatter down the ladder. Then his arm was gripped and Grinnel's voice muttered in his ear: "When you hear me bitch about the coffee, sing out: 'Aircraft 265, DX 3,000'. Good and loud. No, don't stop looking. Repeat it."

Orsino said, his eyes crossing on double images of the meaningless, luminous blobs: "Aircraft 265, DX 3,000. Good and loud. When you bitch about the coffee."

"Right. Don't forget it."

He heard the feet on the ladder again. "Coffee, sir."

"Thanks, sailor." A long sip and then another. "I always said the pigboats drink the lousiest joe in the Navy."

"Aircraft 265, DX 3,000!" Orsino yelled.

A thunderous alarm began to sound. "Take her down!" yelled Commander Grinnel.

"Take her down, sir!" the helmsman echoed. "But sir, the skipper —"

Orsino remembered him too then, dead asleep in his cot on the deck, the muscle twitching the left side of his face every few seconds.

"God-damn it, those were aircraft! *Take her down!*"

The luminous blobs and numbers and arrows swirled before Orsino's eyes as the trim of the ship changed, hatches clanged to and water thundered into the ballast tanks. He staggered and caught himself as the deck angled sharply underfoot.

He knew what Grinnel had meant by saying he was uncommitted, and he knew now that it was no longer true.

He thought for a moment that he might be sick into the face-fitting box, but it passed.

Minutes later, Grinnel was on the mike, his voice sounding metallically through the ship: "To all hands. To all hands. This is Commander Grinnel. We lost the skipper in that emergency dive-but you and I know that that's the way he would have wanted it. As senior line officer aboard, I'm assuming command for the rest of the voyage. We will remain submerged until dark. Division officers report to the wardroom. That's all."

He tapped Orsino on the shoulder. "Take off," he said. Orsino realized that the green blobs-clouds, were they? —no longer showed, and recalled that radar didn't work through water.

He wasn't in on the wardroom meeting, and wandered rather forlornly through the ship, incredibly jammed as it was with sleeping men, coffee-drinking men and booty. Half a dozen times he had to turn away close questioning about his radar experience and the appearance of the aircraft on the radar scope. Each time he managed it, with the feeling that one more question would have cooked his goose.

The men weren't sentimental about the skipper they had lost. Mostly they wondered how much of a cut Grinnel would allot them from the booty of Cape Cod.

At last the word passed for "Wyman" to report to the captain's cabin. He did, sweating after a fifteen-minute chat with a radar technician.

Grinnel closed the door of the minute cabin and smirked at him. "You have trouble, Wyman?" he asked.

"Yes."

"You'd have worse trouble if they found out for sure that you don't know radar. I'd be in the clear. I could tell them you claimed to be a qualified radar man. That would make me out to be pretty gullible, but it would make you out to be a murderer. Who's backing you, Wyman? Who told you to get rid of the skipper?"

"Quite right, sir," Orsino said. "You've really got me there."

"Glad you realize it, Wyman. I've got you and I can use you. It was a great bit of luck, the skipper corking off on deck. But I've always had a talent for improvisation. If you're determined to be a leader, Wyman, nothing is more valuable. Do you know, I can relax with you? It's a rare feeling. For once I can be certain that the man I'm talking to isn't one of Loman's stooges, or one of Clinch's N.A.B.I. ferrets or anything else but what he says he is —

"But that's beside the point. I have something else to tell you. There are two sides to working for me, Wyman. One of them's punishment if you get off the track. That's been made clear to you. The other is reward if you stay on. I have plans, Wyman, that are large-scale. They simply eclipse the wildest hopes of Loman, Clinch, Baggot and the rest. And yet, they're not wild. How'd you like to be on the inside when the North American Government returns to the mainland?"

Orsino uttered an authentic gasp and Commander Grinnel looked satisfied.

CHAPTER IX.

The submarine docked at an indescribably lovely bay in the south of Ireland. Orsino asked Grinnel whether the Irish didn't object to this, and was met with a blank stare. It developed that the Irish consisted of a few hundred wild men in the woods-maybe a few thousand. The stupid shore-bound personnel couldn't seem to clean them out. Grinnel didn't know anything about them, and he cared less.

Ireland appeared to be the naval base. The government proper was located on Iceland, vernal again after a long, climatic swing. The Canaries and Ascencion were outposts.

Orsino had learned enough on the voyage to recognize the Government for what it was. It had happened before in history; Uncle Frank had pointed it out. Big-time Caribbean piracy had grown from very respectable origins. Gentlemen-skippers had been granted letters of marque and reprisal by warring governments, which made them a sort of contract navy. Periods of peace had found these privateers unwilling to give up their hard earned complicated profession and their investments in it. When they could no longer hoist the flag of England or France or Spain, they simply hoisted the Jolly Roger and went it alone.

Confusing? Hell, yes! The famous Captain Kidd thought he was a gallant privateer and sailed trustingly into New York. Somewhere he had failed to touch third base; they shipped him to London for trial and hanged him as a pirate. The famous Henry Morgan had never been anything but a pirate and a super-pirate; as admiral of a private fleet he executed a brilliant amphibious operation and sacked the city of Panama. He was knighted, made governor of a fair-sized English island in the West Indies and died loved and respected by all.

Charles Orsino found himself a member of a pirate band that called itself the North American Government.

More difficult to learn were the ins and outs of pirate politics, which were hampered with an archaic, structurally-inappropriate nomenclature and body of tradition. Commander Grinnel was a Sociocrat, which meant that he was in the same gang as President Loman. The late sub commander had been a Constitutionist, which meant that he was allied with the currently-out "southern bloc." The southern bloc did not consist of southerners at this stage of the North American Government's history but of a clique that tended to include the engineers and main-tenance men of the Government. That had been the reason for the sub commander's erasure.

The Constitutionists traditionally commanded pigboats and aircraft while surface vessels and the shore establishments were in the hands of the Sociocrats-the fruit of some long-forgotten compromise.

Commander Grinnel cheerfully explained to Charles that there was a crypto-Sociocrat naval officer primed and waiting to be appointed to the command of the sub. The Constitutionist gang would back him to the hilt and the Sociocrats would growl and finally assent. If, thereafter, the Constitutionists ever counted on the sub in a coup, they would be quickly disillusioned.

There wasn't much voting. Forty years before there had been a bad deadlock following the death by natural causes of President Powell after seventeen years in office. An ad hoc bipartisan conference called a session of the Senate and the Senate elected a new president.

It was little information to be equipped with when you walked out into the brawling streets of New Portsmouth on shore leave.

* * * * *

The town had an improvised look which was strange to Orsino. There was a sanitation reactor every hundred yards or so, but he mistrusted the look of the ground-level mains that led to it from, the houses. There were house flies from which he shied violently. Every other shack on the waterfront was a bar or a notch joint. He sampled the goods at one of the former and was shocked by the quality and price. He rolled out, his ears still ringing from the belt of raw booze; as half a dozen sweatered Guards rolled in, singing some esoteric song about their high morale and even higher venereal rate. A couple of them looked at him appraisingly, as though they wondered what kind of a noise he'd make if they jumped on his stomach real hard, and he hurried away from them.

The other entertainment facilities of the waterfront were flatly ruled out by a quick inspection of the wares. He didn't know what to make of them. Joints back in Syndic Territory if you were a man, made sense. You went to learn the ropes, or because you were afraid of getting mixed up in something intense when you didn't want to, or because you wanted a change, or because you were too busy, lazy or shy to chase skirts on your own. If you were a woman and not too particular, a couple of years in a joint left you with a considerable amount of money and some interesting memories which you were under no obligation to discuss with your husbands or husband.

But the sloppy beasts who called to him from the windows of the joints here on the waterfront, left him puzzled and disgusted. He reflected, strolling up Washington Street with eyes straight ahead, that women must be in short supply if they could make a living-or that the male citizens of the Government had no taste.

A whiff from one of those questionable sewer mains sent him reeling. He ducked into another saloon in self-defense and leaned groggily against the bar. A pretty brunette demanded: "What'll you have?"

"Gin, please." He peeled a ten off the roll Grinnel had given him. When the girl poured his gin he looked at her and found her fair. In all innocence, he asked her a question, as he might have asked a barmaid back home. She could have answered, "Yes," "No," "Maybe," or "What's in it for me?"

Instead she called him a lousy bastard, picked up a beer mug and was about to shatter it on his head when a hand caught her and a voice warned: "Hold it, Mabel! This guy's off my ship.

"He's just out of the States; he doesn't know any better. You know what it's like over there."

Mabel snarled: "You better wise him up, then, friend. He can't go around talking like that to decent women." She slapped down another glass, poured gin and flounced down the bar.

Charles gulped his gin and turned shakily to his deliverer, a little reactor specialist he had seen on the sub once or twice. "Thanks," he said feeling inadequate. "Maybe you better wise me up. All I said was, 'Darling, do you —'"

The reactor man held up his hand. "That's enough," he said. "You don't talk that way over here unless you want your scalp parted."

Charles, buzzing a little with the gin, protested hotly: "But what's the harm? All she had to say was no; I wasn't going to throw her down on the floor!"

It was all very confusing.

A shrug. "I heard about things in the States-Wyman, isn't it? I guess I didn't really believe it. You mean I could go up to any woman and just ask her how's about it?"

"Within reason, yes."

"And *do* they?"

"Some do, some don't—like here."

"Like hell, like here! Last liberty—" and the reactor man told him a long, confusing story about how he had picked up this pig, how she had dangled it in front of him for one solid week while he managed to spend three hundred and eighty-six dollars on her, and how finally she had bawled that she couldn't, she just hated herself but she couldn't do anything like *that* and bang went the door in his face, leaving him to finish out the evening in a notch joint.

"Good God!" Charles said, appalled. "Was she out of her mind?"

"No," the reactor man said glumly, "but I must have been. I should of got her drunk and raped her the first night."

Charles was fully conscious that values were different here. Choking down something like nausea, he asked carefully: "Is there much rape?"

The little man signalled for another gin and downed it. "I guess so. Once when I was a kid a dame gave me this line about her cousin raped her when she was little so she was frigid. I had more ambition then, so I said: 'Then this won't be anything new to you, baby,' I popped her on the button —"

"I've got to go now," Charles said, walking straight out of the saloon. He was beginning to understand the sloppy beasts in the windows of the notch joint and why men could bring themselves to settle for nothing better. He was also overwhelmed by a great wave of home sickness.

The ugly pattern was beginning to emerge. Prudery, rape, frigidity, intrigue for power-and assassination? Beyond the one hint, Grinnel had said nothing that affected Syndic Territory.

But nothing would be more logical than for this band of brigands to lust after the riches of the continent.

Back of the waterfront were shipfitting shops and living quarters. Work was being done by a puzzling combination of mechanization and musclepower. In one open shed he saw a lathe-hand turning a gunbarrel out of a forging; the lathe was driven by one of those standard 18-inch ehrenhaft rotors Max Wyman knew so well. But a vertical drillpress next to it-Orsino blinked. Two men, sweating and panting, were turning a stubborn vertical drum as tall as they were, and a belt drive from the drum whirled the drill bit as it sank into a hunk of bronze. The men were in rags, dirty rags. And it came to Orsino with a stunning shock when he realized what the dull, clanking things were that swung from their wrists. They were chained to the handles of the wheel.

He walked on, almost dazed, comprehending now some cryptic remarks that had been passed aboard the sub.

"No Frog has staying power. Give a Limey his beef once a day and he'll outsweat a Frog."

"Yeah, but you can't whip a Limey. They just go bad when you whip a Limey."

"They just get sullen for awhile. But let me tell you, friend, don't ever whip a Spig. You whip a Spig, he'll wait twenty years if he has to but he'll *get* you, right between the ribs."

"If a Spig wants to be boiled, I should worry."

It had been broken up in laughter.

Boiled! Could such things be?

Sixteen ragged, filth-crusted sub-humans were creeping down the road, each straining at a rope. An inch at a time, they were dragging a skid loaded with one huge turbine gear whose tiny herringbone teeth caught the afternoon sun.

The Government had reactors, the Government had vehicles-why this? He slowly realized that the Government's metal and machinery and atomic power went into its warships; that there was none left over for consumers, and the uses of peace. The Government had degenerated into a dawn-age monster, specialized all to teeth and claws and muscles to drive them with. The Government was now, whatever it had been, a graceless, humorless incarnate ferocity. Whatever lightness or joy survived was the meaningless vestigial twitching of an obsolete organ.

Somewhere a child began to bawl and Charles was surprised to feel a profound pity welling up in him. Like a sedentary man who after a workout aches in muscles he never knew he owned, Charles was discovering that he had emotions which had never been poignantly evoked by the bland passage of the hours in Syndic Territory.

Poor little bastard, he thought, growing up in this hellhole. I don't know what having slaves to kick around will do to you, but I don't see how you can grow up a human being. I don't know what fear of love will do to you-make you a cheat? Or a graceful rutting animal with a choice only between graceless rutting violence and a stinking scuffle with a flabby and abstracted stranger in a strange unloved room? We have our guns to play with and they're good toys, but I don't know what kind of monster you'll become when they give you a gun to live with and violence for a god.

Reiner was right, he thought unhappily. *We've got to do something about this mess.*

A man and a woman were struggling in an alley as he passed. Old habit almost made him walk on, but this wasn't the playful business of ripping clothes as practiced during hilarious moments in Mob Territory. It was a grim and silent struggle —

The man wore the sweater of the Guards. Nevertheless, Charles walked into the alley and tore him away from the woman; or rather, he yanked at the man's rock-like arm and the man, in surprise, let go of the woman and spun to face him.

"Beat it," Charles said to the woman, not looking around. He saw from the corner of his eye that she was staying right there.

The man's hand was on his sheath knife. He told Charles: "Get lost. Now. You don't mess with the Guards."

Charles felt his knees quivering, which was good. He knew from many a chukker of polo that it meant that he was strung to the breaking point, ready to explode into action. "Pull that knife," he said, "and the next thing you know you'll be eating it."

The man's face went dead calm and he pulled the knife and came in low, very fast. The knife was supposed to catch Charles in the middle. If Charles stepped inside it, the man would grab him in a bear hug and knife him in the back.

There was only one answer.

He caught the thick wrist from above with his left hand as the knife flashed toward his middle and shoved out. He felt the point catch and slice his cuff. The Guardsman tried a furious and ill-advised kick at his crotch; with his grip on the knife-hand, Charles toppled him into the filthy alley as he stood one-legged and off balance. He fell on his back, floundering, and for a black moment, Charles thought his weight was about to tear the wrist loose from his grip. The moment passed, and Charles put his right foot in the socket of the Guardsman's elbow, reinforced his tiring left hand with his right and leaned, doubling the man's forearm over the fulcrum of his boot. The man roared and dropped the knife. It had taken perhaps five seconds.

Charles said, panting: "I don't want to break your arm or kick your head in or anything like that. I just want you to go away and leave the woman alone." He was conscious of her, vaguely hovering in the background. He thought angrily: *She might at least get his knife.*

The Guardsman said thickly: "You give me the boot and I swear to God I'll find you and cut you to ribbons if it takes me the rest of my life."

Good, Charles thought. *Now he can tell himself he scared me. Good.* He let go of the forearm, straightened and took his foot from the man's elbow, stepping back. The Guardsman got up stiffly, flexing his arm, and stooped to pick up and sheath his knife without taking his eyes off Charles. Then he spat in the dust at Charles' feet. "Yellow crud," he said. "If the goddam crow was worth it, I'd cut your heart out." He walked off down the alley and Charles followed him with his eyes until he turned the corner into the street.

Then he turned, irritated that the woman had not spoken.

She was Lee Falcaro.

"Lee!" he said, thunderstruck. "What are you doing here?" It was the same face, feature for feature, and between her brows appeared the same double groove he had seen before. But she didn't know him.

"You know me?" she asked blankly. "Is that why you pulled that ape off me? I ought to thank you. But I can't place you at all. I don't know many people here. I've been ill, you know."

There was a difference apparent now. The voice was a little querulous. And Charles would have staked his life that never could Lee Falcaro have said in that slightly smug, slightly pro-prietary, slightly aren't-I-interesting tone: "I've been ill, you know."

"But what are you *doing* here? Damn it, don't you know me? I'm Charles Orsino!"

He realized then that he had made a horrible mistake.

"Orsino," she said. And then she spat: "*Orsino!* Of the *Syndic!*" There was black hatred in her eyes.

She turned and raced down the alley. He stood there stupidly, for almost a minute, and then ran after her, as far as the alley's mouth. She was gone. You could run almost anywhere in New Portsmouth in almost a minute.

A weedy little seaman wearing crossed quills on his cap was lounging against a building. He snickered at Charles. "Don't chase that one, sailor," he said. "She is the property of O.N.I."

"You know who she is?"

The yeoman happily spilled his inside dope to the fleet gob: "Lee Bennet. Smuggled over here couple months ago by D.A.R. The hottest thing that ever hit Naval Intelligence. Very small potato in the Syndic-knows all the families, who does what, who's a figurehead and who's a worker. Terrific! Inside stuff! Hates the Syndic. A gang of big-timers did her dirt."

"Thanks," Charles said, and wandered off down the street.

It wasn't surprising. He should have *expected* it.

Noblesse oblige.

Pride of the Falcaro line. She wouldn't send anybody into deadly peril unless she were ready to go herself.

Only somehow the trigger that would have snapped neurotic, synthetic Lee Bennet into Lee Falcaro hadn't worked.

He wandered on aimlessly, wondering whether it would be minutes or hours before he'd be picked up and executed as a spy.

PART II.

CHAPTER X.

It took minutes only.

He had headed back to the waterfront, afraid to run, with some vague notion of stealing a boat. Before he reached the row of saloons and joints, a smart-looking squad of eight tall men overtook him.

"Hold it, mister," a sergeant said. "Are you Orsino?"

"No," he said hopelessly. "That crazy woman began to yell at me that I was Orsino, but my name's Wyman. What's this about?"

The other men fell in beside and behind him. "We're stepping over to O.N.I.," the sergeant said.

"There's the son of a bitch!" somebody bawled. Suddenly there were a dozen sweatered Guardsmen around them. Their leader was the thug Orsino had beaten in a fair fight. He said silkily to the sergeant: "We want that boy, leatherneck. Blow."

* * * * *

The sergeant went pale. "He's wanted for questioning by the O.N.I.," he said stolidly.

"Get the marine three-striper!" the Guardsman chortled. He stuck his jaw into the sergeant's face. "Tell your squad to blow. You marines ought to know by now that you don't mess with the Guard."

A very junior officer appeared. "What's going on here, you men?" he shrilled. "Atten-*shun!*" He was ignored as Guardsman and marines measured one another with their eyes. "I said *attention!* Dammit, sergeant, *report!*" There was no reaction. The officer yelled: "You men may think you can get away with this but by God, you're wrong!" He strode away, his fists clenched and his face very red.

Orsino saw him stride through a gate into a lot marked *Bupers Motor Pool.* And he felt a sudden wave of communal understanding that there were only seconds to go. The sergeant played for time: "I'll be glad to surrender the prisoner," he started, "if you have anything to show in the way of —"

The Guardsman kicked for the pit of the sergeant's stomach. He was a sucker Orsino thought abstractedly as he saw the sergeant catch his foot, dump him and pivot to block another Guardsman. Then he was fighting for his life himself, against three bellowing Guardsmen.

A ripping, hammering noise filled the air suddenly. Like cold magic, it froze the milling mob where it stood. Fifty-caliber noise.

The jaygee was back, this time in a jeep with a twin fifty. And he was glaring down its barrels into the crowd. People were beginning to stream from the saloons, joints and shipfitting shops.

The jaygee cocked his cap rakishly over one eye. *"Fall in!"* he rasped, and a haunting air of familiarity came over Orsino.

The waiting jeep, almost bucking in its eagerness to be let loose-Orsino on the ground, knees trembling with tension —a perfect change of mount scene in a polo match. He reacted automatically.

There was a surrealist flash of the jaygee's face before he clipped him into the back of the square little truck. There was another flash of spectators scrambling as he roared the jeep down the road.

From then on it was just a question of hanging onto the wheel with one hand, trying to secure the free-traversing twin-fifty with the other, glancing back to see if the jaygee was still out, avoiding yapping dogs and pedestrians, staying on the rutted road, pushing all possible speed out of the jeep, noting landmarks, estimating the possibility of dangerous pursuit. For a two-goal polo player, a dull little practice session.

The road, such as it was, wound five miles inland through scrubby woodland and terminated at a lumber camp where chained men in rags were dragging logs.

Orsino back tracked a quarter-mile from the camp and jolted overland in a kidney-cracking hare and hounds course at fifty per.

The jeep took it for an hour in the fading afternoon light and then bucked to a halt. Orsino turned for an overdue check on the jaygee and found him conscious, but greenly clinging to the sides of the vehicle. But he saw Orsino staring and gamely struggled to his feet, standing in the truck bed. "You're under arrest, sailor," he said. "Striking an officer, abuse of government property, driving a government vehicle without a trip-ticket —" His legs betrayed him and he sat down, hard.

Orsino thought very briefly of letting him have a burst from the twin-fifty, and abandoned the idea.

He seemed to have bitched up everything so far, but he was still on a mission. He had a commissioned officer of the Government approximately in his power. He snapped: "Nonsense. *You're* under arrest."

The jaygee seemed to be reviewing rapidly any transgressions he may have committed, and asked at last, cautiously: "By what authority?"

"I represent the Syndic."

It was a block-buster. The jaygee stammered: "But you can't —But there isn't any way- But how —"

"Never mind how."

"You're crazy. You must be, or you wouldn't stop here. I don't believe you're from the continent and I don't believe the jeep's broken down." He was beginning to sound just a little hysterical. "It can't break down here. We must be more than thirty miles inland."

"What's special about thirty miles inland?"

"The natives, you fool!"

The natives again. "I'm not worried about natives. Not with a pair of fifties."

"You don't understand," the jaygee said, forcing calm into his voice. "This is The Outback. They're in charge here. We can't do a thing with them. They jump people in the dark and skewer them. Now fix this damn jeep and let's get rolling!"

"Into a firing squad? Don't be silly, lieutenant. I presume you won't slug me while I check the engine?"

The jaygee was looking around him. "My God, no," he said. "You may be a gangster, but —" He trailed off.

Orsino stiffened. Gangster was semi-dirty talk. "Listen, pirate," he said nastily, "I don't believe —"

"*Pirate?*" the jaygee roared indignantly, and then shut his mouth with a click, looking apprehensively about. The gesture wasn't faked; it alarmed Orsino.

"Tell me about your wildmen," he said.

"Go to hell," the jaygee said sulkily.

"Look, you called me a gangster first. What about these natives? You were trying to trick me, weren't you?"

"Kiss my royal North American eyeball, gangster."

"Don't be childish," Charles reproved him, feeling adult and superior. (The jaygee looked a couple of years younger than he.) He climbed out of his seat and lifted the hood. The damage was trivial; a shear pin in the transmission had given way. He reported mournfully: "Cracked block. The jeep's through forever. You can get on your way, lieutenant. I won't try to hold you."

The jaygee fumed: "You couldn't hold me if you wanted to, gangster. If you think I'm going to try and hoof back to the base alone in the dark, you're crazy. We're sticking together. Two of us may be able to hold them off for the night. In the morning, we'll see."

Well, maybe the officer did *believe* there were wildmen in the woods. That didn't mean there *were.*

The jaygee got out and looked under the hood uncertainly. It was obvious that in the first place he was no mechanic and in the second place he couldn't conceive of anybody voluntarily risking the woods rather than the naval base. "Uh-huh," he said. "Dismount that gun while I get a fire started."

"Yes, sir," Charles said sardonically, saluting. The jaygee absently returned the salute and began to collect twigs.

Orsino asked: "How do these aborigines of yours operate?"

"Sneak up in the dark. They have spears and a few stolen guns. Usually they don't have cartridges for them but you can't count on that. But they have ...witches."

Orsino snorted. He was getting very hungry indeed. "Do you know any of the local plants we might eat?"

The jaygee said confidently: "I guess we can get by on roots until morning."

Orsino dubiously pulled up a shrub, dabbed clods off its root and tasted it. It tasted exactly like a root. He sighed and changed the subject. "What do we do with the fifties when I get them both off the mount?"

"The jeep mount breaks down some damn way or other into two low-mount tripods. See if you can figure it out while I get the fire going."

The jaygee had a small, smoky fire barely going in twenty minutes. Orsino was still struggling with the jeep gun mount. It came apart, but it couldn't go together again. The jaygee strolled over at last contemptuously to lend a hand. He couldn't make it work either.

Two lost tempers and four split fingernails later it developed the "elevating screw" really held the two front legs on and that you elevated by adjusting the rear tripod leg. "A hell of an officer you are," Orsino sulked.

It began to rain, putting the fire out with a hiss. They wound up prone under the jeep, not on speaking terms, each tending a gun, each presumably responsible for 180 degrees of perimeter.

* * * * *

Charles was fairly dry, except for a trickle of icy water following a contour that meandered to his left knee. After an hour of eye-straining —nothing to be seen-and ear-straining —only the patter of rain-he heard a snore and kicked the jaygee.

The jaygee cursed wearily and said: "I guess we'd better talk to keep awake."

"*I'm* not having any trouble, pirate."

"Oh, knock it off-where do you get that pirate bit, gangster?"

"You're outlaws, aren't you?"

"Like hell we are. *You're* the outlaws. You rebelled against the lawfully constituted North American Government. Just because you won-for the time being-doesn't mean you were right."

"The fact that we won does mean that we were right. The fact that your so-called Government lives by raiding and scavenging off us means you were wrong. God, the things I've seen since I joined up with you thugs!"

"I'll bet. Respect for the home, sanctity of marriage, sexual morality, law and order-you never saw anything like that back home, did you gangster?" He looked very smug.

Orsino clenched his teeth. "Somebody's been telling you a pack of lies," he said. "There's just as much home and family life and morality and order back in Syndic Territory as there is here. And probably a lot more."

"Bull. I've seen intelligence reports; I know how you people live. Are you telling me you don't have sexual promiscuity? Polygamy? Polyandry? Open gambling? Uncontrolled liquor trade? Corruption and shakedowns?"

Orsino squinted along the barrel of the gun into the rain. "Look," he said, "take me as an average young man from Syndic Territory. I know maybe a hundred people. I know just three women and two men who are what you'd call promiscuous. I know one family with two wives and one husband. I don't really know any people personally who go in for polyandry, but I've met three casually. And the rest are ordinary middle-aged couples."

"Ah-*hah*! Middle-aged! Do you mean to tell me you're just leaving out anybody under middle age when you talk about morality?"

"Naturally," Charles said, baffled. "Wouldn't you?"

The only answer was a snort.

"What are bupers?" Charles asked.

"Bu-Pers," the jaygee said distinctly. "Bureau of Personnel, North American Navy."

"What do you do there?"

"What *would* a personnel bureau do?" the jaygee said patiently. "We recruit, classify, assign, promote and train personnel."

"Paperwork, huh? No wonder you don't know how to shoot or drive."

"If I didn't need you to cover my back, I'd shove this MG down your silly throat. For your information, gangster, all officers do a tour of duty on paperwork before they're assigned to their permanent branch. I'm going into the pigboats."

"Why?"

"Family. My father commands a sub. He's Captain Van Dellen."

Oh, God. Van Dellen. The sub commander Grinnel-and he-had murdered. The kid hadn't heard yet that his father had been "lost" in an emergency dive.

* * * * *

The rain ceased to fall; the pattering drizzle gave way to irregular, splashing drops from leaves and branches.

"Van Dellen," Charles said. "There's something you ought to know."

"It'll keep," the jaygee answered in a grim whisper. The bolt of his gun clicked. "I hear them out there."

CHAPTER XI.

She felt the power of the goddess working in her, but feebly. Dark ...so dark ...and so tired ... how old was she? More than eight hundred moons had waxed and waned above her head since birth. And she had run at the head of her spearmen to the motor sounds. A motor meant the smithymen from the sea, and you killed smithymen when you could.

She let out a short shrill chuckle in the dark. There was a rustling of branches. One of the spearmen had turned to stare at the sound. She knew his face was worried. "Tend to business, you fool!" she wheezed. "Or by Bridget —" His breath went in with a hiss and she chuckled again. You had to let them know who was the cook and who was the potatoes every now and then. Kill the fool? Not now; not when there were smithymen with guns waiting to be taken.

The power of the goddess worked stronger in her withered breast as her rage grew at their impudence. Coming into *her* woods with their stinking metal!

There were two of them. A grin slit her face. She had not taken two smithymen together for thirty moons. For all her wrinkles and creaks, what a fine vessel she was for the power, to be sure! Her worthless, slow-to-learn niece could run and jump and she had a certain air, but she'd never be such a vessel. Her sister-the crone spat-these were degenerate days. In the old days, the sister would have been spitted when she refused the ordeal in her youth. The little one now, whatever her name was, she would make a *fine* vessel for the power when she was gathered to the goddess. If her sister or her niece didn't hold her head under water too long, or have a spear shoved too deep into her gut or hit her on the head with too heavy a rock.

These were degenerate days. She had poisoned her own mother to become the vessel of power.

The spearmen to her right and left shifted uneasily. She heard a faint mumble of the two smithymen talking. Let them talk! Doubtless they were cursing the goddess obscenely; doubtless that was what the smithymen all did when their mouths were not stuffed with food.

She thought of the man called Kennedy who forged spearheads and arrowpoints for her people-he was a strange one, touched by the goddess, which proved her infinite power. She could touch and turn the head of even a smithyman. He was a strange one. Well now, to get on with it. She wished the power were working stronger in her; she was tired and could hardly see. But by the grace of the goddess there would be two new heads over her holy hut come dawn. She could hardly see, but the goddess wouldn't fail her....

She quavered like a screech-owl, and the spearmen began to slip forward through the brush. She was not allowed to eat honey lest its sweetness clash with the power in her, but the taste of power was sweeter than the taste of honey.

* * * * *

With frightful suddenness there was an ear-splitting shriek and a trampling rush of feet. By sheer reflex, Orsino clamped down on the trigger of his fifty, and his brain rocked at its thunder. Shadowy figures were blotted out by the orange muzzle-flash. You're supposed to fire neat, spaced bursts of eight he told himself. I wonder what old Gilby would say if he could see his star pupil burning out a barrel and swinging his gun like a fire hose?

The gun stopped firing; end of the belt. Twenty, fifty or a hundred rounds? He didn't remember. He clawed for another belt and smoothly, in the dark, loaded again and listened.

"You all right, gangster?" the jaygee said behind him, making him jump.

"Yes," he said. "Will they come back?"

"I don't know."

"You filthy swine," an agonized voice wheezed from the darkness. "Me back is broke, you stinking lice." The voice began to sob.

They listened to it in silence for perhaps a minute. At last he said to the jaygee: "If the rest are gone maybe we can at least-make him comfortable."

"Too risky," the jaygee said after a long pause.

The sobbing went on. As the excitement of the attack drained from Orsino, he felt deathly tired, cramped and thirsty. The thirst he could do something about. He scooped water from the muddy runnel by his knee and sucked it from his palms twice. The third time, he thought of the thirst that the sobbing creature out in the dark must be feeling, and his hand wouldn't go to his mouth.

"I'm going to get him," he whispered to the jaygee.

"Stay where you are! That's an order!"

He didn't answer, but began to work his cramped and aching body from under the jeep. The jaygee, a couple of years younger and lither than he, slid out first from his own side. Orsino sighed and relaxed as he heard his footsteps cautiously circle the jeep.

"Finish me off!" the wounded man was sobbing. "For the love of the goddess, finish me off, you bitches' bastards! You've broke me back —*ah!*" That was a cry of savage delight.

There was a strangled noise from the jaygee and then only a soft, deadly thrashing noise from the dark. Hell, Orsino thought bitterly. It was my idea. He snaked out from under the jeep and raced through wet brush.

The two of them were a tangled knot of darkness rolling on the ground. A naked back came uppermost; Orsino fell on it and clawed at its head. He felt a huge beard, took two hand-fulls of it and pulled as hard as he could. There was a wild screech and a flailing of arms. The jaygee broke away and stood up, panting hoarsely. Charles heard a sharp crunch and a snap, and the flailing sweaty figure, beneath him lay still.

"Back to the guns," the jaygee choked. He swayed, and Orsino took him by the arm....On the way back to the jeep, they stumbled over something that was certainly a body.

Orsino's flesh shrank from lying down again in the mud behind his gun, but he did, shivering. He heard the jaygee thud wearily into position. "What did you do to him?" he asked. "Is he dead?"

"Kicked him," the jaygee choked. "His head snapped back and there was that crack. I guess he's dead. I never heard of that broken-wing trick before. I guess he wanted to take one more with him. They have a kind of religion."

The jaygee sounded as though he was teetering on the edge of breakdown. Make him mad, intuition said to Orsino. He might go howling off among the trees unless he snaps out of it.

"It's a hell of way to run an island," he said nastily. "You beggars were chased out of North America because you couldn't run it right and now you can't even control a lousy little island for more than five miles inland." He added with deliberate, superior amusement: "Of course, they've got witches."

"Shut your mouth, gangster —*I'm warning you.*" The note of hysteria was still there. And then the jaygee said dully: "I didn't mean that. I'm sorry. You did come out and help me after all."

"Surprised?"

"Yes. Twice. First time when you wanted to go out yourself. I suppose you can't help being born where you were. Maybe if you came over to us all the way, the Government would forgive and forget. But no —I suppose not." He paused, obviously casting about for a change of subject. He still seemed sublimely confident that they'd get back to the naval base with him in charge of the detail. "What ship did you cross in?"

"Atom sub *Taft*," Orsino said. He could have bitten his tongue out.

"*Taft?* That's my father's pigboat! Captain Van Dellen. How is he? I was going down to the dock when —"

"He's dead," Orsino said flatly. "He was caught on deck during an emergency dive."

The jaygee said nothing for a while and then uttered an unconvincing laugh of disbelief. "You're lying," he said. "His crew'd never let that happen. They'd let the ship be blown to hell before they took her down without the skipper."

"Grinnel had the con. He ordered the dive and roared down the crew when they wanted to get your father inboard. I'm sorry."

"Grinnel," the jaygee whispered. "Grinnel. Yes, I know Commander Grinnel. He's —he's a good officer. He must have done it because he had to. Tell me about it, please."

It was more than Orsino could bear. "Your father was murdered," he said harshly. "I know because Grinnel put me on radar watch-and I don't know a God-damned thing about reading a radarscope. He told me to sing out 'enemy planes' and I did because I didn't know what the hell was going on. He used that as an excuse to crash-dive while your father was sleeping on deck. Your good officer murdered him."

He heard the jaygee sobbing hoarsely. At last he asked Orsino in a dry, choked voice: "Politics?"

"Politics," Orsino said.

Orsino jumped wildly as the jaygee's machine gun began to roar a long burst of twenty, but he didn't fire himself. He knew that there was no enemy out there in the dark, and that the bullets were aimed only at an absent phantom.

"We've got to get to Iceland," the jaygee said at last, soberly. "It's our only chance."

"Iceland?"

"This is one for the C.C. of the Constitutionists. The Central Committee. It's a breach of the Freiberg Compromise. It means we call the Sociocrats, and if they don't make full restitution-war."

"What do you mean, *we?*"

"You and I. You're the source of the story; you're the one who'd be lie-tested."

You've got him, Orsino told himself, but don't be fool enough to count on it. He's been light-headed from hunger and no sleep and the shock of his father's death. You helped him in a death struggle and there's team spirit working on him. The guy covering my back, how can I fail to trust him, how could I dare not to trust him? But don't be fool enough to count on it after he's slept. Meanwhile, push it for all it's worth.

"What are your plans?" he asked gravely.

"We've got to slip out of Ireland by sub or plane," the jaygee brooded. "We can't go to the New Portsmouth or Com-Surf organizations; they're Sociocrat, and Grinnel will have passed the word to the Sociocrats that you're out of control."

"What does that mean?"

"Death," the jaygee said.

Commander Grinnel, after reporting formally, had gone straight to a joint. It wasn't until midnight that he got The Word, from a friendly O.N.I. lieutenant who had dropped into the house.

"What?" Grinnel roared. "Who is this woman? Where is she? Take me to her at once!"

"Commander!" the lieutenant said aghast. "I just got here!"

"You heard me, mister! At once!"

While Grinnel dressed he demanded particulars. The lieutenant dutifully scoured his memory. "Brought in on some cloak-and-dagger deal, Commander. The kind you usually run. Lieutenant-Commander Jacobi was in Syndic Territory on a recruiting, sabotage and reconnaissance mission and one of the D.A.R. passed the girl on him. A real Syndic member. Priceless. And, as I said, she identified this fellow as Charles Orsino, another Syndic. Why are you so interested, if I may ask?"

The Commander dearly wanted to give him a grim: "You may not," but didn't dare. Now was the time to be frank and open. One hint that he had anything to hide or cover up would put his throat to the knife. "The man's my baby, lieutenant," he said. "Either your girl's mistaken or Van Dellen and his polygraph tech and I were taken in by a brand-new technique." *That* was nice work, he congratulated himself. Got in Van Dellen and the tech....Maybe, come to think of it, the tech *was* crooked? No; there was the way Wyman had responded perfectly under scop.

O.N.I.'s building was two stories and an attic, wood-framed, beginning to rot already in the eternal Irish damp.

"We've got her on the third floor, Commander," the lieutenant said. "You get there by a ladder."

"In God's name, why?" They walked past the Charge of Quarters, who snapped to a guilty and belated attention, and through the deserted offices of the first and second floors.

"Frankly, we've had a little trouble hanging on to her."

"She runs away?"

"No, nothing like that-not yet, at least. Marine G-2 and Guard Intelligence School have both tried to snatch her from us. First with requisitions, then with muscle. We hope to keep her until the word gets to Iceland. Then, naturally, *we'll* be out in the cold."

The lieutenant laughed. Grinnel, puffing up the ladder, did not.

The door and lock on Lee Bennet's quarters were impressive. The lieutenant rapped. "Are you awake, Lee? There's an officer here who wants to talk to you."

"Come in," she said.

The lieutenant's hands flew over the lock and the door sprang open. The girl was sitting in the dark.

"I'm Commander Grinnel, my dear," he said. After eight hours in the joint, he could feel authentically fatherly to her. "If the time isn't quite convenient —"

"It's all right," she said listlessly. "What do you want to know?"

"The man you identify as Orsino-it was quite a shock to me. Commander Van Dellen, who died a hero's death only days ago accepted him as authentic and so, I must admit, did I. He passed both scop and polygraph."

"I can't help that," she said. "He came right up to me and told me who he was. I recognized him, of course. He's a polo player. I've seen him play on Long Island often enough, the damned snob. He's not much in the Syndic, but he's close to F. W. Taylor. Orsino's an orphan. I don't know whether Taylor's actually adopted him or not. I think not."

"No-possible-mistake?"

"No possible mistake." She began to tremble. "My God, Commander Whoever-You-Are, do you think I could forget one of those damned sneering faces. Or what those people did to me? Get the lie detector again! Strap me into the lie detector! I insist on it! I won't be called a liar! Do you hear me? Get the lie detector!"

"Please," the Commander soothed. "I do believe you, my dear. Nobody could doubt your sincerity. Thank you for helping us, and good night." He backed out of the room with the lieutenant. As the door closed he snapped at him: "Well, mister?"

The lieutenant shrugged. "The lie detector always bears her out. We've stopped using it on her. We're convinced that she's on our side. Almost deserving of citizenship."

"Come, now," the Commander said. "You know better than that."

Behind the locked door, Lee Bennet had thrown herself on the bed, dry-eyed. She wished she could cry, but tears never came. Not since those three roistering drunkards had demonstrated their virility as males and their immunity as Syndics on her ... she couldn't cry any more.

Charles Orsino-another one of them. She hoped they caught him and killed him, slowly. She knew all this was true. Then why did she feel like a murderess? Why did she think incessantly of suicide? Why, why, why?

* * * * *

Dawn came imperceptibly. First Charles could discern the outline of treetops against the sky and then a little of the terrain before him and at last two twisted shadows that slowly became sprawling half-naked bodies. One of them was a woman's, mangled by fifty-caliber slugs. The other was the body of a bearded giant-the one with whom they had struggled in the dark.

Charles crawled out stiffly. The woman was-had been —a stringy, white haired crone. Some animal's skull was tied to her pate with sinews as a head-dress, and she was tattooed with blue crescents. The jaygee joined him standing over her and said: "One of their witches. Part of the religion, if you can call it that."

"A brand-new religion?" Charles asked dubiously. "Made up out of whole cloth?"

"No," the jaygee said. "I understand it's an *old* religion-pre-Christian. It kept going underground until the Troubles. Then it flared up again all over Europe. A filthy business. Animal sacrifices every new moon. Human sacrifices twice a year. What can you expect from people like that?"

Charles reminded himself that the jaygee's fellow-citizens boiled recalcitrant slaves. "I'll see what I can do about the jeep," he said.

The jaygee sat down on the wet grass. "What the hell's the use?" he mumbled wearily. "Even if you get it running again. Even if we get back to the base. They'll be gunning for you. Maybe they'll be gunning for me if they killed my father." He tried to smile. "You got any aces in the hole, gangster?"

"Maybe," Orsino said slowly. "What do you know about a woman named Lee-Bennet? Works with O.N.I.?"

"Smuggled over here by the D.A.R. A goldmine of information. She's a little nuts, too. What have you got on her?"

"Does she swing any weight? *Is she a citizen?*"

"No weight. They're just using her over at Intelligence to fill out the picture of the Syndic. And she couldn't be a citizen. A woman has to marry a citizen to be naturalized. What have you got to do with her, for God's sake? Did you know her on the other side? She's death to the Syndic; she can't do anything for you."

Charles barely heard him. That had to be it. The trigger on Lee Falcaro's conditioning had to be the oath of citizenship as it was for his. And it hadn't been tripped because this pirate gang didn't particularly want or need women as first-class, all-privileges citizens. A small part of the Government's cultural complex-but one that could trap Lee Falcaro forever in the shell of her synthetic substitute for a personality. Lie-tests, yes. Scopolamine, yes. But for a woman, no subsequent oath.

"I ran into her in New Portsmouth. She knew me from the other side. She turned me in...." He knelt at a puddle and drank thirstily; the water eased hunger cramps a little. "I'll see what I can do with the jeep."

He lifted the hood and stole a look at the jaygee. Van Dellen was dropping off to sleep on the wet grass. Charles pried a shear pin from the jeep's winch, punched out the shear pin that had given way in the transmission and replaced it. It involved some hammering. Cracked block, he thought contemptuously. An officer and he couldn't tell whether the block was cracked or not. If I ever get out of this we'll sweep them from the face of the earth-or more likely just get rid of their tom-fool Sociocrats and Constitutionists. The rest are probably all right. Except maybe for those bastards of Guardsmen. A bad lot. Let's hope they get killed in the fighting.

The small of his back tickled; he reached around to scratch it and felt cold metal.

"Turn slowly or you'll be spitted like a pig," a bass voice growled.

He turned slowly. The cold metal now at his chest, was the leaf-shaped blade of a spear. It was wielded by a red-haired, red-bearded, barrel-chested giant whose blue-green eyes were as cold as death.

"Tie that one," somebody said. Another half-naked man jerked his wrists behind him and lashed them together with cords.

"Hobble his feet." It was a woman's voice. A length of cord or sinew was knotted to his ankles with a foot or two of play. He could walk but not run. The giant lowered his spear and stepped aside.

The first thing Charles saw was that Lieutenant (j.g.) Van Dellen of the North American Navy had escaped forever from his doubts and confusions. They had skewered him to the turf while he slept. Charles hoped he had not felt the blow.

The second thing he saw was a supple and coltish girl of perhaps 20 tenderly removing the animal skull from the head of the slain witch and knotting it to her own red-tressed head. Even to Orsino's numbed understanding, it was clearly an act of the highest significance. It subtly changed the composition of the six-men group in the little glade. They had been a small mob until she put on the skull, but the moment she did they moved instinctively-one a step or two, the other merely turning a bit, perhaps-to orient on her. There was no doubt that she was in charge.

A witch, Orsino thought. "It kept going underground until the Troubles." "A filthy business-human sacrifices twice a year."

She approached him and, like the shifting of a kaleidoscope, the group fell into a new pattern of which she was still the focus. Charles thought he had never seen a face so humorlessly conscious of power. The petty ruler of a few barbarians, she carried herself as though she were empress of the universe. Nor did a large gray louse that crawled from her hairline across her forehead and back again affect her in the slightest. She wore a greasy animal hide as though it were royal purple. It added up to either insanity or a limitless pretension to religious authority. And her eyes were not mad.

"You," she said coldly. "What about the jeep and the guns? Do they go?"

He laughed suddenly and idiotically at these words from the mouth of a stone-age goddess. A raised spear sobered him instantly. "Yes," he said.

"Show my men how," she said, and squatted regally on the turf.

"Please," he said, "could I have something to eat first?"

She nodded indifferently and one of the men loped off into the brush.

* * * * *

His hands untied and his face greasy with venison fat, Charles spent the daylight hours instructing six savages in the nomenclature, maintenance and operation of the jeep and the twin-fifty machine gun.

They absorbed it with utter lack of curiosity. They more or less learned to start and steer and stop the jeep. They more or less learned to load, point and fire the gun.

Through the lessons the girl sat absolutely motionless, first in shadow, then in noon and afternoon sun and then in shadow again. But she had been listening. She said at last: "You are telling them nothing new now. Is there no more?"

Charles noted that a spear was poised at his ribs. "A great deal more," he said hastily. "It takes months."

"They can work them now. What more is there to learn?"

"Well, what to do if something goes wrong."

She said, as though speaking from vast experience: "When something goes wrong, you start over again. That is all you can do. When I make death-wine for the spear blades and the death-wine does not kill, it is because something went wrong —a word or a sign or picking a plant at the wrong time. The only thing to do is make the poison again. As you grow in experience you make fewer mistakes. That is how it will be with my men when they work the jeep and the guns."

She nodded ever so slightly at one of the men and he took a firmer grip on his spear.

Death swooped low.

"No!" Charles exploded. "You don't understand! This isn't like anything you do at all!" He was sweating, even in the late afternoon chill. "You've got to have somebody who knows how to repair the jeep and the gun. If they're busted they're busted and no amount of starting over again will make them work!"

She nodded and said: "Tie his hands. We'll take him with us." Charles was torn between relief and wonder at the way she spoke. He realized that he had never, literally *never*, seen any person concede a point in quite that fashion. There had been no hesitation, there had been no reluctance in the voice, not a flicker of displeasure in the face. Simply, without forcing, she had said: "We'll take him with us." It was as though-as though she had re-made the immediate past, un-making her opposition to the idea, nullifying it. She was a person who was not at war with herself in any respect whatever, a person who knew exactly who she was and what she was —

The girl rose in a single flowing motion, startling after her day spent in immobility. She led the way, flanked by two of the spearmen. The other four followed in the jeep, at a crawl. Last of all came Charles, and nobody had to urge him. In his portable trap his hours would be numbered if he got separated from his captors.

Stick with them, he told himself, stumbling through the brush. Just stay alive and you can outsmart these savages. He fell, cursed, picked himself up, stumbled on after the growl of the jeep.

Dawn brought them to a collection of mud-and-wattle huts, a corral enclosing a few dozen head of wretched diseased cattle, a few adults and a few children. The girl was still clear-eyed and supple in her movements. Her spearmen yawned and stretched stiffly. Charles was a walking dead man, battered by countless trees and stumbles on the long trek. With red and swollen eyes he watched while half-naked brats swarmed over the jeep and grownups made obeisances to the girl-all but one.

This was an evil-faced harridan who said to her with cool insolence: "I see you claim the power of the goddess now, my dear. Has something happened to my sister?"

"The guns killed a certain person. I put on the skull. You know what I am; do not say 'claim to be.' I warn you once."

"Liar!" shrieked the harridan. "You killed her and stole the skull! St. Patrick and St. Bridget shrivel your guts! Abaddon and Lucifer pierce your eyes!"

An arena formed about them as the girl said coldly: "I warn you the second time."

The harridan made signs with her fingers, glaring at her; there was a moan from the watchers; some turned aside and a half-grown girl fainted dead away.

The girl with the skull on her pate said, as though speaking from a million years and a million miles away: "This is the third warning; there are no more. Now the worm is in your backbone gnawing. Now the maggots are at your eyes, devouring them. Your bowels turn to water; your heart pounds like the heart of a bird; soon it will not beat at all." As the eerie, space-filling whisper drilled on the watchers broke and ran, holding their hands over their ears, white-faced, but the harridan stood as if rooted to the earth. Charles listened dully as the curse was droned, nor was he surprised when the harridan fell, blasted by it. Another sorceress, aided it is true by pentothal, had months ago done the same to him.

The people trickled back, muttering and abject.

Just stay alive and you can outsmart these savages, he repeated ironically to himself. It had dawned on him that these savages lived by an obscure and complicated code harder to master than the intricacies of the Syndic or the Government.

A kick roused him to his feet. One of the spearmen grunted: "I'm putting you with Kennedy."

"All right," Charles groaned. "You take these cords off me?"

"Later." He prodded Charles to a minute, ugly block house of logs from which came smoke and an irregular metallic clanging. He cut the cords, rolled great boulders away from a crawl-hole and shoved him through.

The place was about six by nine feet, hemmed in by ten-inch logs. The light was very bad and the smell was too. A few loopholes let in some air. There was a latrine pit and an open stone hearth and a naked brown man with wild hair and a beard.

Rubbing his wrists, Charles asked uncertainly: "Are you Kennedy?"

The man looked up and croaked: "Are you from the Government?"

"Yes," Charles said, hope rekindling. "Thank God they put us together. There's a jeep. Also a twin-fifty. If we play this right the two of us can bust out —"

He stopped, disconcerted. Kennedy had turned to the hearth and the small, fierce fire glowing on it and began to pound a red-hot lump of metal. There were spear heads and arrow heads about in various stages of completion, as well as files and a hone.

"What's the matter?" he demanded. "Aren't you interested?"

"Of course I'm interested," Kennedy said. "But we've got to begin at the beginning. You're too *general*." His voice was mild, but reproving.

"You're right," Charles said. "I guess you've made a try or two yourself. But now that there are two of us, what do you suggest? Can you drive a jeep? Can you fire a twin-fifty?"

The man poked the lump of metal into the heart of the fire again, picked up a black-scaled spear head and began to file an edge into it. "Let's get down to essentials," he suggested apologetically. "What is escape? Getting from an undesirable place to a desirable place, opposing and neutralizing things or persons adverse to the change of state in the process. But I'm not being specific, am I? Let's say, then, escape is getting *us* from a relatively undesirable place to a relatively desirable place, opposing and neutralizing the aborigines." He put aside the file and reached for the hone, sleeking it along the bright metal ribbon of the new edge. He looked up with a pleased smile and asked: "How's that for a plan?"

"Fine," Charles muttered. Kennedy beamed proudly as he repeated: "Fine, fine," and sank to the ground, born down by the almost physical weight of his depression. His hoped-for ally was stark mad.

CHAPTER XIII.

Kennedy turned out to have been an armorer-artificer of the North American Navy, captured two years ago while deer-hunting too far from the logging-camp road to New Portsmouth. Fed on scraps of gristle, isolated from his kind, beaten when he failed to make his daily task of spear heads and arrow points, he had shyly retreated into beautifully interminable labyrinths of abstraction. Now and then, Charles Orsino got a word or two of sense from him before the rosy clouds closed in. When attempted conversation with the lunatic palled, Charles could watch the aborigines through chinks in the palisade. There were about fifty of them. There would have been more if they hadn't been given to infanticide-for what reason, Charles could not guess.

He had been there a week when the boulders were rolled away one morning and he was roughly called out. He said to Kennedy before stooping to crawl through the hole: "Take it easy, friend. I'll be back, I hope."

Kennedy looked up with a puzzled smile: "That's such a *general* statement, Charles. Exactly what are you implying —"

The witch girl was there, flanked by spearmen. She said abruptly: "I have been listening to you. Why are you untrue to your brothers?"

He gawked. The only thing that seemed to fit was: "That's such a *general* statement," but he didn't say it.

"Answer," one of the spearmen growled.

"I —I don't understand. I have no brothers."

"Your brothers in Portsmouth, on the sea. Whatever you call them, they are your brothers, all children of the mother called Government. Why are you untrue to them?"

He began to understand. "They aren't my brothers. I'm not a child of the government. I'm a child of another mother far away, called Syndic."

She looked puzzled-and almost human-for an instant. Then the visor dropped over her face again as she said: "That is true. Now you must teach a certain person the jeep and the guns. Teach her well. See that she gets her hands on the metal and into the grease." To a spearman she said: "Bring Martha."

The spearman brought Martha, who was trying not to cry. She was a half-naked child of ten!

The witch girl abruptly left them. Her guards took Martha and bewildered Charles to the edge of the village where the jeep and its mounted guns stood behind a silly little museum exhibit rope of vine. Feathers and bones were knotted into the vine. The spearmen treated it as though it were a high-tension transmission line.

"*You* break it," one of them said to Charles. He did, and the spearmen sighed with relief. Martha stopped scowling and stared.

The spearman said to Charles: "Go ahead and teach her. The firing pins are out of the guns, and if you try to start the jeep you get a spear through you. Now teach her." He and the rest squatted on the turf around the jeep. The little girl shied violently as he took her hand, and tried to run away. One of the spearmen slung her back into the circle. She brushed against the jeep and froze, white-faced.

"Martha," Charles said patiently, "there's nothing to be afraid of. The guns won't go off and the jeep won't move. I'll teach you how to work them so you can kill everybody you don't like with the guns and go faster than a deer in the jeep —"

He was talking into empty air as far as the child was concerned. She was muttering, staring at the arm that had brushed the jeep: "That did it, I guess. There goes the power. May the goddess blast her-no. The power's out of me now. I felt it go." She looked up at Charles, quite calmly, and said: "Go on. Show me all about it. Do a good job."

"Martha, what are you talking about?"

"She was afraid of me, my sister, so she's robbing me of the power. Don't you know? I guess not. The goddess hates iron and machines. I had the power of the goddess in me, but it's gone now; I felt it go. Now nobody'll be afraid of me any more." Her face contorted and she said: "Show me how you work the guns."

* * * * *

He taught her what he could while the circle of spearmen looked on and grinned, cracking raw jokes about the child as anybody anywhere, would about a tyrant deposed. She pretended to ignore them, grimly repeating names after him and imitating his practiced movements in loading drill. She was very bright, Charles realized. When he got a chance he muttered, "I'm sorry about this, Martha. It isn't my idea."

She whispered bleakly: "I know. I liked you. I was sorry when the other outsider took your dinner." She began to sob uncontrollably. "I'll never see anything again! Nobody'll ever be afraid of me again!" She buried her face against Charles' shoulder.

He smoothed her tangled hair mechanically and said to the watching, grinning circle: "Look, hasn't this gone far enough? Haven't you got what you wanted?"

The headman stretched and spat. "Guess so," he said. "Come on, girl." He yanked Martha from the seat and booted her toward the huts.

Charles scrambled down just ahead of a spear. He let himself be led back to the smithy block house and shoved through the crawl hole.

"I was thinking about what you said the other day," Kennedy beamed, rasping a file over an arrowhead. "When I said that to change one molecule in the past you'd have to change *every* molecule in the past, and you said, 'Maybe so.' I've figured that what you were driving at was —"

"Kennedy," Charles said, "please shut up just this once. I've got to think."

"In what sense do you mean that, Charles? Do you mean that you're a rational animal and therefore that your *being* rather than *essense* is —"

"*Shut up or I'll pick up a rock and bust your head in with it!*" Charles roared. He more than half meant it. Kennedy hunched down before his hearth looking offended and scared. Charles squatted with his head in his hands.

I have been listening to you.

Repeated drives of the Government to wipe out the aborigines. Drives that never succeeded.

I'll never see anything again.

The way the witch girl had blasted her rival-but that was suggestion. But —

I have been listening to you. Why are you untrue to your brothers?

He'd said nothing like that to anybody, not to her or poor Kennedy.

He thought vaguely of *psi* force, a fragment in his memory. An old superstition, like the id-ego-superego triad of the sick-minded psychologists. Like vectors of the mind, exploded nonsense. But —

I have been listening to you. Why are you untrue to your brothers?

Charles smacked one fist against the sand floor in impotent rage. He was going as crazy as Kennedy. Did the witch girl-and Martha-have hereditary *psi* power? He mocked himself savagely: that's such a *general* question!

Neurotic adolescent girls in kerosene-lit farmhouses, he thought vaguely. Things that go bump-and crash and blooie and *whoo-oo-oo!* in the night. Not in electric lit city apartments. Not around fleshed-up middle-aged men and women. You take a hyperthyroid virgin, isolate her from power machinery and electric fields, put on the pressures that make her feel alone and tense to the bursting point-and naturally enough, something bursts. A chamberpot sails from under the bed and shatters on the skull of stepfather-tyrant. The wide-gilt-framed portrait of thundergod-grandfather falls with a crash. Sure, the nail crystallized and broke —*who crystallized it?*

Neurotic adolescent girls speaking in tongues, reading face-down cards and closed books, screaming aloud when sister or mother dies in a railroad wreck fifty miles away, of cancer a hundred miles away, in a bombing overseas.

Sometimes they made saints of them. Sometimes they burned them. Burned them and *then* made saints of them.

A blood-raw hunk of venison came sailing through one of the loopholes and flopped on the sand.

I was sorry when the other outsider took your dinner.

Three days ago he'd dozed off while Kennedy broiled the meat over the hearth. When he woke, Kennedy had gobbled it all and was whimpering with apprehension. But he'd done nothing and said nothing; the man wasn't responsible. He'd said nothing, and yet somehow the child knew about it.

His days were numbered; soon enough the jeep would be out of gas and the guns would be out of ammo or an unreplaceable part lost or broken. Then, according to the serene logic that ruled the witch girl, he'd be surplus.

But there was a key to it somehow.

He got up and slapped Kennedy's hand away from the venison. "Naughty," he said, and divided it equally with a broad spearblade.

"Naughty," Kennedy said morosely. "The naught-class, the null-class. I'm the null-class. I plus the universe equal one, the universe-class. If you could transpose-but you can't transpose." Silently they toasted their venison over the fire.

* * * * *

It was a moonless night with one great planet, Jupiter he supposed, reigning over the star-powdered sky. Kennedy slept muttering feebly in a corner. The hearthfire was out. It had to be out by dark. The spearmen took no chance of their trying to burn down the place. The village had long since gone to sleep, campfires doused, skin flaps pulled to across the door holes. From the corral one of the spavined, tick-ridden cows mooed uneasily and then fell silent.

* * * * *

Charles then began the hardest job of his life. He tried to think, straight and uninterrupted, of Martha, the little girl. Some of the things that interrupted him were:

The remembered smell of fried onions; they didn't have onions here;

Salt;

I wonder how the old 101st Precinct's getting along;

That fellow who wanted to get married on a hundred dollars;

Lee Falcaro, damn her!

This, is damn foolishness; it can't possibly work;

Poor old Kennedy;

I'll starve before I eat another mouthful of that greasy deer-meat;

The Van Dellen kid, I wonder if I could have saved him;

Reiner's right; we've got to clean up the Government and then try to civilize these people;

There must be something wrong with my head, I can't seem to concentrate;

That terrific third-chukker play in the Finals, my picture all over town;

Would Uncle Frank laugh at this?

It was hopeless. He sat bolt upright, his eyes squeezed tensely together, trying to visualize the child and call her and it couldn't be done. Skittering images of her zipped through his mind, only to be shoved aside. It was damn foolishness, anyway....

He unkinked himself, stretched and lay down on the sand floor thinking bitterly: why try? You'll be dead in a few days or a few weeks; kiss the world good-bye. Back in Syndic Territory, fat, sloppy, happy Syndic Territory, did they know how good they had it? He wished he could tell them to cling to their good life. But Uncle Frank said it didn't do any good to cling; it was a matter of tension and relaxation. When you stiffen up a way of life and try to fossilize it so it'll stay that way forever, then you find you've lost it.

Little Martha wouldn't understand it. Magic, ritual, the power of the goddess, fear of iron, fear of the jeep's vine enclosure-cursed, no doubt-what went on in such a mind? Could she throw things like a poltergeist-girl? They didn't have 'em any more; maybe it had something to do with electric fields or even iron. Or were they all phonies? An upset adolescent girl is a hell of a lot likelier to fake phenomena that produce them. Little Martha hadn't been faking her despair, though. The witch-girl—her sister, wasn't she?—didn't fake her icy calm and power. Martha'd be better off without such stuff—

"*Charles*," a whisper said.

He muttered stupidly: "My God. She heard me," and crept to the palisade. Through a chink between the logs she was just visible in the starlight.

She whispered: "I thought I wasn't going to see anything or hear anything ever again but I sat up and I heard you calling and you said you wanted to help me if I'd help you so I came as fast as I could without waking anybody up-you *did* call me, didn't you?"

"Yes, I did. Martha, do you want to get out of here? Go far away with me?"

"You bet I do. *She's* going to take the power of the goddess out of me and marry me to Dinny, he stinks like a goat and he has a cockeye, and then she'll kill all our babies. Just tell me what to do and I'll do it." She sounded very grim and decided.

"Can you roll the boulders away from the hole there?" He was thinking vaguely of teleportation; each boulder was a two-man job.

She said no.

He snarled: "Then why did you bother to come here?"

"Don't talk like that to me," the child said sharply-and he remembered what she thought she was.

"Sorry," he said.

"What I came about," she said calmly, "was the ex-plosion. Can you make an ex-plosion like you said? Back there at the jeep?"

What in God's name was she talking about?

"Back there," she said with exaggerated patience, "you was thinking about putting all the cartridges together and blowing up the whole damn shebang. Remember?"

He did, vaguely. One of a hundred schemes that had drifted through his head.

"I'd sure like to see that ex-plosion," she said. "The way *she* got things figured, I'd almost just as soon get exploded myself as not."

"I might blow up the logs here and get out," he said slowly. "I think you'd be a mighty handy person to have along, too. Can you get me about a hundred of the machine gun cartridges?"

"They'll miss 'em."

"Sneak me a few at a time. I'll empty them, put them together again and you sneak them back."

She said, slow and troubled: *"She* set the power of the goddess to guard them."

"Listen to me, Martha," he said. "I mean *listen.* You'll be doing it for me and they told me the power of the goddess doesn't work on outsiders. Isn't that right?"

There was a long pause, and she said at last with a sigh: "I sure wish I could see your eyes, Charles. I'll try it, but I'm damned if I would if Dinny didn't stink so bad." She slipped away and Charles tried to follow her with his mind through the darkness, to the silly little rope of vine with the feathers and bones knotted in it-but he couldn't. Too tense again.

Kennedy stirred and muttered complainingly as an icy small breeze cut through the chinks of the palisade, whispering.

His eyes, tuned to the starlight, picked up Martha bent almost double, creeping toward the smithy-prison. She wore a belt of fifty-caliber cartridges around her neck like a stole. Looked like about a dozen of them. He hastily scooped out a bowl of clean sand and whispered: "Any trouble?"

He couldn't see the grin on her face, but knew it was there. "It was easy," she bragged. "One bad minute and then I checked with you and it was okay."

"Good kid. Pull the cartridges out of the links the way I showed you and pass them through."

She did. It was a tight squeeze.

He fingered one of the cartridges. The bullet fitted nicely into the socket of an arrowhead. He jammed the bullet in and wrenched at the arrowhead with thumb and forefinger-all he could get onto it. The brass neck began to spread. He dumped the powder into his little basin in the sand and reseated the bullet.

Charles shifted hands on the second cartridge. On the third he realized that he could put the point of the bullet on a hearth-stone and press on the neck with both thumbs. It went faster then; in perhaps an hour he was passing the re-assembled cartridges back through the palisade.

"Time for another load?" he asked.

"Nope," the girl said. "Tomorrow night."

"Good kid."

She giggled. "It's going to be a hell of a big bang, ain't it, Charles?"

CHAPTER XIV.

"Leave the fire alone," Charles said sharply to Kennedy. The little man was going to douse it for the night.

There was a flash of terrified sense: "They beat you. If the fire's on after dark they beat you. Fire and dark are equal and opposite." He began to smile. "Fire is the negative of dark. You just change the sign, in effect rotate it through 180 degrees. But to rotate it through 180 degrees you have to first rotate it through one degree. And to rotate it through one degree you first have to rotate it through half a degree." He was beaming now, having forgotten all about the fire. Charles banked it with utmost care, heaping a couple of flat stones for a chimney that would preserve the life of one glowing coal invisibly.

He stretched out on the sand, one hand on the little heap beneath which five pounds of smokeless powder was buried. Kennedy continued to drone out his power-series happily.

Through the chinks in the palisade a man's profile showed against the twilight. "Shut up," he said.

Kennedy shivering, rolled over and muttered to himself. The spearman laughed and went on.

Charles hardly saw him. His whole mind was concentrated on the spark beneath the impro-vised chimney. He had left such a spark seven nights running. Only twice had it lived more than an hour. Tonight-tonight, it *had* to last. Tonight was the last night of the witch-girl's monthly courses, and during them she lost-or thought she lost, which was the same thing-the power of the goddess.

Primitive aborigines, he jeered silently at himself. A life time wasn't long enough to learn the intricacies of their culture-as occasional executions among them for violating magical law proved to the hilt. His first crude notion-blowing the palisade apart and running like hell-was replaced by a complex escape plan hammered out in detail between him and Martha.

Martha assured him that the witch girl could track him through the dark by the power of the goddess except for four days a month-and he believed it. Martha herself laid a matter-of-fact claim to keener second sight than her sister because of her virginity. With Martha to guide him through the night and the witch-girl's power disabled, they'd get a day's head start. His hand strayed to a pebble under which jerked venison was hidden and ready.

"But Martha. Are you sure you're not-not kidding yourself? Are you *sure?*"

He felt her grin on the other side of the palisade. "You're sure wishing Uncle Frank was here so you could ask him about it, don't you, Charles?"

He sure was. He wiped his brow, suddenly clammy.

Kennedy couldn't come along. One, he wasn't responsible. Two, he might have to be Charles' cover-story. They weren't too dissimilar in build, age, or coloring. Charles had a beard by now that sufficiently obscured his features, and two years absence should have softened recollections of Kennedy. Interrogated, Charles could take refuge in an imitation of Kennedy's lunacy.

"Charles, the one thing I don't get is this Lee dame. She got a spell on her? You don't want to mess with that."

"Listen, Martha, we've *got* to mess with her. It isn't a spell-exactly. Anyway I know how to take it off and then she'll be on our side."

"Can I set off the explosion? If you let me set off the explosion, I'll quit my bitching."

"We'll see," he said.

She chuckled very faintly in the dark. "Okay," she told him. "If I can't, I can't."

He thought of being married to a woman who could spot your smallest lie or reservation, and shuddered.

Kennedy was snoring by now and twilight was deepening into blackness. There was a quarter-moon, obscured by over-cast. He hitched along the sand and peered through a chink at a tiny noise. It was the small scuffling feet of a woods-rat racing through the grass from one morsel of food to the next. It never reached it. There was a soft rush of wings as a great dark owl plummeted to earth and struck talons into the brown fur. The rat squealed its life away while the owl lofted silently to a tree branch where it stood on one leg, swaying drunkenly and staring with huge yellow eyes.

As sudden as that, it'll be, Charles thought abruptly weighted with despair. A half-crazy kid and yours truly trying to outsmart and out-Tarzan these wild men. If only the little dope would let me take the jeep! But the jeep was out. She rationalized her retention of the power even after handling iron by persuading herself that she was only acting for Charles; there was some obscure precedent in a long, memorized poem which served her as a text-book of magic. But riding in the jeep was *out*.

By now she should be stringing magic vines across some of the huts and trails. "They'll see 'em when they get torches and it'll scare 'em. Of course I don't know how to do it right, but they don't know that. It'll slow 'em down. If *she* comes out of her house-and maybe she won't—she'll know they don't matter and send the men after us. But we'll be on our way. Charles, you *sure* I can't set off the explosion? Yeah, I guess you are. Maybe I can set off one when we get to New Portsmouth?"

"If I can possibly arrange it."

She sighed: "I guess that'll have to do."

It was too silent; he couldn't bear it. With feverish haste he uncovered the caches of powder and meat. Under the sand was a fat clayey soil. He dug up hands-full of it, wet it with the only liquid available and worked it into paste. He felt his way to the logs decided on for blasting, dug out a hole at their bases in the clay. After five careful trips from the powder cache to the hole, the mine was filled. He covered it with clay and laid on a roof of flat stones from the hearth. The spark of fire still glowed, and he nursed it with twigs.

She was there, whispering: "Charles?"

"Right here. Everything set?"

"All set. Let's have that explosion."

He took the remaining powder and with minute care, laid a train across the stockade to the mine. He crouched into a ball and flipped a burning twig onto the black line that crossed the white sand floor.

The blast seemed to wake up the world. Kennedy charged out of sleep, screaming, and a million birds woke with a squawk. Charles was conscious more of the choking reek than the noise as he scooped up the jerked venison and rushed through the ragged gap in the wall. A hand caught his —a small hand.

"You're groggy," Martha's voice said, sounding far away. "Come on-fast. *Man*, that was a great ex-plosion!"

She towed him through the woods and underbrush-fast. As long as he hung on to her he didn't stumble or run into a tree once. Irrationally embarrassed by his dependence on a child, he tried letting go for a short time-very short-and was quickly battered into changing his mind. He thought dizzily of the spearmen trying to follow through the dark and could almost laugh again.

* * * * *

Their trek to the coast was marked by desperate speed. For twenty-four hours, they stopped only to gnaw at their rations or snatch a drink at a stream. Charles kept moving because it was unendurable to let a ten-year-old girl exceed him in stamina. Both of them paid terribly for the murderous pace they kept. The child's face became skull-like and her eyes red; her lips dried and cracked. He gasped at her as they pulled their way up a bramble-covered 45-degree slope: "How do you do it? Isn't this ever going to end?"

"Ends soon," she croaked at him. "You know we dodged 'em three times?"

He could only shake his head.

She stared at him with burning red eyes. "This ain't hard," she croaked. "You do this with a gut-full of poison, *that's* hard."

"*Did* you?"

She grinned crookedly and chanted something he did not understand:

She added matter-of-factly: "Last year. Prove I have the power of the goddess. Run, climb, with your guts falling out. This year, starve for a week and run down a deer of seven points."

He had lost track of days and nights when they stood on the brow of a hill at dawn and looked over the sea. The girl gasped: "'Sall right now. *She* wouldn't let them go on. She's a bitch, but she's no fool." The child fell in her tracks. Charles, too tired for panic, slept too.

* * * * *

Charles woke with a wonderful smell in his nostrils. He followed it hungrily down the reverse slope of the hill to a grotto.

Martha was crouched over a fire on which rocks were heating. Beside it was a bark pot smeared with clay. As he watched, she lifted a red-hot rock with two green sticks and rolled it into the pot. It boiled up and continued to boil for an astonishing number of minutes. That was the source of the smell.

"Breakfast?" he asked unbelievingly.

"Rabbit stew," she said. "Plenty of runways, plenty of bark, plenty of green branches. I made snares. Two tough old bucks cooking in there for an hour."

They chewed the meat from the bones in silence. She said at last: "We can't settle down here. Too near to the coast. And if we move further inland, there's *her*. And others. I been thinking." She spat a string of tough meat out. "There's England. Work our way around the coast. Make a raft or steal a canoe and cross the water. *Then* we could settle down. You can't have me for three times thirteen moons yet or I'd lose the power. But I guess we can wait. I heard about England and the English. They have no hearts left. We can take as many slaves as we want. They cry a lot but they don't fight. And none of their women has the power." She looked up anxiously. "You wouldn't want one of their women, would you? Not if you could have somebody with the power just by waiting for her?"

He looked down the hill and said slowly: "You know that's not what I had in mind, Martha. I have my own place with people far away. I want to get back there. I thought—I thought you'd like it too." Her face twisted. He couldn't bear to go on, not in words. "Look into my mind, Martha," he said. "Maybe you'll see what it means to me."

She stared long and deep. At last she rose, her face inscrutable, and spat into the fire. "Think I saved you for that?" she asked. "And for *her*? Not me. Save yourself from now on, mister. I'm going to beat my way south around the coast. England for me, and I don't want any part of you."

She strode off down the hill, gaunt and ragged, but with arrogance in her swinging, space-eating gait. Charles sat looking after her, stupefied, until she had melted into the underbrush. "Think I saved you for that? And for *her*?" She'd made some kind of mistake. He got up stiffly and ran after her, but he could not pick up an inch of her woods-wise trail. Charles slowly climbed to the grotto again and sat in its shelter.

He spent the morning trying to concoct simple springs out of bark strips and whippy branches. He got nowhere. The branches broke or wouldn't bend far enough. The bark shredded, or wouldn't hold a knot. Without metal, he couldn't shape the trigger to fit the bow so that it would be both sensitive and reliable.

At noon he drank enormously from a spring and looked morosely for plants that might be edible. He decided on something with a bulbous, onion-like root. For a couple of hours after that he propped rocks on sticks here and there. When he stepped back and surveyed them, he decided that any rabbit he caught with them would be, even for a rabbit, feeble-minded. He could think of nothing else to do.

First he felt a slight intestinal qualm and then a far from slight nausea. Then the root he had eaten took over with drastic thoroughness. He collapsed, retching, and only after the first spasms had passed was he able to crawl to the grotto. The shelter it offered was mostly psychological, but he had need of that. Under the ancient, mossy stones, he raved with delirium until dark.

Sometimes he was back in Syndic Territory, Charles Orsino of the two-goal handicap and the flashing smile. Sometimes he was back in the stinking blockhouse with Kennedy spinning interminable, excruciatingly boring strands of iridescent logic. Sometimes he was back in the psychology laboratory with the pendulum beating, the light blinking, the bell ringing and sense-impressions flooding him and drowning him with lies. Sometimes he raced in panic down the streets of New Portsmouth with sweatered Guardsmen pounding after him, their knives flashing fire.

But at last he was in the grotto again, with Martha sponging his head and cursing him in a low, fluent undertone for being seven times seven kinds of fool.

She said tartly as recognition came into his eyes: "Yes, for the fifth time, I'm back. I should be making my way to England and a band of my own, but I'm back and I don't know why. I heard you in pain and I thought it served you right for not knowing deathroot when you see it, but I turned around and came back."

"Don't go," he said hoarsely.

She held a bark cup to his lips and made him choke down some nauseating brew. "Don't worry," she told him bitterly. "I won't go. I'll do everything you want, which shows that I'm as big a fool as you are, or bigger because I know better. I'll help you find her and take the spell off her. And may the goddess help me because I can't help myself."

* * * * *

"... things like sawed tree-trunks, shells you call them ... a pile of them ... he looks at them and he thinks they're going bad and they ought to be used soon ... under a wooden roof they are ... a thin man with death on his face and hate in his heart ... he wears blue and gold ... he sticks the gold, you call a coat's wrist the cuff, he sticks the cuff under the nose of a fellow and yells his hate out and the fellow feels ready to strangle on blood ... it's about a boat that sank ... this fellow, he's a fat little man and he kills and kills, he'd kill the man if he could...."

A picket boat steamed by the coast twice a day, north after dawn and south before sunset. They had to watch out for it; it swept the coast with powerful glasses.

"... it's the man with the bellyache again but now he's sleepy ... he's cursing the skipper ... sure there's nothing on the coast to trouble us ... eight good men aboard and that one bastard of a skipper...."

Sometimes it jumped erratically, like an optical lever disturbed by the weight of a hair.

"... board over the door painted with a circle, a zig-zag on its side, an up-and-down line ... they call it office of intelligent navels ... the lumber camp ... machine goes chug-rip, chug-rip ... and the place where they cut metal like wood on machines that spin around ... a deathly-sick little fellow loaded down and chained ... fell on his face, he can't get up, his bowels are water, his muscles are stiff, like dry branches and he's afraid ... they curse him, they beat him, they take him to a machine that spins ... *they ... they —they —*"

She sat bolt upright, screaming. Her eyes didn't see Charles. He drew back one hand and slammed it across her cheek in a slap that reverberated like a pistol shot. Her head rocked to the blow and her eyes snapped back from infinity-focus.

She never told Charles what they had done to the sick slave in the machine shop, and he never asked her.

Without writing equipment, for crutches, Charles doubted profoundly that he'd be able to hang onto any of the material she supplied. He surprised himself; his memory developed with exercise.

The shadowy ranks of the New Portsmouth personnel became solider daily in his mind; the chronically-fatigued ordnance-man whose mainspring was to get by with the smallest possible effort; the sex-obsessed little man in Intelligence who lived only for the brothels where he selected older women-women who looked like his mother; the human weasel in BuShips who was impotent in bed and a lacerating tyrant in the office; the admiral who knew he was dying and hated his juniors proportionately to their youth and health.

And —

"... this woman of yours ... she ain't at home there ... she ain't at ... at home ... *anywhere.* ... the fat man, the one that kills, he's talking to her but she isn't ... yes she is ... no she isn't —she's answering him, talking about over-the-sea...."

"Lee Falcaro," Charles whispered. "Lee Bennet."

The trance-frozen face didn't change; the eerie whisper went on without interruption: "... Lee Bennet on her lips, Lee Falcaro down deep in her guts ... and the face of Charles Orsino down there too...."

An unexpected pang went through him.

He sorted and classified endlessly what he had learned. He formed and rejected a dozen plans. At last there was one he could not reject.

CHAPTER XV.

Commander Grinnel was officer of the day, and sore as a boil about it. O.N.I. wasn't supposed to catch the duty. You risked your life on cloak-and-dagger missions; let the shore-bound fancy dans do the drudgery. But there he was, nevertheless, in the guard house office with a .45 on his hip, the interminable night stretching before him, and the ten-man main guard snoring away outside.

He eased his bad military conscience by reflecting that there wasn't anything to guard, that patrolling the shore establishment was just worn out tradition. The ships and boats had their own watch. At the very furthest stretch of the imagination, a tarzan might sneak into town and try to steal some ammo. Well, if he got caught he got caught. And if he didn't, who'd know the difference with the accounting as sloppy as it was here? They did things differently in Iceland.

* * * * *

They crept through the midnight dark of New Portsmouth's outskirts. As before, she led with her small hand. Lights flared on a wharf where, perhaps, a boat was being serviced. A slave screamed somewhere under the lash or worse.

"Here's the doss house," Martha whispered. It was smack between paydays-part of the plan-and the house was dark except for the hopefully-lit parlor. They ducked down the alley that skirted it and around the back of Bachelor Officer Quarters. The sentry, if he were going his rounds at all, would be at the other end of his post when they passed-part of the plan.

Lee Falcaro was quartered alone in a locked room of the O.N.I. building. Martha had, from seventy miles away, frequently watched the lock being opened and closed.

They dove under the building's crumbling porch two minutes before a late crowd of drinkers roared down the street and emerged when they were safely gone. There was a charge of quarters, a little yeoman, snoozing under a dim light in the O.N.I. building's lobby.

"Anybody else?" Charles whispered edgily.

"No. Just her. She's asleep. Dreaming about-never mind. Come on Charles. He's out."

The little yeoman didn't stir as they passed him and crept up the stairs. Lee Falcaro's room was part of the third-floor attic, finished off specially. You reached it by a ladder from a second-floor one-man office.

The lock was an eight-button piccolo-very rare in New Portsmouth and presumably loot from the mainland. Charles' fingers flew over it: 1-7-5-4-, 2-2-7-3-, 8-2-6-6- and it flipped open silently.

But the door squeaked.

"She's waking up!" Martha hissed in the dark. "She'll yell!"

Charles reached the bed in two strides and clamped his hand over Lee Falcaro-Bennet's mouth. Only a feeble "mmm!" came out, but the girl thrashed violently in his grip.

"Shut up, lady!" Martha whispered. "Nobody's going to rape you."

There was an astonished "mmm?" and she subsided, trembling.

"Go ahead," Martha told him. "She won't yell."

He took his hand away nervously. "We've come to administer the oath of citizenship," he said.

The girl answered in the querulous voice that was hardly hers: "You picked a strange time for it. Who are you? What's all the whispering for?"

He improvised. "I'm Commander Lister. Just in from Iceland aboard atom sub *Taft*. They didn't tell you in case it got turned down, but I was sent for authorization to give you citizenship. You know how unusual it is for a woman."

"Who's this child? And why did you get me up in the dead of night?"

He dipped deeply into Martha's probings of the past week. "Citizenship'll make the Guard Intelligence gang think twice before they try to grab you again. Naturally they'd try to block us if we administered the oath in public. Ready?"

"Dramatic," she sneered. "Oh, I suppose so. Get it over with."

"Do you, Lee Bennet, solemnly renounce all allegiances previously held by you and pledge your allegiance to the North American Government?"

"I do," she said.

There was a choked little cry from Martha. "Hell's fire," she said. "Like breaking a leg!"

"What are you talking about, little girl?" Lee asked, coldly alert.

"It's all right," Charles said wearily. "Don't you know my voice? I'm Orsino. You turned me in back there because they don't give, citizenship to women and so your de-conditioning didn't get triggered off. I managed to break for the woods. A bunch of natives got me. I busted loose with the help of Martha here. Among her other talents, the kid's a mind reader. I remember the triggering shocked me out of a year's growth; how do you feel?"

Lee was silent, but Martha answered in a voice half puzzled and half contemptuous: "She feels fine, but she's crying."

"Am not," Lee Falcaro gulped.

Charles turned from her, embarrassed. In a voice that strove to be normal, he whispered to Martha: "What about the boat?"

"Still there," she said.

Lee Falcaro said tremulously: "Wh-wh-what boat?"

"Martha's staked out a reactor-driven patrol speedboat at a wharf. One guard aboard. She-watched it in operation and I have some small-boat time. I really think we can grab it. If we get a good head-start, they don't have anything based here that'll catch up with it. If we get a break on the weather, their planes won't be able to pick us up."

Lee Falcaro stood up, dashing tears from her eyes. "Then let's go," she said evenly.

"How's the C.Q. —that man downstairs, Martha?"

"Still sleepin'. The way's as clear now as it'll ever be."

They closed the door behind them and Charles worked the lock. The Charge of Quarters looked as though he couldn't be roused by anything less than an earthquake as they passed-but Martha stumbled on one of the rotting steps after they were outside the building.

"Patrick and Bridget rot my clumsy feet off!" she whispered. "He's awake."

"Under the porch," Charles said. They crawled into the dank space between porch floor and ground. Martha kept up a scarcely-audible volleyfire of maledictions aimed at herself.

When they stopped abruptly Charles knew it was bad.

Martha held up her hand for silence, and Charles imagined in the dark that he could see the strained and eerie look of her face. After a pause she whispered: "He's using the-what do you call it? You talk and somebody hears you far away? A prowler he says to them. A wild man from the woods. The bitches bastard must have seen you in your handsome suit of skin and dirt, Charles. Oh, we're *for* it! May my toe that stumbled grow the size of a boulder! May my cursed eyes that didn't see the step fall out!"

They huddled down in the darkness and Charles took Lee Falcaro's hand reassuringly. It was cold. A moment later his other hand was taken, with grim possessiveness, by the child.

Martha whispered: "The fat little man. The man who kills, Charles."

He nodded. He thought he had recognized Grinnel from her picture.

"And ten men waking up. Charles, do you remember the way to the wharf?"

"Sure," he said. "But we're net going to get separated."

"They're mean, mad men," she said. "Bloody-minded. And the little man is the worst."

They heard the stomping feet and a babble of voices, and Commander Grinnel's clear, fat-man's tenor: "Keep it quiet, men. He may still be in the area." The feet thundered over their heads on the porch.

In the barest of whispers Martha said: "The man that slept tells them there was only one, and he didn't see what he was like except for the bare skin and the long hair. And the fat man says they'll find him and-and-and says they'll find him." Her hand clutched Charles' desperately and then dropped it as the feet thudded overhead again.

Grinnel was saying: "Half of you head up the street and half down. Check the alleys, check open window-hell, I don't have to tell you. If we don't find the bastard on the first run we'll have to wake up the whole Guard Battalion and patrol the whole base with them all the goddam night, so keep your eyes open. Take off."

"Remember the way to the wharf, Charles," Martha said. "Good-bye lady. Take care of him. Take good care of him." She wrenched her hand away and darted out from under the porch.

Lee muttered some agonized monosyllable. Charles started out after the child instinctively and then collapsed weakly back onto the dirt. They heard the rest.

"Hey, you-it's him, by God! Get him! Get him!"

"Here he is, down here! Head him off!"

"Over there!" Grinnel yelled. "Head him off! Head him-good work!"

"For God's sake. It's a girl."

"Those goddam yeomen and their goddam prowlers."

Grinnel: "Where are you from, kid?"

"That's no kid from the base, commander. Look at her!"

"I just was, sarge. Looks good to me, don't it to you?"

Grinnel, tolerant, fatherly, amused: "Now, men, have your fun but keep it quiet."

"Don't be afraid, kid —" There was an animal howl from Martha's throat that made Lee Falcaro shake hysterically and Charles grind his fingernails into his palms.

Grinnel: "Sergeant, you'd better tie your shirt around her head and take her into the O.N.I. building."

"Why, commander! And let that lousy little yeoman in on it?"

Grinnel, amused, a good Joe, a man's man: "That's up to you, men. Just keep it quiet."

"Why, commander, sometimes I like to make a little noise —"

"Ow!" a man yelled. There was a scuffle of feet and babbling voices. "Get her, you damn fool!" "She bit my hand —" "There she goes —" and a single emphatic shot.

Grinnel's voice said into the silence that followed: "That's that, men."

"Did you *have* to shoot, Commander?" an aggrieved Guardsman said.

"Don't blame me, fellow. Blame the guy that let her go."

"God-dammit, she bit me —"

Somebody said as though he didn't mean it: "We ought to take her someplace."

"The hell with that. Let 'em get her in the morning."

"Them as wants her." A cackle of harsh laughter.

Grinnel, tolerantly: "Back to the guardhouse, men. And keep it quiet."

They scuffled off and there was silence again for long minutes. Charles said at last: "We'll go down to the wharf." They crawled out and looked for a moment from the shelter of the building at the bundle lying in the road.

Lee muttered: "Grinnel."

"Shut up," Charles said. He led her down deserted alleys and around empty corners, strictly according to plan.

The speedboat was a twenty-foot craft at Wharf Eighteen, bobbing on the water safely removed from other moored boats and ships. Lee Falcaro let out a small, smothered shriek when she saw a uniformed sailor sitting in the cockpit, apparently staring directly at them.

"It's all right," Charles said. "He's a drunk. He's always out cold by this time of night." Smoothly Charles found the rope locker, cut lengths with the sailor's own knife and bound and gagged him. The man's eyes opened, weary, glazed and red while this was going on and closed again. "Help me lug him ashore," Charles said. Lee Falcaro took the sailor's legs and they eased him onto the wharf.

They went back into the cockpit. "This is deep water," Charles said, "so you'll have no trouble with pilotage. You can read a compass and charts. There's an automatic dead reckoner. My advice is just to pull the moderator rods out quarter-speed, point the thing west, pull the rods out as far as they'll go-and relax. Either they'll overtake you or they won't."

She was beginning to get the drift. She said nervously: "You're talking as though you're not coming along."

"I'm not," he said, playing the lock of the arms rack. The bar fell aside and he pulled a .45 pistol from its clamp. He thought back and remembered where the boat's diminutive magazine was located, broke the feeble lock and found a box of short, fat, heavy little cartridges. He began to snap them into the pistol's magazine.

"What do you think you're up to?" Lee Falcaro demanded.

"Appointment with Commander Grinnel," he said. He slid the heavy magazine into the pistol's grip and worked the slide to jack a cartridge into the chamber.

"Shall I cast off for you?" he asked.

"Don't be a fool," she said. "You sound like a revival of a Mickey Spillane comedy. You can't bring her back to life and you've got a job to do for the Syndic."

"You do it," he said, and snapped another of the blunt, fat, little cartridges into the magazine. She cast off, reached for the moderator-rod control and pulled it hard.

"Gee," he gasped, "you'll sink us!" and dashed for the controls. You had seconds before the worm-gears turned, the cadmium rods withdrew from their slots, the reactor seethed and sent boiling metal cycling through the turbine —

He slammed down manual levers that threw off the fore and aft mooring lines, spun the wheel, bracing himself, and saw Lee Falcaro go down to the deck in a tangle, the .45 flying from her hand and skidding across the knurled plastic planking. But by then the turbine was screaming an alarm to the whole base and they were cutting white water through the buoy-marked gap in the harbor net.

Lee Falcaro got to her feet. "I'm not proud of myself," she said to him. "But she told me to take care of you."

He said grimly: "We could have gone straight to the wharf without that little layover to pick you up. Take the wheel."

"Charles, I —"

He snarled at her.

"Take the wheel."

She did, and he went aft to stare through the darkness. The harbor lights were twinkling pin-points; then his eyes misted so he could not see them at all. He didn't give a damn if a dozen corvettes were already slicing the bay in pursuit. He had failed.

CHAPTER XVI.

It was a dank fog-shrouded morning. Sometime during the night the quill of the dead reckoner had traced its fine red line over the 30th meridian. Roughly half-way, Charles Orsino thought, rubbing the sleep from his eyes. But the line was straight as a string for the last four hours of their run. The damn girl must have fallen asleep on watch. He glared at her in the bow and broke open a ration. Blandly oblivious to the glare, she said: "Good morning."

Charles swallowed a mouthful of chocolate, half-chewed, and choked on it. He reached hastily for water and found the tall plastic column of the ion-exchange apparatus empty. "Damn it," he snarled, "why didn't you refill this thing when you emptied it? And why didn't you zig-zag overnight? You're utterly irresponsible." He hurled the bucket overside, hauled it up and slopped seawater into the apparatus. Now there'd be a good twenty minutes before a man-sized drink accumulated.

"Just a minute," she told him steadily. "Let's straighten this out. I haven't had any water on the night watch so I didn't have any occasion to refill the tube. You must have taken the last of the water with your dinner. And as for the zig-zag, you said we should run a straightaway now and then to mix it up. I decided that last night was as good a time as any."

He took a minute drink from the reservoir, stalling. There was something-yes; he had *meant* to refill the apparatus after his dinner ration. And he *had* told her to give it a few hours of straightaway some night....

He said formally: "You're quite right on both counts. I apologize." He bit into a ration.

"That's not good enough," she said. "I'm not going to have you tell me you're sorry and then go scowling and sulking about the boat. In fact I don't like your behavior at all."

He said, enormously angry: *"Oh, you don't do you?"* and hated her, the world and himself for the stupid inadequacy of the comeback.

"No. I don't. I'm seriously worried. I'm afraid the conditioning you got didn't fall away completely when they swore you in. You've been acting irrationally and inconsistently."

"What about you?" he snapped. "You got conditioned too."

"That's right," she said. "That's another reason why you're worrying me. I find impulses in myself that have no business there. I simply seem to do a better job of controlling them than you're doing. For instance: we've been quarreling and at cross-purposes ever since you and Martha picked me up. That couldn't be unless I were contributing to the friction."

The wheel was fixed; she took a step or two aft and said professorially: "I've never had trouble getting along with people. I've had differences, of course, and at times I've allowed myself displays of temper when it was necessary to assert myself. But I find that you upset me; that for some reason or other your opinion on a matter is important to me, that if it differs with mine there should be a reconciliation."

He put down the ration and said wonderingly: "Do you know, that's the way I feel about you? And you think it's the conditioning or-or something?" He took a couple of steps forward, hesitantly.

"Yes," she said in a rather tremulous voice. "The conditioning or something. For instance, you're inhibited. You haven't made an indecent proposition to me, not even as a matter of courtesy. Not that I care, of course, but —" In stepping aft, she tripped over the water bucket and went down to the deck with a faint scream.

He said: "Here, let me help you." He picked her up and didn't let go.

"Thanks," she said faintly. "The conditioning technique can't be called faulty, but it has inherent limitations...." She trailed off and he kissed her. She kissed back and said more faintly still: "Or it might be the drugs we used....Oh, Charles, what *took* you so long?"

He said, brooding: "You're way out of my class, you know. I'm just a bagman for the New York police. I wouldn't even be that if it weren't for Uncle Frank, and you're a Falcaro. It's just barely thinkable that I could make a pass at you. I guess that held me off and I didn't want to admit it so I got mad at you instead. Hell, I could have swum back to the base and made a damned fool of myself trying to find Grinnel, but down inside I knew better. The kid's *gone*."

"We'll make a psychologist of you yet," she said.

"Psychologist? Why? You're joking."

"No. It's not a joke. You'll *like* psychology, darling. You can't go on playing polo forever, you know."

Darling! What was he getting into? Old man Gilby was four-goal at sixty, wasn't he? Good God, was he hooked into marriage at twenty-three? Was she married already? Did she know or care whether he was? Had she been promiscuous? Would she continue to be? He'd never know; that was the one thing you never asked; your only comfort, if you needed comfort, was that she could never dream of asking you. What went on here? Let me out!

It went through his mind in a single panicky flash and then he said: "The hell with it," and kissed her again.

She wanted to know: "The hell with what, darling?"

"Everything. Tell me about psychology. I can't go on playing polo forever."

It was an hour before she got around to telling him about psychology: "The neglect has been criminal-and inexplicable. For about a century it's been *assumed* that psychology is a dead fallacy. Why?"

"All right," he said amiably, playing with a lock of her hair. "Why?"

"Lieberman," she said. "Lieberman of Johns-Hopkins. He was one of the old-line topological psychology men-don't let the lingo throw you, Charles; it's just the name of a system. He wrote an attack on the *mengenlehre* psychology school-point-sets of emotions, class-inclusions of reactions and so on. He blasted them to bits by proving that their constructs didn't correspond to the emotions and reactions of random-sampled populations. And then came the pay-off: he tried the same acid test on his *own* school's constructs and found out that they didn't correspond either. It didn't frighten him; he was a scientist. He published, and then the jig was up. Everybody, from full professors to undergraduate students went down the roster of the schools of psychology and wrecked them so comprehensively that the field was as dead as palmistry in twenty years. The miracle is that it hadn't happened before. The flaws were so glaring! Textbooks of the older kind solemnly described syndromes, psychoses, neuroses that simply couldn't be found in the real world! And that's the way it was all the way down the line."

"So where does that leave us?" Charles demanded. "Is it or isn't it a science?"

"It is," she said simply. "Lieberman and his followers went too far. It became a kind of hysteria. The experimenters must have been too eager. They misread results, they misinterpreted statistics, they misunderstood the claims of a school and knocked down not its true claims but straw-man claims they had set up themselves."

"But —*psychology*!" Charles protested, obscurely embarrassed at the thought that man's mind was subject to scientific study-not because he knew the first thing about it, but because *everybody* knew psychology was phony.

She shrugged. "I can't help it. We were doing physiology of the sensory organs, trying to settle the oldie about focusing the eye, and I got to grubbing around the pre-Lieberman texts looking for light in the darkness. Some of it sounded so-not sensible, but *positive* that I ran off one of Lieberman's population checks. And the old boy had been dead wrong. *Mengenlehre* constructs correspond quite nicely to the actual way people's minds work. I kept checking and the schools that were destroyed as hopelessly fallacious a century ago checked out, some closely and some not so closely, as good descriptions of the way the mind works. Some have predictive value. I used *mengenlehre* psychology algorithms to compute the conditioning on you and me, including the trigger release. It worked. You see, Charles? We're on the rim of something tremendous!"

"When did this Lieberman flourish?"

"I don't have the exact dates in my head. The breakup of the schools corresponded roughly with the lifetime of John G. Falcaro."

That pin-pointed it rather well. John G. succeeded Rafael, who succeeded Amadeo Falcaro, first leader of the Syndic in revolt. Under John G., the hard-won freedom was enjoyed, the bulging store-houses were joyously emptied, craft union rules went joyously out the window and builders *worked*, the dollar went to an all-time high and there was an all-time number of dollars in circulation. It had been an exhuberant time still fondly remembered; just the time for over-enthusiastic rebels against a fusty scholasticism to joyously smash old ways of thought without too much exercise of the conscience. It all checked out.

She started and he got to his feet. A hardly-noticed discomfort was becoming acute; the speedboat was pitching and rolling quite seriously, for the first time since their escape. "Dirty weather coming up," he said. "We've been too damned lucky so far." He thought, but didn't remark, that there was much to worry about in the fact that there seemed to have been no pursuit. The meager resources of the North American Navy wouldn't be spent on chasing a single minor craft-not if the weather could be counted on to finish her off.

"I thought we were unsinkable?"

"In a way. Seal the boat and she's unsinkable the way a corked bottle is. But the boat's made up of a lot of bits and pieces that go together just so. Pound her for a few hours with waves and the bits and pieces give way. She doesn't sink, but she doesn't steam or steer either. I wish the Syndic had a fleet on the Atlantic."

"Sorry," she said. "The nearest fleet I know of is Mob ore boats on the great lakes and they aren't likely to pick us up."

The sea-search radar pinged and they flew to the screen. "*Something* at 273 degrees, about eight miles," he said. "It can't be pursuit. They couldn't have any reason at all to circle around us and come at us from ahead." He strained his eyes into the west and thought he could see a black speck on the gray.

Lee Falcaro tried a pair of binoculars and complained: "These things won't work."

"Not on a rolling, pitching platform they won't —not with an optical lever eight miles long. I don't suppose this boat would have a gyro-stabilized signal glass." He spun the wheel to 180; they staggered and clung as the bow whipped about, searched and steadied on the new course. The mounting waves slammed them broadside-to and the rolling increased. They hardly noticed; their eyes were on the radarscope. Fogged as it was with sea return, they nevertheless could be sure after several minutes that the object had changed course to 135. Charles made a flying guess at her speed, read their own speed off and scribbled for a moment.

He said nothing, but spun the wheel to 225 and went back to the radarscope. The object changed course to 145. Charles scribbled again and said at last, flatly: "They're running collision courses on us. Automatically computed, I suppose, from a radar. We're through."

He spun the wheel to 180 again, and studied the crawling green spark on the radarscope. "This way we give 'em the longest run for their money and can pray for a miracle. The only way we can use our speed to outrun them is to turn around and head back into Government Territory-which isn't what we want. Relax, Lee. Maybe if the weather thickens they'll lose us-no; not with radar."

They sat together on a bunk, wordlessly, for hours while the spray dashed higher and the boat shivered to hammering waves. Briefly they saw the pursuer, three miles off, low, black and ugly, before fog closed in again.

At nightfall there was the close, triumphant roar of a big reaction turbine and a light stabbed through the fog, flooding the boat with blue-white radiance. A cliff-like black hull loomed alongside as a bull-horn roared at them: "Cut your engines and come about into the wind."

Lee Falcaro read white-painted letters on the black hull: "*Hon. James J. Regan, Chicago.*" She turned to Charles and said wonderingly: "It's an ore boat. From the Mob great lakes fleet."

CHAPTER XVII.

"Here?" Charles demanded. *"Here?"*

"No possible mistake," she said, stunned. "When you're a Falcaro you travel. I've seen 'em in Duluth, I've seen 'em in Quebec, I've seen 'em in Buffalo."

The bull-horn voice roared again, dead in the shroud of fog; "Come into the wind and cut your engines or we'll put a shell into you."

Charles turned the wheel and wound in the moderator rod; the boat pitched like a splinter on the waves. There was a muffled double explosion and two grapnels crunched into the plastic hull, bow and stern. As the boat steadied, sharing the inertia of the ore ship, a dark figure leaped from the blue-white eye of the searchlight to their deck. And another. And another.

"Hello, Jim," Lee Falcaro said almost inaudibly. "Haven't met since Las Vegas, have we?"

The first boarder studied her cooly. He was built for football or any other form of mayhem. He ignored Charles completely. "Lee Falcaro as advised. Do you still think twenty reds means a black is bound to come up? You always were a fool, Lee. And now you're in real trouble."

"What's going on, mister?" Charles snapped. "We're Syndics and I presume you're Mobsters. Don't you recognize the treaty?"

The boarder turned to Charles inquiringly. "Some confusion," he said. "Max Wyman? Charles Orsino? Or just some wild man from outback?"

"Orsino," Charles said formally. "Second cousin of Edward Falcaro, under the guardianship of Francis W. Taylor."

The boarder bowed slightly. "James Regan IV," he said. "No need to list my connections. It would take too long and I feel no need to justify myself to a small-time dago chisler. Watch him gentlemen!"

Charles found his arms pinned by Regan's two companions. There was a gun muzzle in his ribs.

Regan shouted to the ship and a ladder was let down. Lee Falcaro and Charles climbed it with guns at their backs. He said to her: "Who is that lunatic?" It did not even occur to him that the young man was who he claimed to be-the son of the Mob Territory opposite number of Edward Falcaro.

"He's Regan," she said. "And I don't know who's the lunatic, him or me. Charles, I'm sorry, terribly sorry, I got you into this."

He managed to smile. "I volunteered," he said.

"Enough talk," Regan said, following them onto the deck. Dull-eyed sailors watched them incuriously, and there were a couple of anvil-jawed men with a stance and swagger Charles had come to know. Guardsmen-he would have staked his life on it. Guardsmen of the North American Government Navy-aboard a Mob Territory ship and acting as if they were passengers or high-rated crewmen.

Regan smirked: "I'm on the horns of a dilemma. There are no accomodations that are quite right for you. There are storage compartments which are worse than you deserve and there are passenger quarters which are too good for you. I'm afraid it will have to be one of the compartments. Your consolation will be that it's only a short run to Chicago."

Chicago-headquarters for Mob Territory. The ore ship had been on a return trip to Chicago when alerted somehow by the Navy to intercept the fugitives. *Why?*

"Down there," one of the men gestured briskly with a gun. They climbed down a ladder into a dark, oily cavern fitfully lit by a flash in Regan's hand.

"Make yourselves comfortable," Regan told them. "If you get a headache, don't worry. We were carrying some avgas on the outward run." The flash winked out and a door clanged on them.

"I can't believe it," Charles said. "That's a top Mob man? Couldn't you be mistaken?" He groped in the dark and found her. The place did reek of gasoline.

She clung to him and said: "Hold me, Charles....Yes that's Jimmy Regan.

"That's what will become top man in the Mob. Jimmy's a charmer at a Las Vegas Hotel. Jimmy's a gourmet when he orders at the Pump Room and he's trying to overawe you. Jimmy plays polo too, but he's crippled three of his own team-mates because he's not very good at it. I kept telling myself whenever I ran into him that he was just an accident, the Mob could survive him. But his father acts-funny. There's something with them, there's some —

"They roll out the carpet when you show up but the people around them are afraid of them. There's a story I never believed-but I believe it now. What would happen if my uncle pulled out a pistol and began screaming and shot a waiter: Jimmy's father did it, they tell me. And nothing happened except that the waiter was dragged away and everybody said it was a good thing Mr. Regan saw him reach for his gun and shot him first. Only the waiter didn't have any gun.

"I saw Jimmy last three years ago. I haven't been in Mob Territory since. I didn't like it there. Now I know why. Give Mob Territory enough time and it'll be like New Portsmouth. Something went wrong with them. We have the Treaty of Las Vegas and a hundred years of peace and there aren't many people going back and forth between Syndic and Mob except for a few high-ups like me who have to circulate. Manners. So you pay duty calls and shut your eyes to what they're really like.

"*This* is what they're like. This dark, damp stinking compartment. And my uncle-and all the Falcaros-and you-and I —we aren't like them. Are we? *Are we?*" Her fingers bit into his arms. She was shaking.

"Easy," he soothed her. "Easy, easy. We're all right. We'll be all right. I think I've got it figured out. This must be some private gun-running Jimmy's gone in for. Loaded an ore boat with avgas and ammo and ran it up the Seaway. If anybody in Syndic Territory gave a damn they thought it was a load of ore for New Orleans via the Atlantic and the Gulf. But Jimmy ran his load to Ireland or Iceland, H.Q. A little private flier of his. He wouldn't dare harm us. There's the Treaty and you're a Falcaro."

"Treaty," she said. "I tell you they're all in it. Now that I've seen the Government in action I understand what I saw in Mob Territory. They've gone rotten, that's all. They've gone rotten. The way he treated you, because he thought you didn't have his rank! Sometimes my uncle's high-handed, sometimes he tells a person off, sometimes he lets him know he's top man in the Syndic and doesn't propose to let anybody teach him how to suck eggs. But the spirit's different. In the Syndic it's parent to child. In the Mob it's master to slave. Not based on age, not based on achievement, but based on the accident of birth. You tell me 'You're a Falcaro' and that packs weight. Why? Not because I was born a Falcaro but because they let me stay a Falcaro. If I hadn't been brainy and quick, they'd have adopted me out before I was ten. They don't do that in Mob Territory. Whatever chance sends a Regan is a Regan then and forever. Even if it's a paranoid constitutional inferior like Jimmy's father. Even if it's a giggling pervert like Jimmy.

"God, Charles, I'm scared.

"At last I know these people and I'm scared. You'd have to see Chicago to know why. The lakefront palaces, finer than anything in New York. Regan Memorial Plaza, finer than Scratch Sheet Square-great gilded marble figures, a hundred running yards of heroic frieze. But the hovels you see only by chance! Gray brick towers dating from the Third Fire! The children with faces like weasels, the men with faces like hogs, the women with figures like beer barrels and all of them glaring at you when you drive past as if they could cut your throat with joy. I never understood the look in their eyes until now, and you'll never begin to understand what I'm talking about until you see their eyes...."

Charles revolted against the idea. It was too gross to go down. It didn't square with his acquired picture of life in North America and therefore Lee Falcaro must be somehow mistaken or hysterical. "There," he murmured, stroking her hair. "We'll be all right. We'll be all right." He tried to soothe her.

She twisted out of his arms and raged: "I *won't* be humored. They're mad, I tell you. Dick Reiner was right. We've got to wipe out the Government. But Frank Taylor was right too. We've got to blast the Mob before they blast us. They've died and decayed into something too horrible to bear. If we let them stay on the continent, with us their stink will infect us and poison us to death. We've got to do something. We've got to do something."

"What?"

It stopped her cold. After a minute she uttered a shaky laugh. "The fat, sloppy, happy Syndic," she said, "sitting around while the wolves overseas and the maniacs across the Mississippi are waiting to jump. Yes-do what?"

Charles Orsino was not good at arguments or indeed at any abstract thinking. He knew it. He knew the virtues that had commended him to F. W. Taylor were his energy and an off-hand talent for getting along with people. But something rang terribly false in Lee's words.

"That kind of thinking doesn't get you anywhere, Lee," he said slowly. "I didn't absorb much from Uncle Frank, but I did absorb this: you run into trouble if you make up stories about the world and then act as if they're true. The Syndic isn't somebody sitting around. The Government isn't wolves. The Mobsters aren't maniacs. And they aren't waiting to jump on the Syndic. The Syndic isn't anything that's jumpable. It's some people and their morale and credit."

"Faith is a beautiful thing," Lee Falcaro said bitterly. "Where'd you get yours?"

"From the people I knew and worked with. Numbers-runners, bookies, sluts. Decent citizens."

"And what about the scared and unhappy ones in Riveredge? That sow of a woman in the D.A.R. who smuggled me aboard a coast raider? The neurotics and psychotics I found more and more of when I invalidated the Lieberman findings? Charles, the North American Government didn't scare me especially. But the thought that they're lined up with a continental power does. It scares me damnably because it'll be three against one. Against the Syndic, the Mob, the Government-and our own unbalanced citizens."

Uncle Frank never let that word "citizens" pass without a tirade. "We are not a government!" he always yelled. "We are not a government! We must not think like a government! We must not think in terms of duties and receipts and disbursements. We must think in terms of the old loyalties that bound the Syndic together!" Uncle Frank was sedentary, but he had roused himself once to the point of wrecking a bright young man's newly installed bookkeeping system for the Medical Center. He had used a cane, most enthusiastically, and then bellowed: "The next wise guy who tries to sneak punch-cards into this joint will get them down his throat! What the hell do we need punch-cards for? Either there's room enough and doctors enough for the patients or there isn't. If there is, we take care of them. If there isn't, we put 'em in an ambulance and take them someplace else. And if I hear one goddammed word about 'efficiency' —" he glared the rest and strode out, puffing and leaning on Charles' arm. "Efficiency," he growled in the corridor. "Every so often a wise guy comes to me whimpering that people are getting away with murder, collections are ten per cent below what they ought to be, the Falcaro Fund's being milked because fifteen per cent of the dough goes to people who aren't in need at all, eight per cent of the people getting old-age pensions aren't really past sixty. Get efficient, these people tell me. Save money by triple-checking collections. Save money by tightening up the Fund rules. Save money by a nice big vital-statistics system so we can check on pensioners. Yeah! Have people who might be *working* check on collections instead, and make enemies to boot whenever we catch somebody short. Make the Fund a grudging Scrooge instead of an open-handed sugar-daddy —and let people *worry* about their chances of making the Fund instead of *knowing* it'll take care of them if they're caught short. Set up a vital statistics system from birth to death, with numbers and finger-prints and house registration and maybe the gas-chamber if you forget to report a change of address. You know what's wrong with the wise guys, Charles? Constipation. And they want to constipate the universe." Charles remembered his uncle restored to chuckling good humor by the time he had finished embroidering his spur-of-the-moment theory with elaborate scatological details.

"The Syndic will stand," he said to Lee Falcaro, thinking of his uncle who knew what he was doing, thinking of Edward Falcaro who did the right thing without knowing why, thinking of his good friends in the 101st Precinct, the roaring happy crowds in Scratch Sheet Square, the good-hearted men of Riveredge Breakdown Station 26 who had borne with his sullenness and intolerance simply because that was the way things were and that was the way you acted. "I don't know what the Mob's up to, and I got a shock from the Government, and I don't deny that we have a few miserable people who can't seem to be helped. But you've seen too much of the Mob and Government and our abnormals. Maybe you don't know as much as you should about our ordinary people. Anyway, all we can do is wait."

"Yes," she said. "All we can do is wait. Until Chicago we have each other."

CHAPTER XVIII.

They were too sick with gasoline fumes to count the passing hours or days. Food was brought to them from time to time, but it tasted like avgas. They could not think for the sick headaches that pounded incessantly behind their eyes. When Lee developed vomiting spasms that would not stop, Charles Orsino pounded on the bulkhead with his fists and yelled, his voice thunderous in the metal compartment, for an hour.

Somebody came at last-Regan. The light stabbed Charles' eyes when he opened the door. "Trouble?" Regan asked, smirking.

"Miss Falcaro may be dying," Charles said. His own throat felt as though it had been gone over with a cobbler's rasp. "I don't have to tell you your life won't be worth a dime if she dies and it gets back to Syndic Territory. She's got to be moved and she's got to have medical attention."

"Death threat from the dago?" Regan was amused. "I have it on your own testimony that the Syndic is merely morale and people and credit-not a formidable organization. Yes, there was a mike in here. One reason for your discomfort. You'll be gratified to learn that I thought most of your conversation decidedly dull. However, the lady will be of no use to us dead and we're now in the Seaway entering Lake Michigan. I suppose it can't do any harm to move you two. Pick her up, will you? I'll let you lead the way-and I'll remind you that I may not, as the lady said, be a four-goal polo player but I am a high expert with the handgun. Get moving."

Charles did not think he could pick his own feet up, but the thought of pleading weakness to Regan was unbearable. He could try. Staggering, he got Lee Falcaro over his shoulder and through the door. Regan courteously stood aside and murmured: "Straight ahead and up the ramp. I'm giving you my own cabin. We'll be docking soon enough; I'll make out."

Charles dropped her onto a sybaritic bed in a small but lavishly-appointed cabin. Regan whistled up a deckhand and a ship's officer of some sort, who arrived with a medicine chest. "Do what you can for her, mister," he told the officer. And to the deckhand: "Just watch them. They aren't to touch anything. If they give you trouble, you're free to punch them around a bit." He left, whistling.

The officer fussed unhappily over the medicine chest and stalled by sponging off Lee Falcaro's face and throat. The deckhand watched impassively. He was a six-footer, and he hadn't spent days inhaling casing-head fumes. The trip-hammer pounding behind Charles's eyes seemed to be worsening with the fresher air. He collapsed into a seat and croaked, with shut eyes: "While you're trying to figure out the vomiting, can I have a handful of aspirins?"

"Eh? Nothing was said about you. You were in Number Three with her? I suppose it'll be all right. Here." He poured a dozen tablets into Charles' hand. "Get him some water, you." The deckhand brought a glass of water from the adjoining lavatory and Charles washed down some of the tablets. The officer was reading a booklet, worry written on his face. "Do you know any medicine?" he finally asked.

The hard-outlined, kidney-shaped ache was beginning to diffuse through Charles' head, more general now and less excruciating. He felt deliciously sleepy, but roused himself to answer: "Some athletic trainer stuff. I don't know-morphine? Curare?"

The officer ruffled through the booklet. "Nothing about vomiting," he said. "But it says curare for muscular cramp and I guess that's what's going on. A lipoid suspension to release it slowly into the bloodstream and give the irritation time to subside. Anyway, I can't kill her if I watch the dose...."

Charles, through half-opened eyes, saw Lee Falcaro's arm reach behind the officer's back to his medicine chest. The deckhand's eyes were turning to the bed-Charles heaved himself to his feet, skyrockets going off again through his head, and started for the lavatory. The deckhand grabbed his arm. "Rest, mister! Where do you think you're going?"

"Another glass of water —"

"I'll get it. You heard my orders."

Charles subsided. When he dared to look again, Lee's arm lay alongside her body and the officer was triple-checking dosages in his booklet against a pressurized hypodermic spray. The officer sighed and addressed Lee: "You won't even feel this. Relax." He read his setting on the spray again, checked it again against the booklet. He touched the syringe to the skin of Lee's arm and thumbed open the valve. It hissed for a moment and Charles knew submicroscopic particles of the medication had been blasted under Lee's skin too fast for nerves to register the shock.

His glass of water came and he gulped it greedily. The officer packed the pressurized syringe away, folded the chest and said to both of them, rather vaguely: "That should do it. If, uh, if anything happens-or if it doesn't work-call me and I'll try something else. Morphine, maybe."

He left and Charles slumped in the chair, the pain ebbing and sleep beginning to flow over him. Not yet, he told himself. She hooked something from the chest. He said to the deckhand: "Can I clean the lady and myself up?"

"Go ahead, mister. You can use it. Just don't try anything."

The man lounged in the door-frame of the lavatory alternately studying Charles at the wash-basin and Lee on the bed. Charles took off a heavy layer of oily grease from himself and then took washing tissues to the bed. Lee Falcaro's spasms were tapering off. As he washed her, she managed a smile and an unmistakable wink.

"You folks married?" the deckhand asked.

"No," Charles said. Weakly she held up her right arm for the washing tissue. As he scrubbed the hand, he felt a small cylinder smoothly transferred from her palm to his. He slid it into a pocket and finished the job.

The officer popped in again with a carton of milk. "Any better, miss?" he asked.

"Yes," she whispered.

"Good. Try to drink this." Immensely set up by his success in treatment, he hovered over her for a quarter of an hour getting the milk down a sip at a time. It stayed down. He left trailing a favorable prognosis. Meanwhile, Charles had covertly examined Lee's booty: a pressurized syringe labeled *morphine sulfate sol.* It was full and ready. He cracked off the protective cap and waited his chance.

It came when Lee grimaced at him and called the deckhand in a feeble murmur. She continued to murmur so indistinctly that he bent over trying to catch the words. Charles leaned forward and emptied the syringe at one inch range into the taut seat of the deckhand's pants. He scratched absently and said to Lee: "You'll have to talk up, lady." Then he giggled, looked bewildered and collapsed on the floor, staring, coked to the eyebrows.

Lee painfully sat up on the bed. "Porthole," she said.

Charles went to it and struggled with the locking lugs. It opened-and an alarm bell began to clang through the ship. *Now* he saw the hair-fine, broken wire. An alarm trip-wire.

Feet thundered outside and the glutinous voice of Jimmy Regan was heard: "Wait, you damn fools! You in there-is everything all right? Did they try to pull something?"

Charles kept silent and shook his head at the girl. He picked up a chair and stood by the door. The glutinous voice again, in a mumble that didn't carry through-and the door sprang open. Charles brought the chair down in a murderous chop, conscious only that it seemed curiously light. There was an impact and the head fell.

It was Regan, with a drawn gun. It had been Regan. His skull was smashed before he knew it. Charles felt as though he had all the time in the world. He picked up the gun to a confused roar like a slowed-down sound track and emptied it into the corridor. It had been a full automatic, but the fifteen shots seemed as well-spaced as a ceremonial salute. Regan, in his vanity, wore two guns. Charles scooped up the other and said to Lee: "Come on."

He knew she was following as he raced down the cleared corridor and down the ramp, back to the compartment in which they had been locked. Red danger lights burned on the walls. Charles flipped the pistol to semi-automatic as they passed a red-painted bulkhead with valves and gages sprouting from it. He turned and fired three deliberate shots into it. The last was drowned out by a dull roar as gasoline fumes exploded. Pipe fittings and fragments of plate whizzed about them like bullets as they raced on.

Somebody ahead loomed, yelling querulously: "What the hell was that, Mac? What blew?"

"Where's the reactor room?" Charles demanded, jamming the pistol into his chest. The man gulped and pointed.

"Take me there. Fast."

"Now *look*, Mac —"

Charles told him in a few incisive details where and how he was going to be shot. The man went white and led them down the corridor and into the reactor room. Three white-coated men with the aloof look of reactor specialists stared at them as they bulled into the spotless chamber.

The oldest sniffed: "And what, may I ask, are you crewmen doing in —"

Lee slammed the door behind them and said: "Sound the radiation alarm."

"Certainly not! You must be the couple we —"

"*Sound the radiation alarm.*" She picked up a pair of dividers from the plot board and approached the technician with murder on her face. He gaped until she poised the needle points before his eyes and repeated: "*Sound the radiation alarm.*" Nobody in the room, including Charles, had the slightest doubt that the points would sink into the technician's eyeballs if he refused.

"Do what she says, Will," he mumbled, his eyes crossing on the dividers. "For God's sake, do what she says. She's crazy."

One of the men moved, very cautiously, watching Charles and the gun, to a red handle and pulled it down. A ferro-concrete barrier rose to wall off the chamber and the sine-curve wail of a standard radioactivity warning began to howl mournfully through the ship.

"Dump the reactor metal," Charles said. His eyes searched for the exit, and found it —a red-painted breakaway panel, standard for a hot lab.

A technician wailed: "We *can't* do that! We can't *do* that! A million bucks of thorium with a hundred years of life in it-have a heart, mister! They'll crucify us!"

"They can dredge for it," Charles said. "Dump the metal."

"Dump the metal," Lee said. She hadn't moved.

The senior technician's eyes were still on the bright needle points. He was crying silently. "Dump it," he said.

"Okay, chief. Your responsibility, remember."

"Dump it!" wailed the senior.

The technician did something technical at the control board. After a moment the steady rumbling of the turbines ceased and the ship's deck began to wallow underfoot.

"Hit the panel, Lee," Charles said. She did, running. He followed her through the oval port. It was like an open-bottomed diving bell welded to the hull. There were large, luminous cleats for pulling yourself down through the water, under the rim of the bell. He dropped the pistol into the water, breathed deeply a couple of times and began to climb down. There was no sign of Lee.

He kicked up through the dark water on a long slant away from the ship. It might be worse. With a fire and a hot-lab alarm and a dead chief aboard, the crew would have things on their mind besides looking for bobbing heads.

He broke the surface and treaded water to make a minimum target. He did not turn to the ship. His dark hair would be less visible than his white face. And if he was going to get a burst of machine-gun bullets through either, he didn't want to know about it. Ahead he saw Lee's blonde hair spread on the water for a moment and then it vanished. He breathed hugely, ducked and swam under water toward it.

When he rose next a sheet of flame was lightening the sky and the oily reek of burning hydrocarbons tainted the air. He dove again, and this time caught up with Lee. Her face was bone-white and her eyes blank. Where she was drawing her strength from he could not guess.

Behind them the ship sent up an oily plume and the sine-curve wail of the radioactivity warning could be faintly heard. Before them a dim shore stretched.

He gripped her naked arm, roughened by the March waters of Lake Michigan, bent it around his neck and struck off for the shore. His lungs were bursting in his chest and the world was turning gray-black before his burning eyes. He heaved his tired arm through the water as though each stroke would be his last, but the last stroke, by some miracle, never was the last.

CHAPTER XIX

It hadn't been easy to get time off from the oil-painting factory. Ken Oliver was a little late when he slid into the aseptic-smelling waiting room of the Michigan City Medical Center. A parabolic mike in the ceiling trained itself on the heat he radiated and followed him across the floor to a chair. A canned voice said: "State your business, please."

He started a little and said in the general direction of the mike: "I'm Ken Oliver. A figure man in the Blue Department, Picasso Oils and Etching Corporation. Dr. Latham sent me here for-what do you call it? —a biopsy."

"Thank you, please be seated."

He smiled because he was seated already and picked up a magazine, the current copy of the *Illinois Sporting News*, familiarly known as the Green Sheet. Everybody in Mob Territory read it. The fingers of the blind spelled out its optimism and its selections at Hawthorne in Braille. If you were not only blind but fingerless, there was a talking edition that read itself aloud to you from tape.

He riffled through the past performances and selections to the articles. This month's lead was —*Thank God I am Dying of Throat Cancer*.

He leaned back in the chair dizzily, the waiting room becoming gray mist around him. *No*, he thought. *No*. It couldn't be that. All it could be was a little sore on the back of his throat-no more than that. Just a little sore on the back of his throat. He'd been a fool to go to Latham. The fees were outrageous and he was behind, always a little behind, on his bills. But cancer-so much of it around-and the drugs didn't seem to *help* any more....But Latham had almost promised him it was non-malignant.

"Mr. Oliver," the loudspeaker said, "please go to Dr. Riordan's office, Number Ten."

Riordan was younger than he. That was supposed to be bad in a general practitioner, good in a specialist. And Riordan was a specialist-pathology. A sour-faced young specialist.

"Good morning. Sit here. Open your mouth. Wider than that, and relax. *Relax*; your glottis is locked."

Oliver couldn't protest around the plastic-and-alcohol taste of the tongue depressor. There was a sudden coldness and a metallic *snick* that startled him greatly; then Riordan took the splint out of his mouth and ignored him as he summoned somebody over his desk set. A young man, even younger than Riordan, came in. "Freeze, section and stain this right away," the pathologist said, handing him a forceps from which a small blob dangled. "Have them send up the Rotino charts, three hundred to nine hundred inclusive."

He began to fill out charts, still ignoring Oliver, who sat and sweated bullets for ten minutes. Then he left and was back in five minutes more.

"You've got it," he said shortly. "It's operable and you won't lose much tissue." He scribbled on a sheet of paper and handed it to Oliver. The painter numbly read: "...anterior ...epithelioma ...metastases ...giant cells...."

Riordan was talking again: "Give this to Latham. It's my report. Have him line up a surgeon. As to the operation, I say the sooner the better unless you care to lose your larynx. That will be fifty dollars."

"Fifty dollars," the painter said blankly. "But Dr. Latham told me —" He trailed off and got out his check book. Only thirty-two in the account, but he would deposit his paycheck today which would bring it up. It was after three so his check wouldn't go in today-he wrote out the slip slowly and carefully.

Riordan took it, read it suspiciously, put it away and said: "Good day, Mr. Oliver."

Oliver wandered from the Medical Center into the business heart of the art colony. The Van Gogh Works on the left must have snagged the big order from Mexico-their chimneys were going full blast and the reek of linseed oil and turps was strong in the air. But the poor beggars on the line at Rembrandts Ltd. across the square were out of luck. They'd been laid off for a month now, with no sign of a work call yet. Somebody jostled him off the sidewalk, somebody in a great hurry. Oliver sighed. The place was getting more like Chicago every day. He sometimes thought he had made art his line not because he had any special talent but because artists were relatively easy-going people, not so quick to pop you in the nose, not such aggressive drunks when they *were* drunks.

Quit the stalling, a thin, cold voice inside him said. Get over to Latham. The man said "The sooner the better."

He went over to Latham whose waiting room was crowded with irascible women. After an hour, he got to see the old man and hand him the slip.

Latham said: "Don't worry about a thing. Riordan's a good man. If he says it's operable, it's operable. Now we want Finsen to do the whittling. With Finsen operating, you won't have to worry about a thing. He's a good man. His fee's fifteen hundred."

"Oh, my God!" Oliver gulped.

"What's the matter-haven't you got it?"

To his surprise and terror, Oliver found himself giving Dr. Latham a hysterical stump speech about how he didn't have it and who did have it and how could anybody get ahead with the way prices were shooting up and everybody gouged you every time you turned around and yes, that went for doctors too and if you did get a couple of bucks in your pocket the salesmen heard about it and battered at you until you put down an installment on some piece of junk you didn't want to get them out of your hair and what the hell kind of world was this anyway.

Latham listened, smiling and nodding, with, as Oliver finally realized, his hearing aid turned off. His voice ran down and Latham said briskly: "All right, then. You just come around when you've arranged the financial details and I'll contact Finsen. He's a good man; you won't have to worry about a thing. And remember: the sooner, the better."

Oliver slumped out of the office and went straight to the Mob Building, office of the Regan Benevolent Fund. An acid-voiced woman there turned him down indignantly: "You should be ashamed of yourself trying to draw on the Fund when there are people in actual want who can't be accommodated! No, I don't want to hear any more about it if you please. There are others waiting."

Waiting for what? The same treatment?

Oliver realized with a shock that he hadn't phoned his foreman as promised, and it was four minutes to five. He did a dance of agonized impatience outside a telephone booth occupied by a fat woman. She noticed him, pursed her lips, hung up-and stayed in the booth. She began a slow search of her hand-bag, found coins and slowly dialed a new number. She gave him a malevolent grin as he walked away, crushed. He had a good job record, but that was no way to keep it good. One black mark, another black mark, and one day-bingo.

General Advances was open, of course. Through its window you could see handsome young men and sleek young women just waiting to help you, whatever the fiscal jam. He went in and was whisked to a booth where a big-bosomed honey-voiced blonde oozed sympathy over him. He walked out with a check for fifteen hundred dollars after signing countless papers, with the creamy hand of the girl on his to help guide the pen. What was printed on the papers, God and General Advances alone knew. There were men on the line who told him with resignation that they had been paying off to G.A. for the better part of their lives. There were men who said bitterly that G.A. was owned by the Regan Benevolent Fund, which must be a lie.

The street was full of people-strangers who didn't look like your run-of-the-mill artist. Muscle men, with the Chicago style and if anybody got one in the gut, too goddamned bad about it. They were peering into faces as they passed.

He was frightened. He stepped onto the slidewalk and hurried home, hoping for temporary peace there. But there was no peace for his frayed nerves. The apartment house door opened obediently when he told it: "Regan," but the elevator stood stupidly still when he said: "Seventh Floor." He spat bitterly and precisely: *"Sev-enth Floor."* The doors closed on him with a faintly derisive, pneumatic moan and he was whisked up to the eighth floor. He walked down wearily and said: "Cobalt blue" to his own door after a furtive look up and down the hall. It worked and he went to his phone to flash Latham, but didn't. Oliver sank instead into a dun-colored pneumatic chair, his 250-dollar Hawthorne Electric Stepsaver door mike following him with its mindless snout. He punched a button on the chair and the 600-dollar hi-fi selected a random tape. A long, pure melodic trumpet line filled the room. It died for two beats and than the strings and woodwinds picked it up and tossed it —

Oliver snapped off the music, sweat starting from his brow. It was the Gershwin *Lost Symphony*, and he remembered how Gershwin had died. There had been a little nodule in his brain as there was a little nodule in Oliver's throat.

Time, the Great Kidder. The years drifted by. Suddenly you were middle-aged, running to the medics for this and that. Suddenly they told you to have your throat whittled out or die disgustingly. And what did you have to show for it? A number, a travel pass, a payment book from General Advance, a bunch of junk you never wanted, a job that was a heavier ball and chain than any convict ever wore in the barbarous days of Government. Was this what Regan and Falcaro had bled for?

He defrosted some hamburger, fried it and ate it and then went mechanically down to the tavern. He didn't like to drink every night, but you had to be one of the boys, or word would get back to the plant and you might be on your way to another black mark. They were racing under the lights at Hawthorne too, and he'd be expected to put a couple of bucks down. He never seemed to win. Nobody he knew ever seemed to win. Not at the horses, not at the craps table, not at the numbers.

He stood outside the neon-bright saloon for a long moment, and then turned and walked into the darkness away from town, possessed by impulses he did not understand or want to understand. He had only a vague hope that standing on the Dunes and looking out across the dark lake might somehow soothe him.

In half an hour he had reached the deciduous forest, then the pine, then the scrubby brushes, then the grasses, then the bare white sand. And lying in it he found two people: a man so hard and dark he seemed to be carved from oak and a woman so white and gaunt she seemed to be carved from ivory.

He turned shyly from the woman.

"Are you all right?" he asked the man. "Is there anything I can do?"

The man opened red-rimmed eyes. "Better leave us alone," he said. "We'd only get you into trouble."

Oliver laughed hysterically. "Trouble?" he said. "Don't think of it."

The man seemed to be measuring him with his eyes, and said at last: "You'd better go and not talk about us. We're enemies of the Mob."

Oliver said after a pause: "So am I. Don't go away. I'll be back with some clothes and food for you and the lady. Then I can help you to my place. I'm an enemy of the Mob too. I just never knew it until now."

He started off and then turned. "You won't go away? I mean it. I want to help you. I can't seem to help myself, but perhaps there's something —"

The man said tiredly: "We won't go away."

Oliver hurried off. There was something mingled with the scent of the pine forest tonight. He was half-way home before he identified it: oil smoke.

CHAPTER XX

Lee swore and said: "I can get up if I want to."

"You'll stay in bed whether you want to or not," Charles told her. "You're a sick woman."

"I'm a very bad-tempered woman and that means I'm convalescent. Ask anybody."

"I'll go right out into the street and do that, darling."

She got out of bed and wrapped Oliver's dressing gown around her. "I'm hungry again," she said.

"He'll be back soon. You've left nothing but some frozen-worms, looks like. Shall I defrost them?"

"Please don't trouble. I can wait."

"Window!" he snapped.

She ducked back and swore again, this time at herself. "Sorry," she said. "Which will do us a whole hell of a lot of good if somebody saw me and started wondering."

Oliver came in with packages. Lee kissed him and he grinned shyly. "Trout," he whispered. She grabbed the packages and flew to the kitchenette.

"The way to Lee Falcaro's heart," Charles mused. "How's your throat, Ken?"

"No pain, today," Oliver whispered. "Latham says I can talk as much as I like. And I've got things to talk about." He opened his coat and hauled out a flat package that had been stuffed under his belt. "Stolen from the factory. Brushes, pens, tubes of ink, drawing instruments. My friends, you are going to return to Syndic Territory in style, with passes and permits galore."

Lee returned. "Trout's frying," she said. "I heard that about the passes. Are you *sure* you can fake them?"

His face fell. "Eight years at the Chicago Art Institute," he whispered. "Three years at Original Reproductions, Inc. Eleven years at Picasso Oils and Etchings, where I am now third figure man in the Blue Department. I really think I deserve your confidence."

"Ken, we trust and love you. If it weren't for the difference in your ages I'd marry you *and* Charles. Now what about the Chicagoans? Hold it-the fish!"

Dinner was served and cleared away before they could get more out of Oliver. His throat wasn't ready for more than one job at a time. He told them at last: "Things are quieting down. There are still some strangers in town and the road patrols are still acting very hard-boiled. But nobody's been pulled in today. Somebody told me on the line that the whole business is a lot of foolishness. He said the ship must have been damaged by somebody's stupidity and Regan must have been killed in a brawl-everybody knows he was half crazy, like his father. So my friend figures they made up the story about two wild Europeans to cover up a mess. I said I thought there was a lot in what he said." Oliver laughed silently.

"Good man!" Charles tried not to act over-eager. "When do you think you can start on the passes, Ken?"

Oliver's face dropped a little. "Tonight," he whispered. "I don't suppose the first couple of tries will be any good so-let's go."

Lee put her hand on his shoulder. "We'll miss you too," she said. "But don't ever forget this: we're coming back. Hell won't stop us. We're coming back."

Oliver was arranging stolen instruments on the table. "You have a big order," he whispered sadly. "I guess you aren't afraid of it because you've always been rich and strong. Anything you want to do you think you can do. But those Government people? And after them the Mob? Maybe it would be better if you just let things take their course, Lee. I've found out a person can be happy even here."

"We're coming back," Lee said.

Oliver took out his own Michigan City-Chicago travel permit. As always, the sight of it made Charles wince. Americans under such a yoke! Oliver whispered: "I got a good long look today at a Michigan City Buffalo permit. The foreman's. He buys turps from Carolina at Buffalo. I sketched it from memory as soon as I got by myself. I don't swear to it, not yet, but I have the sketch to practice from and I can get a few more looks later."

He pinned down the drawing paper, licked a ruling pen and filled it, and began to copy the border of his own pass. "I don't suppose there's anything I can do?" Lee asked.

"You can turn on the audio," Oliver whispered. "They have it going all the time at the shop. I don't feel right working unless there's some music driving me out of my mind."

Lee turned on the big Hawthorne Electric set with a wave of her hand; imbecillic music filled the air and Oliver grunted and settled down.

Lee and Charles listened, fingers entwined, to half an hour of slushy ballads while Oliver worked. The news period announcer came on with some anesthetic trial verdicts, sports results and society notes about which Regan had gone where. Then —

"The local Mobsters of Michigan City, Indiana, today welcomed Maurice Regan to their town. Mr. Regan will assume direction of efforts to apprehend the two European savages who murdered James Regan IV last month aboard the ore boat *Hon. John Regan* in waters off Michigan City. You probably remember that the Europeans did some damage to the vessel's reactor room before they fled from the ship. How they boarded the ship and their present whereabouts are mysteries-but they probably won't be mysteries long. Maurice Regan is little-known to the public, but he has built an enviable record in the administration of the Chicago Police Department. Mr. Regan on taking charge of the case, said this: 'We know by traces found on the Dunes that they got away. We know from the logs of highway patrols that they didn't get out of the Michigan City area. The only way to close the books on this matter fast is to cover the city with a fine-tooth comb. Naturally and unfortunately this will mean inconvenience to many citizens. I hope they will bear with the inconveniences gladly for the sake of confining those two savages in a place where they can no longer be a menace. I have methods of my own and there may be complaints. Reasonable suggestions will be needed, but with crackpots I have no patience.'"

The radio began to spew more sports results. Oliver turned and waved at it to be silent. "I don't like that," he whispered. "I never heard of this Regan in the Chicago Police."

"They said he wasn't in the public eye."

"I wasn't the public. I did some posters for the police and I knew who was who. And that bit at the end. I've heard things like it before. The Mob doesn't often admit it's in the wrong, you know. When they try to disarm criticism in advance ... this Regan must be a rough fellow."

Charles and Lee Falcaro looked at each other in sudden fear. "We don't want to hurry you, Ken," she said. "But it looks as though you'd better do a rush job."

Nodding, Oliver bent over the table. "Maybe a week," he said hopefully. With the finest pen he traced the curlicues an engraving lathe had evolved to make the passes foolproof. Odd, he thought-the lives of these two hanging by such a weak thing as the twisted thread of color that feeds from pen to paper. And, as an afterthought —I suppose mine does too.

* * * * *

Oliver came back the next day to work with concentrated fury, barely stopping to eat and not stopping to talk. Lee got it out of him, but not easily. After being trapped in a half dozen contradictions about feeling well and having a headache, about his throat being sore and the pain having gone, he put down his pen and whispered steadily: "I didn't want you to worry friends. But it looks bad. There is a new crowd in town. Twenty couples have been pulled in by them —*couples* to prove who they were. Maybe fifty people have been pulled in for questioning-what do you know about this, what do you know about that. And they've begun house searches. Anybody you don't like, you tell the new Regan about him. Say he's sheltering Europeans. And his people pull them in. Why, everybody wants to know, are they pulling in couples who are obviously American if they're looking for Europeans? And, everybody says, they've never seen anything like it. Now —I think I'd better get back to work."

"Yes," Lee said. "I think you had."

Charles was at the window, peering around the drawn blind. "Look at that," he said to Lee. She came over. A big man on the street below was walking, very methodically down the street.

"I will bet you," Charles said, "that he'll be back this way in ten minutes or so-and so on through the night."

"I won't take the bet," she said. "He's a sentry, all right. The Mob's learning from their friends across the water. Learning too damned much. They must be all over town."

They watched at the window and the sentry was back in ten minutes. On his fifth tour he stopped a young couple going down the street studied their faces, drew a gun on them and blew a whistle. A patrol came and took them away; the girl was hysterical. At two in the morning, the sentry was relieved by another, just as big and just as dangerous looking. At two in the morning they were still watching and Oliver was still hunched over the table tracing exquisite filigree of color.

* * * * *

In five days, virtually without sleep, Oliver finished two Michigan City-Buffalo travel permits. The apartment house next door was hit by raiders while the ink dried; Charles and Lee Falcaro stood waiting grotesquely armed with kitchen knives. But it must have been a tip rather than part of the search plan crawling nearer to their end of town. The raiders did not hit their building.

Oliver had bought clothes according to Lee's instructions-including two men's suits, Oliver's size. One she let out for Charles; the other she took in for herself. She instructed Charles minutely in how he was to behave, on the outside. First he roared with incredulous laughter; Lee, wise, in psychology assured him that she was perfectly serious. Oliver, puzzled by his naivete, assured him that such things were not uncommon-not at least in Mob Territory. Charles then roared with indignation and Lee roared him down. His last broken protest was: "But what'll I do if somebody takes me up on it?"

She shrugged, washing her hands of the matter, and went on trimming and dying her hair.

It was morning when she kissed Oliver good-bye, said to Charles: "See you at the station. Don't say good-bye," and walked from the apartment, a dark-haired boy with a slight limp. Charles watched her down the street. A cop turned to look after her and then went on his way.

Half an hour later Charles shook hands with Oliver and went out.

Oliver didn't go to work that day. He sat all day at the table, drawing endless slow sketches of Lee Falcaro's head.

Time the Great Kidder, he thought. He opens the door that shows you in the next room tables of goodies, colorful and tasty, men and women around the tables pleasantly surprised to see you, beckoning to you to join the feast. We have roast beef if you're serious, we have caviar if you're experimental, we have baked alaska if you're frivolous-join the feast; try a little bit of everything. So you start toward the door.

Time, the Great Kidder, pulls the rug from under your feet and slams the door while the guests at the feast laugh their heads off at your painful but superficial injuries.

Oliver slowly drew Lee's head for the fifteenth time and wished he dared to turn on the audio for the news. Perhaps he thought, the next voice you hear will be the cops at the door.

CHAPTER XXI.

Charles walked down the street and ran immediately into a challenge from a police sergeant.

"Where you from, mister?" the cop demanded, balanced and ready to draw.

Charles gulped and let Lee Falcaro's drilling take over. "Oh, around, sergeant. I'm from around here."

"What're you so nervous about?"

"Why, sergeant, you're such an exciting type, really. Did anybody ever tell you you look well in uniform?"

The cop glared at him and said: "If I wasn't in uniform, I'd hang one on you sister. And if the force wasn't all out hunting the lunatics, that killed Mr. Regan I'd pull you in for spitting on the sidewalk. Get to hell off my beat and stay off. I'm not forgetting your face."

Charles scurried on. It had worked.

It worked once more with a uniformed policeman. One of the Chicago plain-clothes imports was the third and last. He socked Charles in the jaw and sent him on his way with a kick in the rear. He had been thoroughly warned that it would probably happen: "Count on them to over-react. That's the key to it. You'll make them so eager to assert their own virility, that it'll temporarily bury their primary mission. It's quite likely that one or more pokes will be taken at you. All you can do is take them. If you get —*when* you get through, they'll be cheap at the price."

The sock in the jaw hadn't been very expert. The kick in the pants was negligible, considering the fact that it had propelled him through the gate of the Michigan City Transport Terminal.

By the big terminal clock the Chicago-Buffalo Express was due in fifteen minutes. Its gleaming single rail, as tall as a man crossed the far end of the concourse. Most of the fifty-odd people in the station were probably Buffalo-bound ... safe geldings who could be trusted to visit Syndic Territory, off the leash and return obediently. Well-dressed, of course, and many past middle-age, with a stake in the Mob Territory stronger than hope of freedom. One youngster, though-oh. It was Lee, leaning, slack-jawed, against a pillar and reading the Green Sheet.

Who were the cops in the crowd? The thickset man with restless eyes, of course. The saintly-looking guy who kept moving and glancing into faces.

Charles went to the newsstand and put a coin in the slot for *The Mob —A Short History*, by the same Arrowsmith Hunde who had brightened and misinformed his youth.

Nothing to it, he thought. Train comes in, put your money in the turnstile, show your permit to the turnstile's eye, get aboard and that-is-that. Unless the money is phony, or the pass is phony in which case the turnstile locks and all hell breaks loose. His money was just dandy, but the permit now-there hadn't been any way to test it against a turnstile's template, or time to do it if there had been a way. Was the probability of boarding two to one?

The probability abruptly dropped to zero as a round little man flanked by two huge men entered the station.

Commander Grinnel.

The picture puzzle fell into a whole as the two plainclothesmen circulating in the station eyed Grinnel and nodded to him. The big one absent-mindedly made a gesture that was the start of a police salute.

Grinnel was Maurice Regan-the Maurice Regan mysteriously unknown to Oliver, who knew the Chicago police. Grinnel was a bit of a lend-lease from the North American Navy, called in because of his unique knowledge of Charles Orsino and Lee Falcaro, their faces, voices and behavior. Grinnel was the expert in combing the city without any nonsense about rights and mouthpieces. Grinnel was the expert who could set up a military interior guard of the city. Grinnel was the specialist temporarily invested with the rank of a Regan so he could do his job.

The round little man with the halo of hair walked briskly to the turnstile and there stood at a military parade rest with a look of resignation on his face.

How hard on me it is, he seemed to be saying, that I have such dull damn duty. How hard that an officer of my brilliance must do sentry-go for every train to Syndic Territory.

The slack-jawed youth who was Lee Falcaro looked at him over her Green Sheet and nodded before dipping into the Tia Juana past performances again. She knew.

Passengers were beginning to line up at the turnstile, smoothing out their money and fiddling with their permits. In a minute he and Lee Falcaro would have to join the line or stand conspicuously on the emptying floor. The thing was dead for twenty-four hours now, until the next train-and then Grinnel headed across the floor looking very impersonal. The look of a man going to the men's room. The station cops and Grinnel's two bruisers drifted together at the turnstile and began to chat.

Charles followed Grinnel, wearing the same impersonal look, and entered the room almost on his heels.

Grinnel saw him in a wash-bowl mirror; simultaneously he half turned, opened his mouth to yell and whipped his hand into his coat. A single round-house right from Charles crunched into the soft side of his neck. He fell with his head twisted at an odd angle. Blood began to run from the corner of his mouth onto his shirt.

"Remember Martha?" Charles whispered down at the body. "That was for murder." He looked around the tiled room. There was a mop closet with the door ajar, and Grinnel's flabby body fitted in it.

Charles walked from the washroom to the line of passengers across the floor. It seemed to go on for miles. Lee Falcaro was no longer lounging against the past. He spotted her in line, still slack-jawed, still gaping over the magazine. The monorail began to sing shrilly with the vibration of the train braking a mile away, and the turnstile "unlocked" light went on.

There was the usual number of fumblers, the usual number of "please unfold your currency" flashes. Lee carried through to the end with her slovenly pose. For her the sign said: "incorrect denominations." Behind her a man snarled: "for Christ's sake, kid, we're all waiting on you!" The cops only half noticed; they were talking. When Charles got to the turnstile one of the cops was saying: "Maybe it's something he ate. How'd *you* like somebody to barge in —"

The rest was lost in the clicking of the turnstile that let him through.

* * * * *

He settled in a very pneumatic chair as the train accelerated evenly to a speed of three hundred and fifty miles per hour. A sign in the car said that the next stop was Buffalo. And there was Lee, lurching up the aisle against the acceleration. She spotted him, tossed the Green Sheet in the Air and fell into his lap.

"Disgusting!" snarled a man across the aisle. "Simply disgusting!"

"You haven't seen anything yet," Lee told him, and kissed Charles on the mouth.

The man choked: "I shall certainly report this to the authorities when we arrive in Buffalo!"

"Mmm," said Lee, preoccupied. "Do that, mister. Do that."

CHAPTER XXII

"I didn't like his reaction," Charles told her in the anteroom of F. W. Taylor's office. "I didn't talk to him long on the phone, but I don't like his reaction at all. He seemed to think I was exaggerating. Or all wet. Or a punk kid."

"I can assure him you're not that," Lee Falcaro said warmly. "Call on me any time."

He gave her a worried smile. The door opened then and they went in.

Uncle Frank looked up. "We'd just about written you two off," he said. "What's it like?"

"Bad," Charles said. "Worse than anything you've imagined. There's an underground, all right, and they are practicing assassination."

"Too bad," the old man said. "We'll have to shake up the bodyguard organization. Make 'em de rigeur at all hours, screen 'em and see that they really know how to shoot. I hate to meddle, but we can't have the Government knocking our people off."

"It's worse than that," Lee said. "There's a tie-up between the Government and the Mob. We got away from Ireland aboard a speed boat and we were picked up by a Mob lakes ore ship. It had been running gasoline and ammunition to the Government. Jimmy Regan was in charge of the deal. We jumped into Lake Michigan and made our way back here. We were in Mob Territory-down among the small-timers —long enough to establish that the Mob and Government are hand in glove. One of these day's they're going to jump us."

"Ah," Taylor said softly. "I've thought so for a long time."

Charles burst out: "Then for God's sake, Uncle Frank, why haven't you *done* anything? You don't know what it's like out there. The Government's a nightmare. They have slaves. And the Mob's not much better. Numbers! Restrictions! Permits! Passes! And they don't call it that, but they have taxes!"

"They're mad," Lee said. "Quite mad. And I'm talking technically. Neurotics and psychotics swarm in the streets of Mob Territory. The Government, naturally-but the Mob was a shock. We've got to get ready, Mr. Taylor. Every psychotic or severe neurotic in Syndic Territory is a potential agent of theirs."

"Don't just check off the Government, darling," Charles said tensely. "They've got to be smashed. They're no good to themselves or anybody else. Life's a burden there if only they knew it. And they're holding down the natives by horrible cruelty."

Taylor leaned back and asked: "What do you recommend?"

Charles said: "A fighting fleet and an army."

Lee said: "Mass diagnosis of the unstable. Screening of severe cases and treatment where it's indicated. Riveredge must be a plague-spot of agents."

Taylor shook his head and told them: "It won't do."

Charles was aghast. "It won't *do*? Uncle Frank, what the hell do you mean, it won't do? Didn't we make it clear? They want to invade us and loot us and subject us!"

"It won't do," Taylor said. "I choose the devil we know. A fighting fleet is out. We'll arm our merchant vessels and hope for the best. A full-time army is out. We'll get together some-kind of militia. And a roundup of the unstable is out."

"Why?" Lee demanded. "My people have worked out perfectly effective techniques —"

"Let me talk, please. I have a feeling that it won't be any good, but hear me out.

"I'll take your black art first, Lee. As you know, I have played with history. To a historian, your work has been very interesting. The sequence was this: study of abnormal psychology collapsed under Lieberman's findings, study of abnormal psychology revived by you when you invalidated Lieberman's findings. I suggest that Lieberman and his followers were correct-and that you were correct. I suggest that what changed was the makeup of the population. That would mean that before Lieberman there were plenty of neurotics and psychotics to study, that in Lieberman's time there were so few that earlier generalizations were invalidated, and that now-in our time, Lee-neurotics and psychotics are among us again in increasingly ample numbers."

The girl opened her mouth, shut it again and thoughtfully studied her nails.

"I will not tolerate," Taylor went on, "a roundup or a registration, or mass treatment or any such violation of the Syndic's spirit."

Charles exploded: "Damn it, this is a matter of life or death to the Syndic!"

"No, Charles. Nothing can be a matter of life or death to the Syndic. When anything becomes a matter of life or death to the Syndic, the Syndic is already dead, its morale, is already disintegrated, its credit already gone. What is left is not the Syndic but the Syndic's dead shell. I am not placed so that I can say objectively now whether the Syndic is dead or alive. I fear it is dying. The rising tide of neurotics is a symptom. The suggestion from you two, who should be imbued with the old happy-go-lucky, we-can't-miss esprit of the Syndic that we cower behind mercenaries instead of trusting the people who made us-that's another symptom. Dick Reiner's rise to influence on a policy of driving the Government from the seas is another symptom.

"I mentioned the devil we know as my choice. That's the status quo, even though I have reason to fear it's crumbling beneath our feet. If it is, it may last out our time. We'll shore it up with armed merchantmen and a militia. If the people are with us now as they always have been, that'll do it. The devil we don't know is what we'll become if we radically dislocate Syndic life and attitudes.

"I can't back a fighting fleet. I can't back a regular army. I can't back any restrictive measure on the freedom of anybody but an apprehended criminal. Read history. It has taught me not to meddle, it has taught me that no man should think himself clever enough or good enough to dare it. *That* is the lesson history teaches us.

"Who can know what he's doing when he doesn't even know why he does it? Bless the bright Cromagnon for inventing the bow and damn him for inventing missile warfare. Bless the stubby little Sumerians for miracles in gold and lapis lazuli and damn them for burying a dead queen's hand-maidens living in her tomb. Bless Shih Hwang-Ti for building the Great Wall between northern barbarism and southern culture, and damn him for burning every book in China. Bless King Minos for the ease of Cnossian flush toilets and damn him for his yearly tribute of Greek sacrificial victims. Bless Pharaoh for peace and damn him for slavery. Bless the Greeks for restricting population so the well-fed few could kindle a watch-tower in the west, and damn the prostitution and sodomy and wars of colonization by which they did it. Bless the Romans for their strength to smash down every wall that hemmed their building genius, and damn them for their weakness that never broke the bloody grip of Etruscan savagery on their minds. Bless the Jews who discovered the fatherhood of God and damn them who limited it to the survivors of a surgical operation. Bless the Christians who abolished the surgical preliminaries and damn them who substituted a thousand cerebral quibbles. Bless Justinian for the Code of Law and damn him for his countless treacheries that were the prototype of the wretched Byzantine millenium. Bless the churchmen for teaching and preaching, and damn, them for drawing a line beyond which they could only teach and preach in peril of the stake.

"Bless the navigators who, opened the new world to famine-ridden Europe, and damn them for syphillis. Bless the red-skins who bred maize, the great preserver of life and damn them for breeding maize the great destroyer of topsoil. Bless the Virginia planters for the solace of tobacco and damn them for the red gullies they left where forests had stood. Bless the obstetricians with forceps who eased the agony of labor and damn them for bringing countless monsters into the world to reproduce their kind. Bless the Point Four boys who slew the malaria mosquitoes of Ceylon and damn them for letting more Sinhalese be born then five Ceylons could feed.

"Who knows what he is doing, why he does it or what the consequences will be?

"Let the social scientists play with their theories if they like; I'm fond of poetry myself. The fact is that they have not so far solved what I call the two-billion-body problem. With brilliant hindsight some of them tell us that more than a dozen civilizations have gone down into the darkness before us. I see no reason why ours should not go down into the darkness with them, nor do I see any reason why we should not meanwhile enjoy ourselves collecting sense-impressions to be remembered with pleasure in old age. No; I will not agitate for exter-mination of the Government and hegemony over the Mob. Such a policy would automatically, inevitably and immediately entail many, many violent deaths and painful wounds. The wrong kind of sense-impressions. I shall, with fear and trembling, recommend the raising of a mili-tia —a purely defensive, extremely sloppy militia-and pray that it will not Involve us in a war of aggression."

He looked at the two of them and shrugged. "Lee, so stern, Charles so grim," he said. "I suppose you're dedicated now." He looked at the desk.

He thought: *I have a faint desire to take the pistol from my desk and shoot you both. I have a nervous feeling that you're about to embark on a crusade to awaken Syndic Territory to its perils. You think the fate of civilization hinges on you. You're right, of course. The fate of civilization hinges on every one of us at any given moment. We are all components in the two-billion-body problem. Somehow for a century we've achieved in Syndic Territory for almost everybody the civil liberties, peace of mind and living standards that were enjoyed by the middle classes before 1914 —plus longer life, better health, a more generous morality, increased command over nature; minus the servant problem and certain superstitions. A handful of wonderfully pleasant decades. When you look back over history you wonder who in his right mind could ask for more. And you wonder who would dare to presume to tamper with it.*

He studied the earnest young faces. There was so much that he might say-but he shrugged again.

"Bless you," he said. "Gather ye sense impression while ye may. Some like pointer readings, some like friction on the mucous membranes. Now go about your business; I have work to do."

He didn't really. When he was alone he leaned back and laughed and laughed.

Win, lose or draw, those two would go far and enjoy themselves mightily along the way. Which was what counted.

Wolfbane

Appallingly, the Earth and the Moon had been
kidnapped from the Solar System-but who were
the kidnappers and what ransom did they want?

CHAPTER I.

Roget Germyn, banker, of Wheeling, West Virginia, a Citizen, woke gently from a Citizen's dreamless sleep. It was the third-hour-rising time, the time proper to a day of exceptional opportunity to appreciate.

Citizen Germyn dressed himself in the clothes proper for the appreciation of great works-such as viewing the Empire State ruins against storm clouds from a small boat, or walking in silent single file across the remaining course of the Golden Gate Bridge. Or as today-one hoped-witnessing the Re-creation of the Sun.

Germyn with difficulty retained a Citizen's necessary calm. One was tempted to meditate on improper things: Would the Sun be re-created? What if it were not?

He put his mind to his dress. First of all, he put on an old and storied bracelet, a veritable identity bracelet of heavy silver links and a plate which was inscribed:

PFC Joe Hartmann

Korea

1953

His fellow jewelry-appreciators would have envied him that bracelet-if they had been capable of such an emotion as envy. No other ID bracelet as much as two hundred and fifty years old was known to exist in Wheeling.

His finest shirt and pair of light pants went next to his skin, and over them he wore a loose parka whose seams had been carefully weakened. When the Sun was re-created, every five years or so, it was the custom to remove the parka gravely and rend it with the prescribed graceful gestures ... but not so drastically that it could not be stitched together again. Hence the weakened seams.

This was, he counted, the forty-first day on which he and all of Wheeling had do-nned the appropriate Sun Re-creation clothing. It was the forty-first day on which the Sun-no longer white, no longer blazing yellow, no longer even bright red-had risen and displayed a color that was darker maroon and always darker.

* * * * *

It had, thought Citizen Germyn, never grown so dark and so cold in all of his life. Perhaps it was an occasion for special viewing. For surely it would never come again, this opportunity to see the old Sun so near to death....

One hoped.

Gravely, Citizen Germyn completed his dressing, thinking only of the act of dressing itself. It was by no means his specialty, but he considered, when it was done, that he had done it well, in the traditional flowing gestures, with no flailing, at all times balanced lightly on the ball of the foot. It was all the more perfectly consummated because no one saw it but himself.

He woke his wife gently, by placing the palm of his hand on her forehead as she lay neatly, in the prescribed fashion, on the Woman's Third of the bed.

The warmth of his hand gradually penetrated the layers of sleep. Her eyes demurely opened.

"Citizeness Germyn," he greeted her, making the assurance-of-identity sign with his left hand.

"Citizen Germyn," she said, with the assurance-of-identity inclination of the head which was prescribed when the hands are covered.

He retired to his tiny study.

It was the time appropriate to meditation on the properties of Connectivity. Citizen Germyn was skilled in meditation, even for a banker; it was a grace in which he had schooled himself since earliest childhood.

Citizen Germyn, his young face composed, his slim body erect as he sat but in no way tense or straining, successfully blanked out, one after another, all of the external sounds and sights and feelings that interfered with proper meditation. His mind was very nearly vacant except of one central problem: Connectivity.

Over his head and behind, out of sight, the cold air of the room seemed to thicken and form a —call it a blob; a blob of air.

There was a name for those blobs of air. They had been seen before. They were a known fact of existence in Wheeling and in all the world. They came. They hovered. And they went away-sometimes not alone. If someone had been in the room with Citizen Germyn to look at it, he would have seen a distortion, a twisting of what was behind the blob, like flawed glass, a lens, like an eye. And they were called Eye.

Germyn meditated.

The blob of air grew and slowly moved. A vagrant current that spun out from it caught a fragment of paper and whirled it to the floor. Germyn stirred. The blob retreated.

Germyn, all unaware, disciplined his thoughts to disregard the interruption, to return to the central problem of Connectivity. The blob hovered....

From the other room, his wife's small, thrice-repeated throat-clearing signaled to him that she was dressed. Germyn got up to go to her, his mind returning to the world; and the overhead Eye spun relentlessly, and disappeared.

* * * * *

Some miles east of Wheeling, Glenn Tropile-of a class which found it wisest to give itself no special name, and which had devoted much time and thought to shaking the unwelcome name it had been given-awoke on the couch of his apartment.

He sat up, shivering. It was cold. The damned Sun was still bloody dark outside the window and the apartment was soggy and chilled.

He had kicked off the blankets in his sleep. *Why couldn't* he learn to sleep quietly, like anybody else? Lacking a robe, he clutched the blankets around him, got up and walked to the unglassed window.

It was not unusual for Glenn Tropile to wake up on his couch. This happened because Gala Tropile had a temper, was inclined to exile him from her bed after a quarrel, and-the operative factor-he knew he always had the advantage over her for the whole day following the night's exile. Therefore the quarrel was worth it. An advantage was, by definition, worth anything you paid for it or else it was no advantage.

He could hear her moving about in one of the other rooms and cocked an ear, satisfied. She hadn't waked him. Therefore she was about to make amends. A little itch in his spine or his brain-it was not a physical itch, so he couldn't locate it; he could only be sure that it was there-stopped troubling him momentarily; he was winning a contest. It was Glenn Tropile's nature to win contests ... and his nature to create them.

Gala Tropile, young, dark, attractive, with a haunted look, came in tentatively carrying coffee from some secret hoard of hers.

Glenn Tropile affected not to notice. He stared coldly out at the cold landscape. The sea, white with thin ice, was nearly out of sight, so far had it retreated as the little sun waned.

"Glenn —"

Ah, good! *Glenn.* Where was the proper mode of first-greeting-one's-husband? Where was the prescribed throat-clearing upon entering a room?

Assiduously, he had untaught her the meticulous ritual of manners that they had all of them been brought up to know; and it was the greatest of his many victories over her that sometimes, now, *she* was the aggressor, *she* would be the first to depart from the formal behavior prescribed for Citizens.

Depravity! Perversion!

Sometimes they would touch each other at times which were not the appropriate coming-together times, Gala sitting on her husband's lap in the late evening, perhaps, or Tropile kissing her awake in the morning. Sometimes he would force her to let him watch her dress-no, not now, for the cold of the waning sun made that sort of frolic unattractive, but she had permitted it before; and such was his mastery over her that he knew she would permit it again, when the Sun was re-created....

If, a thought came to him, *if* the Sun was re-created.

* * * * *

He turned away from the cold outside and looked at his wife. "Good morning, darling." She was contrite.

He demanded jarringly: "Is it?" Deliberately he stretched, deliberately he yawned, deliberately he scratched his chest. Every movement was ugly. Gala Tropile quivered, but said nothing.

Tropile flung himself on the better of the two chairs, one hairy leg protruding from under the wrapped blankets. His wife was on her best behavior-in his unique terms; she didn't avert her eyes.

"What've you got there?" he asked. "Coffee?"

"Yes, dear. I thought —"

"Where'd you get it?"

The haunted eyes looked away. Still better, thought Glenn Tropile, more satisfied even than usual; she's been ransacking an old warehouse again. It was a trick he had taught her, and like all of the illicit tricks she had learned from him, a handy weapon when he chose to use it.

It was not prescribed that a Citizen should rummage through Old Places. A Citizen did his work, whatever that work might be-banker, baker or furniture repairman. He received what rewards were his due for the work he did. A Citizen *never* took anything that was not his due-not even if it lay abandoned and rotting.

It was one of the differences between Glenn Tropile and the people he moved among.

I've got it made, he exulted; it was what I needed to clinch my victory over her.

He spoke: "I need you more than I need coffee, Gala."

She looked up, troubled.

"What would I do," he demanded, "if a beam fell on you one day while you were scrambling through the fancy groceries? How can you take such chances? Don't you *know* what you mean to me?"

She sniffed a couple of times. She said brokenly: "Darling, about last night —I'm sorry —" and miserably held out the cup. He took it and set it down. He took her hand, looked up at her, and kissed it lingeringly. He felt her tremble. Then she gave him a wild, adoring look and flung herself into his arms.

A new dominance cycle was begun at the moment he returned her frantic kisses.

Glenn knew, and Gala knew, that he had over her an edge, an advantage-the weather gauge, initiative of fire, percentage, the can't-lose lack of tension. Call it anything, but it was life itself to such as Glenn Tropile. He knew, and she knew, that having the advantage he would press it and she would yield-on and on, in a rising spiral.

He did it because it was his life, the attaining of an advantage over anyone he might encounter; because he was (unwelcomely but justly) called a Son of the Wolf.

* * * * *

A world away, a Pyramid squatted sullenly on the planed-off top of the highest peak of the Himalayas.

It had not been built there. It had not been carried there by Man or Man's machines. It had-come, in its own time; for its own reasons.

Did it wake on that day, the thing atop Mount Everest, or did it ever sleep? Nobody knew. It stood, or sat, there, approximately a tetrahedron. Its appearance was known: constructed on a base line of some thirty-five yards, slaggy, midnight-blue in color. Almost nothing else about it was known-at least, to mankind.

It was the only one of its kind on Earth, though men thought (without much sure knowledge) that there were more, perhaps many thousands more, like it on the unfamiliar planet that was Earth's binary, swinging around the miniature Sun that hung at their common center of gravity like an unbalanced dumbbell. But men knew very little about that planet itself, only that it had come out of space and was now there.

Time was when men had tried to label that binary, more than two centuries before, when it had first appeared. "Runaway Planet." "The Invader." "Rejoice in Messias, the Day Is at Hand." The labels were sense-free; they were Xs in an equation, signifying only that there was *something* there which was unknown.

"The Runaway Planet" stopped running when it closed on Earth.

"The Invader" didn't invade; it merely sent down one slaggy, midnight-blue tetrahedron to Everest.

And "Rejoice in Messias" stole Earth from its sun-with Earth's old moon, which it converted into a miniature sun of its own.

That was the time when men were plentiful and strong-or thought they were-with many huge cities and countless powerful machines. It didn't matter. The new binary planet showed no interest in the cities or the machines.

There was a plague of things like Eyes-dust-devils without dust, motionless air that suddenly tensed and quivered into lenticular shapes. They came with the planet and the Pyramid, so that there probably was some connection. But there was nothing to do about the Eyes. Striking at them was like striking at air-was the same thing, in fact.

While the men and machines tried uselessly to do something about it, the new binary system-the stranger planet and Earth-began to move, accelerating very slowly.

But accelerating.

In a week, astronomers knew something was happening. In a month, the Moon sprang into flame and became a new sun-beginning to be needed, for already the parent Sol was visibly more distant, and in a few years it was only one other star among many.

* * * * *

When the little sun was burned to a clinker, they-whoever "they" were, for men saw only the one Pyramid-would hang a new one in the sky. It happened every five clock-years, more or less. It was the same old moon-turned-sun, but it burned out, and the fires needed to be rekindled.

The first of these suns had looked down on an Earthly population of ten billion. As the sequence of suns waxed and waned, there were changes, climatic fluctuation, all but immeasurable differences in the quantity and kind of radiation from the new source.

The changes were such that the forty-fifth such sun looked down on a shrinking human race that could not muster up a hundred million.

A frustrated man drives inward; it is the same with a race. The hundred million that clung to existence were not the same as the bold, vital ten billion.

The thing on Everest had, in its time, received many labels, too: The Devil, The Friend, The Beast, A Pseudo-living Entity of Quite Unknown Electrochemical Properties.

All these labels were also Xs.

If it did wake that morning, it did not open its eyes, for it had no eyes-apart from the quivers of air that might or might not belong to it. Eyes might have been gouged; therefore it had none. So an illogical person might have argued-and yet it was tempting to apply the "purpose, not function" fallacy to it. Limbs could be crushed; it had no limbs. Ears could be deafened; it had none. Through a mouth, it might be poisoned; it had no mouth. Intentions and actions could be frustrated; apparently it had neither.

It was there. That was all.

It and others like it had stolen the Earth and the Earth did not know why. It was there. And the one thing on Earth you could not do was hurt it, influence it, or coerce it in any way whatever.

It was there-and it, or the masters it represented, owned the Earth by right of theft. Utterly. Beyond human hope of challenge or redress.

CHAPTER II.

Citizen and Citizeness Roget Germyn walked down Pine Street in the chill and dusk of-one hoped —a Sun Re-creation Morning.

It was the convention to pretend that this was a morning like any other morning. It was not proper either to cast frequent hopeful glances at the sky, nor yet to seem disturbed or afraid because this was, after all, the forty-first such morning since those whose specialty was Sky Viewing had come to believe the Re-creation of the Sun was near.

The Citizen and his Citizeness exchanged the assurance-of-identity sign with a few old friends and stopped to converse. This also was a convention of skill divorced from purpose. The conversation was without relevance to anything that any one of the participants might know, or think, or wish to ask.

Germyn said for his friends a twenty-word poem he had made in honor of the occasion and heard their responses. They did line-capping for a while-until somebody indicated unhappiness and a wish to change by frowning the Two Grooves between his brows. The game was deftly ended with an improvised rhymed exchange.

Casually, Citizen Germyn glanced aloft. The sky-change had not begun yet; the dying old Sun hung just over the horizon, east and south, much more south than east. It was an ugly thought, but suppose, thought Germyn, just *suppose* that the Sun were not re-created today? Or tomorrow. Or —

Or ever.

The Citizen got a grip on himself and told his wife: "We shall dine at the oatmeal stall."

The Citizeness did not immediately reply. When Germyn glanced at her with well-masked surprise, he found her almost staring down the dim street at a Citizen who moved almost in a stride, almost swinging his arms. Scarcely graceful.

"That might be more Wolf than man," she said doubtfully.

Germyn knew the fellow. Tropile was his name. One of those curious few who made their homes outside of Wheeling, though they were not farmers. Germyn had had banking dealings with him-or would have had, if it had been up to Tropile.

"That is a careless man," he decided, "and an ill-bred one."

They moved toward the oatmeal stall with the gait of Citizens, arms limp, feet scarcely lifted, slumped forward a little. It was the ancient gait of fifteen hundred calories per day, not one of which could be squandered.

* * * * *

There was a need for more calories. So many for walking, so many for gathering food. So many for the economical pleasures of the Citizens, so many more-oh, many more, these days! —to keep out the cold. Yet there were no more calories; the diet the whole world lived on was a bare subsistence diet.

It was impossible to farm well when half the world's land was part of the time drowned in the rising sea, part of the time smothered in falling snow.

Citizens knew this and, knowing, did not struggle-it was ungraceful to struggle, particularly when one could not win. Only-well, Wolves struggled, wasting calories, lacking grace.

Citizen Germyn turned his mind to more pleasant things.

He allowed himself his First Foretaste of the oatmeal. It would be warm in the bowl, hot in the throat, a comfort in the belly. There was a great deal of pleasure there, in weather like this, when the cold plucked through the loosened seams and the wind came up the sides of the hills. Not that there wasn't pleasure in the cold itself, for that matter. It was proper that one should be cold now, just before the re-creation of the Sun, when the old Sun was smoky-red and the new one not yet kindled.

"—still looks like Wolf to me," his wife was muttering.

"Cadence," Germyn reproved his Citizeness, but took the sting out of it with a Quirked Smile.

The man with the ugly manners was standing at the very bar of the oatmeal stall where they were heading. In the gloom of mid-morning, he was all angles and strained lines. His head was turned awkwardly on his shoulder, peering toward the back of the stall where the vendor was rhythmically measuring grain into a pot. His hands were resting helter-skelter on the counter, not hanging by his sides.

Citizen Germyn felt a faint shudder from his wife. But he did not reprove her again, for who could blame her? The exhibition was revolting.

She said faintly: "Citizen, might we dine on bread this morning?"

He hesitated and glanced again at the ugly man. He said indulgently, knowing that he was indulgent: "On Sun Re-creation Morning, the Citizeness may dine on bread." Bearing in mind the occasion, it was only a small favor and therefore a very proper one.

The bread was good, very good. They shared out the half-kilo between them and ate it in silence, as it deserved. Germyn finished his first portion and, in the prescribed pause before beginning his second, elected to refresh his eyes upward.

He nodded to his wife and stepped outside.

* * * * *

Overhead, the Old Sun parceled out its last barrel-scrapings of heat. It was larger than the stars around it, but many of them were nearly as bright.

A high-pitched male voice said: "Citizen Germyn, good morning."

Germyn was caught off balance. He took his eyes off the sky, half turned, glanced at the face of the person who had spoken to him, raised his hand in the assurance-of-identity sign. It was all very quick and fluid-almost too quick, for he had had his fingers bent nearly into the sign for female friends and this was a man. Citizen Boyne. Germyn knew him well; they had shared the Ice Viewing at Niagara a year before.

Germyn recovered quickly enough, but it had been disconcerting.

He improvised swiftly: "There are stars, but are stars still there if there is no Sun?" It was a hurried effort, he grieved, but no doubt Boyne would pick it up and carry it along. Boyne had always been very good, very graceful.

Boyne did no such thing. "Good morning," he said again, faintly. He glanced at the stars overhead, as though trying to unravel what Germyn was talking about. He said accusingly, his voice cracking sharply: "There isn't any Sun, Germyn. What do you think of that?"

Germyn swallowed. "Citizen, perhaps you —"

"No Sun, you hear me!" the man sobbed. "It's cold, Germyn. The Pyramids aren't going to give us another Sun, do you know that? They're going to starve us, freeze us; they're through with us. We're done, all of us!" He was nearly screaming.

All up and down Pine Street, people were trying not to look at him and some of them were failing.

Boyne clutched at Germyn helplessly. Revolted, Germyn drew back—*bodily contact!*

It seemed to bring the man to his senses. Reason returned to his eyes. He said: "I —" He stopped, stared about him. "I think I'll have bread for breakfast," he said foolishly, and plunged into the stall.

Boyne left behind him a shaken Citizen, caught halfway into the wrist-flip of parting, staring after him with jaw slack and eyes wide, as though Germyn had no manners, either.

All this on Sun Re-creation Day!

What could it mean? Germyn wondered fretfully, worriedly.

Was Boyne on the point of —

Could Boyne be about to —

Germyn drew back from the thought. There was one thing that might explain Boyne's behavior. But it was not a proper speculation for one Citizen to make about another.

All the same-Germyn dared the thought-all the same, it *did* seem almost as though Citizen Boyne were on the point of-well, running amok.

At the oatmeal stall, Glenn Tropile thumped on the counter. The laggard oatmeal vendor finally brought the ritual bowl of salt and the pitcher of thin milk. Tropile took his paper twist of salt from the top of the neatly arranged pile in the bowl. He glanced at the vendor. His fingers hesitated. Then, quickly, he ripped the twist of paper into his oatmeal and covered it to the permitted level with the milk.

He ate quickly and efficiently, watching the street outside.

They were wandering and mooning about, as always-maybe today more than most days, since they hoped it would be the day the Sun blossomed flame once more.

Tropile always thought of the wandering, mooning Citizens as *they*. There was a *we* somewhere for Tropile, no doubt, but Tropile had not as yet located it, not even in the bonds of the marriage contract.

He was in no hurry. At the age of fourteen, Glenn Tropile had reluctantly come to realize certain things about himself-that he disliked being bested, that he had to have a certain advantage in all his dealings, or an intolerable itch of the mind drove him to discomfort. The things added up to a terrifying fear, gradually becoming knowledge, that the only we that could properly include him was one that it was not very wise to join.

He had realized, in fact, that he was a Wolf.

For some years, Tropile had struggled against it, for Wolf was an obscene word; the children he played with were punished severely for saying it, and for almost nothing else.

It was not *proper* for one Citizen to advantage himself at the expense of another; Wolves did that.

It was *proper* for a Citizen to accept what he had, not to strive for more, to find beauty in small things, to accommodate himself, with the minimum of strain and awkwardness, to whatever his life happened to be.

Wolves were not like that. Wolves never meditated, Wolves never Appreciated, Wolves *never* were Translated-that supreme fulfillment, granted only to those who succeeded in a perfect meditation, that surrender of the world and the flesh by taking leave of both, which could never be achieved by a Wolf.

Accordingly, Glenn Tropile had tried very hard to do all the things that Wolves could not do.

He had nearly succeeded. His specialty, Water Watching, had been most rewarding. He had achieved many partly successful meditations on Connectivity.

And yet he was still a Wolf, for he still felt that burning, itching urge to triumph and to hold an advantage. For that reason, it was almost impossible for him to make friends among the Citizens; and gradually he had almost stopped trying.

Tropile had arrived in Wheeling nearly a year before, making him one of the early settlers in point of time. And yet there was not a Citizen in the street who was prepared to exchange recognition gestures with him.

He knew *them*, nearly every one. He knew their names and their wives' names. He knew what northern states they had moved down from with the spreading of the ice, as the sun grew dim. He knew very nearly to the quarter of a gram what stores of sugar and salt and coffee each one of them had put away-for their guests, of course, not for themselves; the well-bred Citizen hoarded only for the entertainment of others.

Tropile knew these things because there was an advantage in knowing them. But there was no advantage in having anyone know him.

A few did-that banker, Germyn; Tropile had approached him only a few months before about a prospective loan. But it had been a chancy, nervous encounter. The idea was so luminously simple to Tropile-organize an expedition to the coal mines that once had flourished nearby, find the coal, bring it to Wheeling, heat the houses. And yet it had seemed blasphemous to Germyn. Tropile had counted himself lucky merely to have been refused the loan, instead of being cried out upon as Wolf.

* * * * *

The oatmeal vendor was fussing worriedly around his neat stack of paper twists in the salt bowl.

Tropile avoided the man's eyes. Tropile was not interested in the little wry smile of self-deprecation which the vendor would make to him, given half a chance. Tropile knew well enough what was disturbing the vendor. Let it disturb him. It was Tropile's custom to take extra twists of salt. They were in his pockets now; they would stay there. Let the vendor wonder why he was short.

Tropile licked the bowl of his spoon and stepped into the street. He was comfortably aware under a double-thick parka that the wind was blowing very cold.

A Citizen passed him, walking alone: odd, thought Tropile. He was walking rapidly and there was a look of taut despair on his face. Still more odd. Odd enough to be worth another look, because that sort of haste, that sort of abstraction, suggested something to Tropile. They were in no way normal to the gentle sheep of the class *They*, except in one particular circumstance.

Glenn Tropile crossed the street to follow the abstracted Citizen, whose name, he knew, was Boyne. The man blundered into Citizen Germyn outside the baker's stall, and Tropile stood back out of easy sight, watching and listening.

Boyne was on the ragged edge of breakdown. What Tropile heard and saw confirmed his diagnosis. The one particular circumstance was close to happening-Citizen Boyne was on the verge of running amok.

Tropile looked at the man with amusement and contempt. Amok! The gentle sheep *could* be pushed too far. He had seen Citizens run amok, the signs were obvious.

There was pretty sure to be an advantage in it for Glenn Tropile. There was an advantage in almost anything, if you looked for it.

He watched and waited. He picked his spot with care, so that he could see Citizen Boyne inside the baker's stall, making a dismal botch of slashing his quarter-kilo of bread from the Morning Loaf.

He waited for Boyne to come racing out....

Boyne did.

A yell-loud, piercing. It was Citizen Germyn, shrilling: "Amok, amok!" A scream. An enraged wordless cry from Boyne, and the baker's knife glinting in the faint light as Boyne swung it. And then Citizens were scattering in every direction-all of the Citizens but one.

One Citizen was under the knife-his own knife, as it happened; it was the baker himself. Boyne chopped and chopped again. And then Boyne came out, roaring, the broad knife whistling about his head. The gentle Citizens fled panicked before him. He struck at their retreating forms and screamed and struck again. Amok.

It was the one particular circumstance when they forgot to be gracious-one of the two, Tropile corrected himself as he strolled across to the baker's stall. His brow furrowed, because there was another circumstance when they lacked grace, and one which affected him nearly.

* * * * *

He watched the maddened creature, Boyne, already far down the road, chasing a knot of Citizens around a corner. Tropile sighed and stepped into the baker's stall to see what he might gain from this.

Boyne would wear himself out-the surging rage would leave him as quickly as it came; he would be a sheep again and the other sheep would close in and capture him. That was what happened when a Citizen ran amok. It was a measure of what pressures were on the Citizens that, at any moment, there might be one gram of pressure too much and one of them would crack. It had happened here in Wheeling twice within the past two months. Glenn Tropile had seen it happen in Pittsburgh, Altoona and Bronxville.

There is a limit to the pressure that can be endured.

Tropile walked into the baker's stall and looked down without emotion at the slaughtered baker. The corpse was a gory mess, but Tropile had seen corpses before.

He looked around the stall, calculating. As a starter, he bent to pick up the quarter-kilo of bread Boyne had dropped, dusted it off and slipped it into his pocket. Food was always useful. Given enough food, perhaps Boyne would not have run amok.

Was it simple hunger they cracked under? Or the knowledge of the thing on Mount Everest, or the hovering Eyes, or the sought-after-dreaded prospect of Translation, or merely the strain of keeping up their laboriously figured lives?

Did it matter? *They* cracked and ran amok, and Tropile never would, and that was what mattered.

He leaned across the counter, reaching for what was left of the Morning Loaf—

And found himself staring into the terrified large eyes of Citizeness Germyn.

She screamed: "Wolf! Citizens, help me! Wolf!"

Tropile faltered. He hadn't even *seen* the damned woman, but there she was, rising up from behind the counter, screaming her head off: "Wolf! Wolf!"

He said sharply: "Citizeness, I beg you —" But that was no good. The evidence was on him and her screams would fetch others.

Tropile panicked. He started toward her to silence her, but that was no good, either. He whirled. She was screaming, screaming, and there were people to hear. Tropile darted into the street, but they were popping out of every doorway now, appearing from each rat's hole in which they had hid to escape Boyne.

"Please!" he cried, sobbing. "Wait a minute!"

But they weren't waiting. They had heard the woman and maybe some of them had seen him with the bread. They were all around him-no, they were all over him; they were clutching at him, tearing at his soft, warm furs.

They pulled at his pockets and the stolen twists of salt spilled accusingly out. They yanked at his sleeves and even the stout, unweakened seams ripped open. He was fairly captured.

"Wolf!" they were shouting. "Wolf!" It drowned out the distant noise from where Boyne had finally been run to earth, a block and more away. It drowned out everything.

It was the other circumstance when *they* forgot to be gracious: when they had trapped a Son of the Wolf.

CHAPTER III.

Engineering had long ago come to an end.

Engineering is possible under one condition of the equation: Total available Calories divided by Population equals Artistic-Technological Style. When the ratio Calories-to-Population is large-say, five thousand or more, five thousand daily calories for every living person-then the Artistic-Technological Style is *big*. People carve Mount Rushmore; they build great foundries; they manufacture enormous automobiles to carry one housewife half a mile for the purchase of one lipstick.

Life is coarse and rich where C:P is large. At the other extreme, where C:P is too small, life does not exist at all. It has starved out.

Experimentally, add little increments to C:P and it will be some time before the right-hand side of the equation becomes significant. But at last, in the 1,000 to 1,500 calorie range, Artistic-Technological Style firmly appears in self-perpetuating form. C:P in that range produces the small arts, the appreciations, the peaceful arrangements of necessities into subtle relationships of traditionally agreed-upon virtue.

Think of Japan, locked into its Shogunate prison, with a hungry population scrabbling food out of mountainsides and beauty out of arrangements of lichens. The small, inexpensive sub-sub-arts are characteristic of the 1,000 to 1,500 calorie range.

And this was the range of Earth, the world of ten billion men, when the planet was stolen by its new binary.

Some few persons inexpensively studied the study of science with pencil and renewable paper, but the last research accelerator had long since been shut down. The juice from its hydro-power dam was needed to supply meager light to a million homes and to cook the pablum for two million brand-new babies.

In those days, one dedicated Byzantine wrote the definitive encyclopedia of engineering (though he was no engineer). Its four hundred and twenty tiny volumes examined exhaustively the engineering feats of ancient Greece and Egypt, the Wall of Shih-Hwang Ti, the Gothic builders, Brunel who changed the face of England, the Roeblings of Brooklyn, Groves of the Pentagon, Duggan of the Shelter System (before C:P dropped to the point where war became vanishingly implausible), Levern of Operation Up. But the encyclopedist could not use a slide rule without thinking, faltering, jotting down his decimals.

And then ... the magnitudes grew less.

Under the tectonic and climatic battering of the great abduction of Earth from its primary, under the sine-wave advances to and retreats from the equator of the ice sheath, as the small successor Suns waxed, waned, died and were replaced, the ratio C:P remained stable. C had diminished enormously; so had P. As the calories to support life grew scarce, so the consuming mouths of mankind grew less in number.

* * * * *

The forty-fifth small Sun shone on no engineers.

Not even on the binary, perhaps. The Pyramids, the things on the binary, the thing on Mount Everest-they were not engineers. They employed a crude metaphysic based on dissection and shoving.

They had no elegant field theories. All they knew was that everything came apart, and that if you pushed a thing, it would move.

If your biggest push would not move a thing, you took it apart and pushed the parts, and then it would move. Sometimes, for nuclear effects, they had to take things apart into 3×10^9 pieces and shove each piece very carefully.

By taking apart and shoving, then, they landed their one spaceship on the burned-out sun-let. Four human beings were on that ship. They meditated briefly on Connectivity and died screaming.

A point of new flame appeared on the sunlet's surface and the spaceship scrambled for the binary. The point of flame went from cherry through orange into the blue-white and began to spread.

* * * * *

At the moment of the Re-creation of the Sun, there was rejoicing on the Earth.

Not quite everywhere, though. In Wheeling's House of the Five Regulations, Glenn Tropile waited unquietly for death. Citizen Boyne, who had run amok and slaughtered the baker, shared Tropile's room and his doom, but not his rage. Boyne, with demure pleasure, was composing his death poem.

"Talk to me!" snapped Tropile. "Why are we here? What did you do and why did you do it? What have I done? Why don't I pick up a bench and kill you with it? You would've killed me two hours ago if I'd caught your eye!"

There was no satisfaction in Citizen Boyne; the passions were burned out of him. He politely tendered Tropile a famous aphorism: "Citizen, the art of living is the substitution of unimportant, answerable questions for important, unanswerable ones. Come, let us appreciate the new-born Sun."

He turned to the window, where the spark of blue-white flame in what had once been the crater of Tycho was beginning to spread across the charred moon.

Tropile was child enough of his culture to turn with him, almost involuntarily. He was silent. That blue-white infinitesimal up there growing slowly-the oneness, the calm rapture of Being in a universe that you shaded into without harsh discontinua, the being one with the great blue-white gem-flower blossoming now in the heavens that were no different stuff than you yourself—

He closed his eyes, calm, and meditated on Connectivity.

He was being Good.

By the time the fusion reaction had covered the whole small disk of the sunlet, a quarter-hour at the most, his meditation began to wear off.

Tropile shrugged out of his torn parka, not bothering to rip it further. It was already growing warm in the room. Citizen Boyne, of course, was carefully opening every seam with graceful rending motions, miming great and smooth effort of the biceps and trapezius.

But the meditation was over, and as Tropile watched his cellmate, he screamed a silent *Why?* Since his adolescence, that wailing syllable had seldom been far from his mind. It could be silenced by appreciation and meditation.

Tropile's specialty was Water Watching and he was so good at it that several beginners had asked him for instruction in the subtle art, in spite of his notorious oddities of life and manner. He *enjoyed* Water Watching. He almost pitied anybody so single-mindedly devoted to, say, Clouds and Odors-great game though it was-that he had never even tried Water Watching. And after a session of Watching, when one was lucky enough to observe the Nine Boiling Stages in classic perfection, one might slip into meditation and be harmonious, feel Good.

But what did one do when the meditations failed, as they had failed him? What did one do when they came farther and farther apart, became less and less intense, could be inspired, finally, only by a huge event like the renewal of the Sun?

One went amok, he had always thought.

But he had not. Boyne had. He had been declared a Son of the Wolf, on no evidence that he could understand. Yet he had not run amok.

Still, the penalties were the same, he thought, uncomfortably aware of an unfamiliar itch-not the inward intolerable itch of needing the advantage, but a localized sensation at the base of his spine. The penalties for all gross crimes-Wolfhood or running amok-were the same, and simply this:

They would perform the Lumbar Puncture. He would make the Donation of Spinal Fluid. He would be dead.

* * * * *

The Keeper of the House of Five Regulations, an old man, Citizen Harmane, looked in on his charges-approvingly at Boyne, with a beclouded expression at Glenn Tropile.

It was thought that even Wolves were entitled to the common human decencies in the brief interval between exposure and the Donation of Fluid. The Keeper would not have dreamed of scowling at the detected Wolf or of interfering with whatever wretched imitation of meditation-before-dying the creature might practice. But he could not, all the same, bring himself to offer even an assurance-of-identity gesture.

Tropile had no such qualms.

He scowled at Keeper Harmane with such ferocity that the old man almost hurried away. He turned an almost equally ugly scowl upon Citizen Boyne. How dared that knife-murderer be so calm, so relaxed!

Tropile said brutally: "They'll kill us! You know that? They'll stick a needle in our spines and drain us dry. It *hurts.* Do you understand me? They're going to drain us, and then they're going to drink our spinal fluid, and it's going to *hurt.*"

He was gently corrected. "We shall make the Donation," Citizen Boyne said calmly. "Is not the difference intelligible to a Son of the Wolf?"

True culture demanded that that remark be accepted as a friendly joke, probably based on a truth-how else could an unpalatable truth be put in words? Otherwise the unthinkable might happen. They might quarrel. They might even come to blows!

The appropriate mild smile formed on Tropile's lips, but harshly he wiped it off. They were going to *kill* him. He would *not* smile for them! And the effort was enormous.

"I'm *not* a Son of the Wolf!" he howled, desperate, knowing he was protesting to the man of all men in Wheeling who didn't care, and who could do least about it if he did. "What's this crazy talk about Wolves? I don't know what a Son of the Wolf is and I don't think you or anybody does. All I know is that I was acting *sensibly.* And everybody began howling! You're supposed to know a Son of the Wolf by his unculture, his ignorance, his violence. But you chopped down three people and I only picked up a piece of bread! And *I'm* supposed to be the dangerous one!"

"Wolves never know they're Wolves," sighed Citizen Boyne. "Fish probably think they're birds and you evidently think you're a Citizen. Would a Citizen speak as you are speaking?"

"But they're going to kill us!"

"Then why aren't you composing your death poem?"

* * * * *

Glenn Tropile took a deep breath. Something was biting him. It was bad enough that he was about to die, bad enough that he had done nothing worth dying for. But what was gnawing at him now had nothing to do with dying.

The percentages were going the wrong way. This pale Citizen was getting an edge on him.

An engorged gland in Tropile's adrenals-it was only a pinhead in Citizen Boyne's —gushed raw hormones into his bloodstream. He could die, yes-that was a skill everyone had to acquire, sooner or later. But while he was alive, he could not stand to be bested in an encounter, an argument, a relationship-not and stay alive. Wolf? Call him Wolf. Call him Operator, or Percentage Player; call him Sharp Article; call him Gamesman.

If there was an advantage to be derived, he would derive it. It was the way he was put together.

He said, for time: "You're right. Stupid of me. I must have lost my head!"

He thought. Some men think by poking problems apart; some think by laying facts side by side to compare. Tropile's thinking was neither of these, but a species of judo. He conceded to his opponent such things as Strength, Armor, Resource. He didn't need these things for himself; to every contest, the opponent brought enough of them to supply two. It was Tropile's

118

habit (and Wolfish, he had to admit) to use the opponent's strength against him, to break the opponent against his own steel walls.

He thought.

The first thing was to make up his mind: He was Wolf. Then let him *be* Wolf. He wouldn't stay around for the spinal tap; he would go from there. But how?

The second thing was to plan. There were obstacles. Citizen Boyne was one. The Keeper of the House of the Five Regulations was another.

Where was the pole which would permit him to vault over these hurdles? There was always his wife, Gala. He owned her; she would do what he wished-provided he made her *want* to do it.

Yes, Gala. He walked to the door and shouted to Citizen Harmane: "Keeper! I must see my wife! Have her brought to me!"

It was impossible for the Keeper to refuse. He called gently, "I will invite the Citizeness," and toddled away.

The third thing was time.

Tropile turned to Citizen Boyne. "Citizen," he said persuasively, "since your death poem is ready and mine is not, will you be gracious enough to go first when they-when they come?"

Citizen Boyne looked temperately at his cellmate and made the Quirked Smile.

"You see?" he said. "Wolf."

And that was true. But what was also true was that Boyne couldn't and didn't refuse.

CHAPTER IV.

Half a world away, the midnight-blue Pyramid sat on its planed-off peak as it had sat since the days when Earth had a real sun of its own.

It was of no importance to the Pyramid that Glenn Tropile was about to receive a slim catheter into his spine, to drain his saps and his life. It didn't matter to the Pyramid that the pretext for the execution was an act which human history had long stopped considering a capital crime. Ritual sacrifice in any guise made no difference to the Pyramid.

The Pyramid saw them come and the Pyramid saw them go-if the Pyramid could be said to "see." One human being more or less, what matter? Who bothers to take a census of the cells in a hangnail?

And yet the Pyramid did have a kind of interest in Glenn Tropile. Or, at least, in the human race of which he was a part.

Nobody knew much about the Pyramids, but everybody knew *that* much. They wanted something-else why would they have bothered to steal the Earth?

The date of the theft was 2027. A great year-the year of the first landings on the Runaway Planet that had come blundering into the Solar System. Maybe those landings were a mistake-although they were a very great triumph, too; but maybe if it hadn't been for the landings, the Runaway Planet might have run right through the ecliptic and away.

However, the triumphal mistake was made and that was the first time a human eye saw a Pyramid.

Shortly after-though not before a radio message was sent-that human eye winked out forever; but by then the damage was done. What passed in a Pyramid for "attention" had been attracted. The next thing that happened set the wireless channels between Palomar and Pernambuco, between Greenwich and the Cape of Good Hope, buzzing and worrying, as astronomers all over the Earth reported and confirmed and reconfirmed the astonishing fact that our planet was on the move. Rejoice in Messias had come to take us away.

A world of ten billion people, some of them brilliant, many of them brave, built and flung the giant rockets of Operation Up at the invader: Nothing.

The first, and only, Interplanetary Expeditionary Force was boosted up to no-gravity and dropped onto the new planet to strike back: Nothing.

Earth moved spirally outward.

If a battle could not be won, then perhaps a migration. New ships were built in haste. But they lay there rusting as the sun grew small and the ice grew thick, because where was there to go? Not Mars. Not the Moon, which was trailing alone. Not choking Venus or crushing Jupiter.

The migration was defeated as surely as the war, there being no place to migrate to.

One Pyramid came to Earth, only one. It shaved the crest off the highest mountain there was and squatted on it. An observer? A warden? Whatever it was, it stayed.

The sun grew too distant to be of use, and out of the old Moon, the Pyramid aliens built a new small sun in the sky —a five-year sun that burned out and was replaced, again and again and endlessly again.

It had been a fierce struggle against unbeatable odds on the part of the ten billion; and when the uselessness of struggle was demonstrated at last, many of the ten billion froze to death, and many of them starved, and nearly all of the rest had something frozen or starved out of them; and what was left, two centuries and more later, was more or less like Citizen Boyne, except for a few —a very few-like Glenn Tropile.

* * * * *

Gala Tropile stared miserably at her husband. "I want to get out of here," he was saying urgently. "They mean to kill me. Gala, you know you can't make yourself suffer by letting them kill me!"

She wailed: "I *can't!*"

Tropile looked over his shoulder. Citizen Boyne was fingering the textured contrasts of a golden watch-case which had been his father's —and soon would be his son's. Boyne's eyes were closed and he wasn't listening.

Tropile leaned forward and deliberately put his hand on his wife's arm. She started and flushed, of course.

"You *can*," he said, "and what's more, you will. You can help me get out of here. I insist on it, Gala, because I must save you that pain."

He took his hand off her arm, content.

He said harshly: "Darling, don't you think I know how much we've always meant to each other?"

She looked at him wretchedly. Fretfully she tore at the billowing filmy sleeve of her summer blouse. The seams hadn't been loosened; there had not been time. She had just been getting into the appropriate Sun Re-creation Day costume, to be worn under the parka, when the messenger had come with the news about her husband.

She avoided his eyes. "If you're really Wolf...."

Tropile's sub-adrenals pulsed and filled him with confident strength. "*You* know what I am—you better than anyone else." It was a sly reminder of their curious furtive behavior together; like the hand on her arm, it had its effect. "After all, why do we quarrel the way we did last night?"

He hurried on; the job of the rowel was to spur her to action, not to inflame a wound. "Because we're *important* to each other. I know that you would count on me to help if you were in trouble. And I know that you'd be hurt —*deeply*, Gala! —if I didn't count on you."

She sniffled and scuffed the bright strap over her open-toed sandal.

Then she met his eyes.

It was the after-effect of the argument, of course. Glenn Tropile knew just how heavily he could rely on the after-spiral of a quarrel. She was submitting.

She glanced furtively at Citizen Boyne and lowered her voice.

"What do I have to do?" she whispered.

* * * * *

In five minutes, she was gone, but that was more than enough time. Tropile had at least thirty minutes left. They would take Boyne first; he had seen to that. And once Boyne was gone —

Tropile wrenched a leg off his three-legged stool and sat precariously balanced on the other two. He tossed the loose leg clattering into a corner.

The Keeper of the House of Five Regulations ambled slack-bodied by and glanced into the room. "Wolf, what happened to your stool?"

Tropile made a left-handed sign of no-importance. "It doesn't matter. Except it *is* hard to meditate, sitting on this thing, with every muscle tensing and fighting against every other to keep my balance...."

The Keeper made an overruling sign of please-let-me-help. "It's your last half-hour, Wolf," he reminded Tropile. "I'll fix the stool for you."

He entered and slammed and banged it together, and left with an expression of mild concern. Even a Son of the Wolf was entitled to the fullest appreciation of that unique opportunity for meditation, the last half-hour before a Donation.

In five minutes, the Keeper was back, looking solemn and yet glad, like a bearer of serious but welcome tidings.

"It is the time for the first Donation," he announced. "Which of you —"

"Him," said Tropile quickly, pointing.

Boyne opened his eyes calmly and nodded. He got to his feet, made a formal leavetaking bow to Tropile, and followed the Keeper toward his Donation and his death. As they were going out, Tropile coughed a would-you-please-grant-me-a-favor cough.

The Keeper paused. "What is it, Wolf?"

Tropile showed him the empty water pitcher-empty, all right; he had emptied it out the window.

"My apologies," the Keeper said, flustered, and hurried Boyne along. He came back almost at once to fill the pitcher, even though he should be there to watch Boyne's ceremonial Donation.

Tropile stood looking at the Keeper, his sub-adrenals beginning to pound like the rolling boil of Well-aged Water. The Keeper was at a disadvantage. He had been neglectful of his charge —a broken stool, no water in the pitcher. And a Citizen, brought up in a Citizen's maze of consideration and tact, could not help but be humiliated, seeking to make amends.

Tropile pressed his advantage home. "Wait," he said to the Keeper. "I'd like to talk to you."

The Keeper hesitated, torn. "The Donation —"

"Damn the Donation," Tropile said calmly. "After all, what is it but sticking a pipe into a man's backbone and sucking out the juice that keeps him alive? It's killing, that's all."

The Keeper turned literally white. Tropile was speaking blasphemy and he wasn't stopping.

"I want to tell you about my wife," Tropile went on, assuming a confidential air. "Now there's a real *woman*. Not one of these frozen-up Citizenesses, you know? Why, she and I used to —" He hesitated. "You're a man of the world, aren't you?" he demanded. "I mean you've seen life."

"I —suppose so," the Keeper said faintly.

"Then you won't be shocked," Tropile lied. "Well, let me tell you, there's a lot to women that these stuffed-shirt Citizens don't know about. Boy! Ever see a woman's knee?" He sniggered. "Ever kiss a woman with —" he winked —"with the *light on*? Ever sit in a big armchair, say, with a woman in your *lap* —all soft and heavy, and kind of warm, and slumped up against your chest, you know, and —"

He stopped and swallowed. He was almost making himself retch, it was so hard to say these things. But he forced himself to go on: "Well, that's what she and I used to do. Plenty. All the time. That's what I call a real *woman*."

He stopped, warned by the Keeper's sudden change of expression, glazed eyes, strangling breath. He had gone too far. He had only wanted to paralyze the man, revolt him, put him out of commission, but he was overdoing it. He jumped forward and caught the Keeper as he fell, fainting.

* * * * *

Tropile callously emptied the water pitcher over the man. The Keeper sneezed and sat up groggily. He focused his eyes on Tropile and agonizedly blushed.

Tropile said harshly: "I wish to see the new sun from the street."

The request was incredible. Even after the unbelievable obscenities he had heard, the Keeper was not prepared for this; he was staggered. Tropile was in detention regarding the Fifth Regulation. That was all there was to it. Such persons were not to be released from their quarters. The Keeper knew it, the world knew it, Tropile knew it.

It was an obscenity even greater than the lurid tales of perverted lust, for Tropile had asked something which was impossible! No one *ever* asked anything that was impossible to grant, for no one could ever refuse anything. That was utterly graceless, unthinkable.

One could only attempt to compromise. The Keeper stammeringly said: "May I —may I let you see the new sun from the corridor?" And even that was wretchedly wrong, but he had to offer something. One always offered something. The Keeper had never since babyhood given a flat no to anybody about anything. No Citizen had. A flat no led to anger, strong words-perhaps even hurt feelings. The only flat no conceivable was the enormous terminal no of an amok. Short of that —

One offered. One split the difference. One was invariably filled with tepid pleasure when, invariably, the offer was accepted, the difference was split, both parties were satisfied.

"That will do for a start," Tropile snarled. "Open, man, open! Don't make me wait."

The Keeper reeled and unlatched the door to the corridor.

"Now the street!"

"I can't!" burst in an anguished cry from the Keeper. He buried his face in his hands and began to sob, hopelessly incapacitated.

"The street!" Tropile said remorselessly. He himself felt wrenchingly ill; he was going against custom that had ruled his own life as surely as the Keeper's.

But he was Wolf. "I *will* be Wolf," he growled, and advanced upon the Keeper. "My wife," he said, "I didn't finish telling you. Sometimes she used to put her arm around me and just snuggle up and —I remember one time she kissed my ear. Broad daylight. It felt funny and warm —I can't describe it."

Whimpering, the Keeper flung the keys at Tropile and tottered brokenly away.

He was out of the action. Tropile himself was nearly as badly off; the difference was that he continued to function. The words coming from him had seared like acid in his throat.

"They call me Wolf," he said aloud, reeling against the wall. "I will be one."

He unlocked the outer door and his wife was waiting, holding in her arms the things he had asked her to bring.

Tropile said strangely to her: "I am steel and fire. I am Wolf, full of the old moxie."

She wailed: "Glenn, are you sure I'm doing the right thing?"

He laughed unsteadily and led her by the arm through the deserted streets.

CHAPTER V.

Citizen Germyn, as was his right by position and status as a connoisseur, helped prepare Citizen Boyne for his Donation. There was nothing much to it-which made it an elaborate and lengthy task, according to the ethic of the Citizens; it had to be protracted, each step being surrounded by fullest dress of ritual.

It was done in the broad daylight of the new Sun, and as many of the three hundred citizens of Wheeling as could manage it were in the courtyard of the old Federal Building to watch.

The nature of the ceremony was this: A man who revealed himself Wolf, or who finally crumbled under the demands of life and ran amok, could not be allowed to live. He was hauled before an audience of his equals and permitted-with the help of regretful force, if that should be necessary, but preferably not-to make the Donation of Spinal Fluid.

Execution was murder and murder was not permitted under the gentle code of Citizens; this was not execution. The draining of a man's spinal fluid did not kill him. It only insured that, after a time and with much suffering, his internal chemistry would so arrange itself that it would continue to function, only not in a way that would sustain life.

Once the Donation was made, the problem was completely altered, of course. Suffering was bad in itself. To save the Donor from the suffering that lay ahead, it was the custom to have the oldest and gentlest Citizen on hand stand by with a sharp-edged knife. When the Donation was complete, the Donor's head was removed-purely to avert suffering. That was not execution, either, but only the hastening of an inevitable end.

The dozen or so Citizens whose rank permitted them to assist then dissolved the spinal fluids in water and ceremoniously sipped them, at which time it was proper to offer a small poem in commentary. All in all, it was a perfectly splendid opportunity for the purest form of meditation for everyone concerned.

Citizen Germyn, whose role was Catheter Bearer, took his place behind the Introducer Bearer, the Annunciators and the Questioner of Purpose. As he passed Citizen Boyne, Germyn assisted him to assume the proper crouched-over position. Boyne looked up gratefully and Germyn found the occasion correct for a commendatory half-smile.

The Questioner of Purpose said solemnly to Boyne: "It is your privilege to make a Donation here today. Do you wish to do so?"

"I do," said Boyne raptly. The anxiety had passed; clearly he was confident of making a good Donation. Germyn approved with all his heart.

The Annunciators, in alternate stanzas, announced the right pause for meditation to the meager crowd, and all fell silent. Citizen Germyn began the process of blanking out his mind, to ready himself for the great opportunity to Appreciate that lay ahead. A sound distracted him; he glanced up irritably. It seemed to come from the House of the Five Regulations, a man's voice, carrying. But no one else appeared to notice it. All of the watchers, all of those on the stone steps, were in somber meditation.

Germyn tried to return his thoughts to where they belonged.

But something was troubling him. He had caught a glimpse of the Donor and there had been something-something —

He angrily permitted himself to look up once more to see just what it had been about Citizen Boyne that had attracted his attention.

Yes, there *was* something. Over the form of Citizen Boyne, silent, barely visible, a flicker of life and motion. Nothing tangible. It was as if the air itself were in motion.

It was, Germyn thought with a bursting heart-it was an Eye!

The veritable miracle of Translation and it was about to take place here and now, upon the person of Citizen Boyne! And no one knew it but Germyn himself!

* * * * *

In this last surmise, Citizen Germyn was wrong. Or was he? True, no other human eyes saw the flawed-glass thing that twisted the air over Boyne's prostrate body, but there was, in a sense, another witness … some thousands of miles away.

The Pyramid on Mount Everest "stirred."

It did not move, but something about it moved, or changed, or radiated. The Pyramid surveyed its-cabbage patch? Wristwatch mine? As much sense, it may be, to say wristwatch patch or cabbage mine. At any rate, it surveyed what to it was a place where intricate mechanisms grew, ripened and were dug up at the moment of usefulness, whereupon they were quick-frozen and wired into circuits.

Through signals perceptible to it, the Pyramids had become "aware" that one of its mechanisms was now ready to be plucked-harvested.

The Pyramid's blood was dielectric fluid. Its limbs were electrostatic charges. Its philosophy was: Unscrew It and Push. Its motive was survival.

Survival today was not what survival once had been, for a Pyramid.

Once survival had merely been gliding along on a cushion of repellent charges, streaming electrons behind for the push, sending h-f pulses out often enough to get a picture of their bounced return to integrate deep inside.

If the picture showed something metabolizable, one metabolized it. One broke it down into molecules by lashing it with the surplus protons left over from the dispersed electrons; one adsorbed the molecules. Sometimes the metabolizable object was an Immobile and sometimes a Mobile —a vague, theoretical, frivolous classification to a philosophy whose basis was that *everything* unscrewed. If it was a Mobile, one sometimes had to move after it.

That was the difference.

The essential was survival, not making idle distinctions. And one small part of survival today was the Everest Pyramid's job.

It sat and waited. It sent out its h-f pulses bouncing and scattering, and it bounced and scattered them additionally on their return. Deep inside, the more-than-anamorphically distorted picture was reintegrated. Deeper inside, it was interpreted and evaluated for its part in survival.

* * * * *

There was a need for certain mechanisms which grew on this planet. At irregular times, the Pyramid evaluated the picture to the effect that a mechanism —a wristwatch, so to speak-was ripe for plucking; and by electrostatic charges, it did so. The electrostatic charges, in forming, produced what humans called an Eye. But the Pyramid had no use for names.

It merely plucked, when a mechanism was ripe. It had found that a mechanism was ripe now.

A world away, before the steps of Wheeling's Federal Building, electrostatic charges gathered above a component whose name was Citizen Boyne. There was a small sound like the clapping of two hands which made the three hundred citizens of Wheeling jerk upright out of their meditations.

The sound was air filling the gap that had once been occupied by Citizen Boyne, who had instantly vanished-who had, in a word, been ripe and therefore been plucked.

CHAPTER VI.

Glenn Tropile and his sobbing wife passed the night in the stubble of a cornfield. Neither of them slept much.

Tropile, numbed by contact with the iron chill of the field-it would be months before the new Sun warmed the Earth enough for it to begin radiating in turn-tossed restlessly, dreaming. He was Wolf. Let it be so, he told himself again and again. I *will* be Wolf. I will strike back at the Citizens. I will —

Always the thought trailed off. He would exactly *What*? What could he do?

Migration was an answer-go to another city. With Gala, he guessed. Start a new life, where he was not known as Wolf.

And then what? Try to live a sheep's life, as he had tried all his years? And there was the question of whether, in fact, he could manage to find a city where he was not known. The human race was migratory, in these years of subjection to the never quite understood rule of the Pyramids.

It was a matter of insulation. When the new Sun was young, it was hot, and there was plenty of warmth; it was possible to spread north and south, away from final line of permafrost which, in North America, came just above the old Mason-Dixon line. When the Sun was dying, the cold spread down. The race followed the seasons. Soon all of Wheeling would be spreading north again, and how was he to be sure that none of Wheeling's Citizens might not turn up wherever he might go?

He could be sure-that was the answer to that.

All right, scratch migration. What remained? He could-with Gala, he guessed-live a solitary life on the fringes of cultivated land. They both had some skill at rummaging the old storehouses of the ancients, and there was still food and other commodities to be found.

But even a Wolf is gregarious by nature and there were bleak hours in that night when Tropile found himself close to sobbing with his wife.

At the first break of dawn, he was up. Gala had fallen into a light and restless sleep; he called her awake.

"We have to move," he said harshly. "Maybe they'll get up enough guts to follow us. I don't want them to find us."

Silently she got up. They rolled and tied the blankets she had bought; they ate quickly from the food she had brought; they made packs and put them on their shoulders and started to walk. One thing in their favor: they were moving fast, faster than any Citizen was likely to follow. All the same, Tropile kept looking nervously behind him.

They hurried north and east, and that was a mistake, because by noon they found themselves blocked by water. Once it had been a river; the melting of the polar ice caps that had submerged the coasts of the old continents had drowned it out and now it was salt water. But whatever it was, it was impassable. They would have to skirt it westward until they found a bridge or a boat.

"We can stop and eat," Tropile said grudgingly, trying not to despair.

They slumped to the ground. It was warmer now. Tropile found himself getting drowsier, drowsier —

He jerked erect and stared around belligerently. Beside him, his wife was lying motionless, though her eyes were open, gazing at the sky. Tropile sighed and stretched out. A moment's rest, he promised himself, and then a quick bite to eat, and then onward....

He was sound asleep when they spotted him.

* * * * *

There was a flutter of iron bird's wings from overhead. Tropile jumped up out of his sleep, awakening to panic. It was outside the possibility of belief, but there it was:

In the sky over him, etched black against a cloud, a helicopter. And men staring out of it, staring down at him.

A helicopter!

But there were no helicopters, or none that flew-if there had been fuel to fly them with-if any man had had the skill to make them fly. It was impossible! And yet there it was, and the men were looking at him, and the impossible great whirling thing was coming down, nearer.

He began to run in the downward wash of air from the vanes. But it was no use. There were three men and they were fresh and he wasn't. He stopped, dropping into the fighter's crouch that is pre-set into the human body, ready to do battle.

The men didn't want to fight. They laughed and one of them said amiably: "*Long* past your bedtime, boy. Get in. We'll take you home."

Tropile stood poised, hands half-clenched. "Take —"

"Take you home. Yeah. Where you belong, Tropile. Not back to Wheeling, if that's what is worrying you."

"Where I —"

"Where you belong."

Then Tropile understood.

He got into the helicopter wonderingly. Home. So there *was* a home for such as he. He wasn't alone. He needn't keep his solitary self apart. He could be with his own kind.

He remembered Gala Tropile and paused. One of the men said with quick understanding: "Your wife? I think we saw her about half a mile from here. Heading back to Wheeling as fast as she could go."

Tropile nodded. That was better, after all. Gala was no Wolf, though he had tried his best to make her one.

One of the men closed the door; another did something with levers and wheels; the vanes whooshed around overhead; the helicopter bounced on its stiff-sprung landing legs and then rocked up and away.

For the first time in his life, Glenn Tropile looked *down* on the land.

They didn't fly high-but Glenn Tropile had never flown at all, and the two or three hundred feet of air beneath made him faint and queasy. They danced through the passes in the West Virginia hills, crossed icy streams and rivers, swung past old empty towns which no longer even had names of their own. They saw no one.

It was something over four hundred miles to where they were going, one of the men told him. They made it easily before dark.

* * * * *

As Tropile walked through the town in the evening light, electricity flared white and violet in the buildings around him. Imagine! Electricity was calories, and calories were to be hoarded.

There were other walkers in the street. Their gait was not the economical shuffle with pendant arms. They burned energy visibly. They swung. They *strode*. It had been chiseled on his brain in earliest childhood that such walking was wrong, reprehensible, debilitating. It wasted calories. These people did not look debilitated and they didn't seem to mind wasting calories.

It was an ordinary sort of town, apparently named Princeton. It did not have the transient look to it of, say, Wheeling, or Altoona, or Gary, in Tropile's experience. It looked like-well, it looked permanent.

Tropile had heard of a town called Princeton, but it happened that he had never passed through it southwarding or northbound. There was no reason why he or anybody should or should not have. Still, there was a possibility, once he thought of it, that things were somehow so arranged that they should not; maybe it was all on purpose. Like every town, it was underpopulated, but not so much so as most. Perhaps one living space in five was used. A high ratio.

The man beside him was named Haendl, one of the men from the helicopter. They hadn't talked much on the flight and they didn't talk much now. "Eat first," Haendl said, and took Tropile to a bright and busy sort of food stall. Only it wasn't a stall. It was a restaurant.

This Haendl-what to make of him? He should have been disgusting, nasty, an abomination. He had no manners whatever. He didn't know, or at least didn't use, the Seventeen Conventional Gestures. He wouldn't let Tropile walk behind him and to his left, though he was easily five years Tropile's senior. When he ate, he *ate*. The Sip of Appreciation, the Pause of First Surfeit, the Thrice Proffered Share meant nothing to him. He laughed when Tropile tried to give him the Elder's Portion.

Cheerfully patronizing, this man Haendl said to Tropile: "That stuffs all right when you don't have anything better to do with your time. Those poor mutts don't. They'd die of boredom without their inky-pinky cults and they don't have the resources to do anything bigger. Yes, I do know the Gestures. Seventeen delicate ways of communicating emotions too refined for words. The hell with them, Tropile. I've got words. You'll learn them, too."

Tropile ate silently, trying to think.

A man arrived, threw himself in a chair, glanced curiously at Tropile and said: "Haendl, the Somerville Road. The creek backed up when it froze. Flooded bad. Ruined everything."

Tropile ventured: "The flood ruined the road?"

"The road? No. Say, you must be the fellow Haendl went after. Tropile, that the name?" He leaned across the table, pumped Tropile's hand. "We had the road nicely blocked," he explained. "The flood washed it clean. Now we have to block it again."

Haendl said: "Take the tractor if you need it."

The man nodded and left.

Haendl said: "Eat up. We're wasting time. About that road-we keep all entrances blocked up, see? Why let a lot of sheep in and out?"

"Sheep?"

"The opposite," said Haendl, "of Wolves."

* * * * *

Take ten billion people and say that, out of every million of them, one-just one-is different. He has a talent for survival; call him Wolf. Ten thousand of him in a world of ten billion.

Squeeze them, freeze them, cut them down. Let old Rejoice in Messias loom in the terrifying sky and so abduct the Earth that the human race is decimated, fractionated, reduced to what is in comparison a bare handful of chilled, stunned survivors. There aren't ten billion people in the world any more. No, not by a factor of a thousand. Maybe there are as many as ten million, more or less, rattling around in the space their enormous Elder Generations made for them.

And of these ten million, how many are Wolf?

Ten thousand.

"You understand, Tropile?" said Haendl. "We survive. I don't care what you call us. The sheep call us Wolves. Me, I kind of call us Supermen. We have a talent for survival."

Tropile nodded, beginning to understand. "The way I survived the House of the Five Regulations."

Haendl gave him a pitying look. "The way you survived thirty years of Sheephood before that. Come on."

It was a tour of inspection. They went into a building, big, looking like any other big and useful building of the ancients, gray stone walls, windows with ragged spears of glass. Inside, though, it wasn't like the others. Two sub-basements down, Tropile winced and turned away from the flood of violet light that poured out of a quartz bull's-eye on top of a squat steel cone.

"Perfectly harmless, Tropile-you don't have to worry," Haendl boomed. "Know what you're looking at? There's a fusion reactor down there. Heat. Power. All the power we need. Do you know what that means?"

He stared soberly down at the flaring violet light of the inspection port.

"Come on," he said abruptly to Tropile.

Another building, also big, also gray stone. A cracked inscription over the entrance read: Orial Hall of Humanities. The sense-shock this time was not light; it was sound. Hammering, screeching, rattling, rumbling. Men were doing noisy things with metal and machines.

"Repair shop!" Haendl yelled. "See those machines? They belong to our man Innison. We've salvaged them from every big factory ruin we could find. Give Innison a piece of metal-any alloy, any shape-and one of those machines will change it into any other shape and damned near any other alloy. Drill it, cut it, plane it, weld it, smelt it, zone-melt it, bond it-you tell him what to do and he'll do it.

"We got the parts to make six tractors and forty-one cars out of this shop. And we've got other shops-aircraft in Farmingdale and Wichita, armaments in Wilmington. Not that we can't make some armaments here. Innison could build you a tank if he had to, complete with 105-millimeter gun."

"What's a tank?" Tropile asked.

Haendl only looked at him and said: "Come on!"

* * * * *

Glenn Tropile's head spun dizzily and all the spectacles merged and danced in his mind. They were incredible. All of them.

Fusion pile, machine shop, vehicular garage, aircraft hangar. There was a storeroom under the seats of a football stadium, and Tropile's head spun on his shoulders again as he tried to count the cases of coffee and canned soups and whiskey and beans. There was another storeroom, only this one was called an armory. It was filled with … guns. Guns that could be loaded with cartridges, of which they had very many; guns which, when you loaded them and pulled the trigger, would fire.

Tropile said, remembering: "I saw a gun once that still had its firing pin. But it was rusted solid."

"These work, Tropile," said Haendl. "You can kill a man with them. Some of us have."

"*Kill* —"

"Get that sheep look out of your eyes, Tropile! What's the difference how you execute a criminal? And what's a criminal but someone who represents a danger to your world? We prefer a gun instead of the Donation of the Spinal Tap, because it's quicker, because it's less messy-and because we don't like to drink spinal fluid, no matter what imaginary therapeutic or symbolic value it has. You'll learn."

But he didn't add "come on." They had arrived where they were going.

It was a small room in the building that housed the armory and it held, among other things, a rack of guns.

"Sit down," said Haendl, taking one of the guns out of the rack thoughtfully and handling it as the doomed Boyne had caressed his watch-case. It was the latest pre-Pyramid-model rifle, anti-personnel, short-range. It would not scatter a cluster of shots in a coffee can at more than two and a half miles.

"All right," said Haendl, stroking the stock. "You've seen the works, Tropile. You've lived thirty years with sheep. You've seen what they have and what we have. I don't have to ask you to make a choice. I know what you choose. The only thing left is to tell you what *we* want from *you*."

A faint pulsing began inside Glenn Tropile. "I expected we'd be getting to that."

"Why not? We're not sheep. We don't act that way. Quid pro quo. Remember that-it saves time. You've seen the quid. Now we come to the quo." He leaned forward. "Tropile, what do you know about the Pyramids?"

"Nothing."

Haendl nodded. "Right. They're all around us and our lives are beggared because of them. And we don't even know why. We don't have the least idea of what they are. Did you know that one of the sheep was Translated in Wheeling when you left?"

"Translated?"

Tropile listened with his mouth open while Haendl told him about what had happened to Citizen Boyne.

"So he didn't make the Donation after all," Tropile said.

"Might have been better if he had," said Haendl. "Still, it gave you a chance to get away. We had heard-never mind how just yet-that Wheeling'd caught itself a Wolf, so we came looking for you. But you were already gone."

* * * * *

Tropile said, faintly annoyed: "You were damn near too late."

"Oh, no, Tropile," Haendl assured him. "We're never too late. If you don't have enough guts and ingenuity to get away from sheep, you're no wolf-simple as that. But there's this Translation. We know it happens, but we don't even know what it is. All we know, people disappear. There's a new sun in the sky every five years or so. Who makes it? The Pyramids. How? We don't know that. Sometimes something floats around in the air and we call it an Eye. It has something to do with Translation, something to do with the Pyramids. What? We don't know that."

"We don't know much of anything," interrupted Tropile, trying to hurry him along.

"Not about the Pyramids, no." Haendl shook his head. "Hardly anyone has ever seen one, for that matter."

"Hardly-You mean you have?"

"Oh, yes. There's a Pyramid on Mount Everest, you know. That's not just a story. It's true. I've been there, and it's there. At least, it was there five years ago, right after the last Sun Re-creation. I guess it hasn't moved. It just sits there."

Tropile listened, marveling. To have seen a real Pyramid! Almost he had thought of them as legends, contrived to account for such established physical facts as the Eyes and Translation, as children with a Santa Claus. But this incredible man had seen it!

"Somebody dropped an H-bomb on it, way back," Haendl continued, "and the only thing that happened is that now the North Col is a crater. You can't move the Pyramid. You can't hurt it. But it's alive. It has been there, alive, for a couple of hundred years; and that's about all we know about the Pyramids. Right?"

"Right."

Haendl stood up. "Tropile, that's what all of this is all about!" He gestured around him. "Guns, tanks, airplanes-we want to know more! We're going to find out more and then we're going to fight."

There was a jarring note and Tropile caught at it, sniffing the air. Somehow-perhaps it was his sub-adrenals that told him-this very positive, very self-willed man was just the slightest bit unsure of himself. But Haendl swept on and Tropile, for a moment, forgot to be alert.

"We had a party up Mount Everest five years ago," Haendl was saying. "We didn't find out a thing. Five years before that, and five years before *that* —every time there's a sun, while it is still warm enough to give a party a chance to climb up the sides-we send a team up there. It's a rough job. We give it to the new boys, Tropile. Like you."

There it was. He was being invited to attack a Pyramid.

Tropile hesitated, delicately balanced, trying to get the *feel* of this negotiation. This was Wolf against Wolf; it was hard. There had to be an advantage —

"There is an advantage," Haendl said aloud.

Tropile jumped, but then he remembered: Wolf against Wolf.

Haendl went on: "What you get out of it is your life, in the first place. You understand you can't get out now. We don't want sheep meddling around. And in the second place, there's a considerable hope of gain." He stared at Tropile with a dreamer's eyes. "We don't send parties up there for nothing, you know. We want to get something out of it. What we want is the Earth."

"The Earth?" It reeked of madness. But this man wasn't mad.

"Some day, Tropile, it's going to be us against them. Never mind the sheep-they don't count. It's going to be Pyramids and Wolves, and the Pyramids won't win. And then —"

It was enough to curdle the blood. This man was proposing to *fight*, and against the invulnerable, the godlike Pyramids.

But he was glowing and the fever was contagious. Tropile felt his own blood begin to pound. Haendl hadn't finished his "and then —" but he didn't have to. The "and then" was obvious: And then the world takes up again from the day the wandering planet first came into view. And then we go back to our own solar system and an end to the five-year cycle of frost and hunger.

And then the Wolves can rule a world worth ruling.

It was a meretricious appeal, perhaps, but it could not be refused. Tropile was lost.

He said: "You can put away the gun, Haendl. You've signed me up."

CHAPTER VII.

The way to Mount Everest, Tropile glumly found, lay through supervising the colony's nursery school. It wasn't what he had expected, but it had the advantages that while his charges were learning, he was learning, too.

One jump ahead of the three-year-olds, he found that the "wolves," far from being predators on the "sheep," existed with them in a far more complicated ecological relationship. There were Wolves all through sheepdom; they leavened the dough of society.

In barbarously simple prose, a primer said: "The Sons of the Wolf are good at numbers and money. You and your friends play money games almost as soon as you can talk, and you can think in percentages and compound interest when you want to. Most people are not able to do this."

True, thought Tropile subvocally, reading aloud to the tots. That was how it had been with him.

"Sheep are afraid of the Sons of the Wolf. Those of us who live among them are in constant danger of detection and death-although ordinarily a Wolf can take care of himself against any number of sheep." True, too.

"It is one of the most dangerous assignments a Wolf can be given to live among the sheep. Yet it is essential. Without us, they would die-of stagnation, of rot, eventually of hunger."

It didn't have to be spelled out any further. Sheep can't mend their own fences.

The prose was horrifyingly bald and the children were horrifyingly-he choked on the word, but managed to form it in his mind —*competitive.* The verbal taboos lingered, he found, after he had broken through the barriers of behavior.

But it was distressing, in a way. At an age when future Citizens would have been learning their Little Pitcher Ways, these children were learning to fight. The perennial argument about who would get to be Big Bill Zeckendorf when they played a strange game called "Zeckendorf and Hilton" sometimes ended in bloody noses.

And nobody-nobody at all-meditated on Connectivity.

Tropile was warned not to do it himself. Haendl said grimly: "We don't understand it and we don't like what we don't understand. We're suspicious animals, Tropile. As the children grow older, we give them just enough practice so they can go into one meditation and get the feel of it-or pretend to, at any rate. If they have to pass as Citizens, they'll need that much. But more than that we do not allow."

"Allow?" Somehow the word grated; somehow his sub-adrenals began to pulse.

"*Allow!* We have our suspicions and we know for a fact that sometimes people disappear when they meditate. We don't want to disappear. We think it's not a good thing to disappear. Don't meditate, Tropile. You hear?"

* * * * *

But later, Tropile had to argue the point. He picked a time when Haendl was free, or as nearly free as that man ever was. The whole adult colony had been out on what they used as a parade ground-it had once been a football field, Haendl said. They had done their regular twice-a-week infantry drill, that being one of the prices one paid for living among the free, progressive Wolves instead of the dull and tepid sheep.

Tropile was mightily winded, but he cast himself on the ground near Haendl, caught his breath and said: "Haendl-about meditation."

"What about it?"

"Well, perhaps you don't really grasp it."

Tropile searched for words. He knew what he wanted to say. How could anything that felt as good as Oneness be bad? And wasn't Translation, after all, so rare as hardly to matter? But he wasn't sure he could get through to Haendl in those terms.

He tried: "When you meditate successfully, Haendl, you're one with the Universe. Do you know what I mean? There's no feeling like it. It's indescribable peace, beauty, harmony, repose."

"It's the world's cheapest narcotic," Haendl snorted.

"Oh, now, really —"

"*And* the world's cheapest religion. The stone-broke mutts can't afford gilded idols, so they use their own navels. That's all it is. They can't afford alcohol; they can't even afford the muscular exertion of deep breathing that would throw them into a state of hyperventilated oxygen drunkenness. Then what's left? Self-hypnosis. Nothing else. It's all they can do, so they learn it, they define it as pleasant and good, and they're all fixed up."

Tropile sighed. The man was so stubborn! Then a thought occurred to him and he pushed himself up on his elbows. "Aren't you leaving something out? What about Translation?"

Haendl glowered at him. "That's the part we don't understand."

"But surely self-hypnosis doesn't account for —"

"Surely it doesn't!" Haendl mimicked savagely. "All right. We don't understand it and we're afraid of it. Kindly do not tell me Translation is the supreme act of Un-willing, Total Disavowal of Duality, Unison with the Brahm-Ground or any such slop. You don't know what it is and neither do we." He started to get up. "All we know is, people vanish. And we want no part of it, so we don't meditate. None of us-including you!"

* * * * *

It was foolishness, this close-order drill. Could you defeat the unreachable Himalayan Pyramid with a squads-right flanking maneuver?

And yet it wasn't all foolishness. Close-order drill and 2500-calorie-a-day diet began to put fat and flesh and muscle on Tropile's body, and something other than that on his mind. He had not lost the edge of his acquisitiveness, his drive-his whatever it was that made the difference between Wolf and sheep.

But he had gained something. Happiness? Well, if "happiness" is a sense of purpose, and a hope that the purpose can be accomplished, then happiness. It was a feeling that had never existed in his life before. Always it had been the glandular compulsion to gain an advantage, and that was gone, or anyway almost gone, because it was permitted in the society in which he now lived.

Glenn Tropile sang as he putt-putted in his tractor, plowing the thawing Jersey fields. Still, a faint doubt remained. Squads right against the Pyramids?

Stiffly, Tropile stopped the tractor, slowed the diesel to a steady *thrum* and got off. It was hot-being midsummer of the five-year calendar the Pyramids had imposed. It was time for rest and maybe something to eat.

He sat in the shade of a tree, as farmers always have done, and opened his sandwiches. He was only a mile or so from Princeton, but he might as well have been in Limbo; there was no sign of any living human but himself. The northering sheep didn't come near Princeton-it "happened" that way, on purpose.

He caught a glimpse of something moving, but when he stood up for a better look into the woods on the other side of the field, it was gone. Wolf? *Real* Wolf, that is? It could have been a bear, for that matter-there was talk of wolves and bears around Princeton; and although Tropile knew that much of the talk was assiduously encouraged by men like Haendl, he also knew that some of it was true.

As long as he was up, he gathered straw from the litter of last "year's" head-high grass, gathered sticks under the trees, built a small fire and put water on to boil for coffee. Then he sat back and ate his sandwiches, thinking.

Maybe it was a promotion, going from the nursery school to labor in the fields. Or maybe it wasn't. Haendl had promised him a place in the expedition that would-maybe-discover something new and great and helpful about the Pyramids. And that might still come to pass, because the expedition was far from ready to leave.

Tropile munched his sandwiches thoughtfully. Now *why* was the expedition so far from ready to leave? It was absolutely essential to get there in the warmest weather possible-otherwise Mt. Everest was unclimbable. Generations of alpinists had proved that. That warmest weather was rapidly going by.

And *why* were Haendl and the Wolf colony so insistent on building tanks, arming themselves with rifles, organizing in companies and squads? The H-bomb hadn't flustered the Pyramid. What lesser weapon could?

Uneasily, Tropile put a few more sticks on the fire, staring thoughtfully into the canteen cup of water. It was a satisfyingly hot fire, he noticed abstractedly. The water was very nearly ready to boil.

* * * * *

Half across the world, the Pyramid in the Himalays felt, or heard, or tasted —a difference.

Possibly the h-f pulses that had gone endlessly wheep, wheep, wheep were now going wheep-*beep*, wheep-*beep*. Possibly the electromagnetic "taste" of lower-than-red was now spiced with a tang of beyond-violet. Whatever the sign was, the Pyramid recognized it.

A part of the crop it tended was ready to harvest.

The ripening bud had a name, of course, but names didn't matter to the Pyramid. The man named Tropile didn't know he was ripening, either. All that Tropile knew was that, for the first time in nearly a year, he had succeeded in catching each stage of the nine perfect states of water-coming-to-a-boil in its purest form.

It was like ... like ... well, it was like nothing that anyone but a Water Watcher could understand. He observed. He appreciated. He encompassed and absorbed the myriad subtle perfections of time, of shifting transparency, of sound, of distribution of ebulliency, of the faint, faint odor of steam.

Complete, Glenn Tropile relaxed all his limbs and let his chin rest on his breast-bone.

It was, he thought with placid, crystalline perception, a rare and perfect opportunity for meditation. He thought of Connectivity. (Overhead, a shifting glassy flaw appeared in the thin, still air.) There wasn't any thought of Eyes in the erased palimpsest that was Glenn Tropile's mind. There wasn't any thought of Pyramids or of Wolves. The plowed field before him didn't exist. Even the water, merrily bubbling itself dry, was gone from his perception.

He was beginning to meditate.

Time passed-or stood still-for Tropile; there was no difference. There was no time. He found himself almost on the brink of Understanding.

Something snapped. An intruding blue-bottle drone, maybe, or a twitching muscle. Partly, Tropile came back to reality. Almost, he glanced upward. Almost, he saw the Eye....

It didn't matter. The thing that really mattered, the only thing in the world, was all within his mind; and he was ready, he knew, to find it.

Once more! Try harder!

He let the mind-clearing unanswerable question drift into his mind:

If the sound of two hands together is a clapping, what is the sound of one hand?

Gently he pawed at the question, the symbol of the futility of mind-and therefore the gateway to meditation. Unawareness of self was stealing deliciously over him.

He was Glenn Tropile. He was more than that. He was the water boiling ...and the boiling water was he. He was the gentle warmth of the fire, which was-which was, yes, itself the arc of the sky. As each thing was each other thing; water was fire, and fire air; Tropile was the first simmering bubble and the full roll of Well-aged Water was Self, was-more than Self-was —

The answer to the unanswerable question was coming clearer and softer to him. And then, all at once, but not suddenly, for there was no time, it was not close-it *was*.

The answer was his, was him. The arc of sky was the answer, and the answer belonged to sky-to warmth, to all warmths that there are, and to all waters, and-and the answer was-was —

Tropile vanished. The mild thunderclap that followed made the flames dance and the column of steam fray; and then the fire was steady again, and so was the rising steam. But Tropile was gone.

CHAPTER VIII.

Haendl plodded angrily through the high grass toward the dull throb of the diesel.

Maybe it had been a mistake to take this Glenn Tropile into the colony. He was more Citizen than Wolf-no, cancel that, Haendl thought; he was more Wolf than Citizen. But the Wolf in him was tainted with sheep's blood. He *competed* like a Wolf, but in spite of everything, he refused to give up some of his sheep's ways. Meditation. He had been cautioned against that. But had he given it up?

He had not.

If it had been entirely up to Haendl, Glenn Tropile would have found himself back among the sheep or dead. Fortunately for Tropile, it was not entirely up to Haendl. The community of Wolves was by no means a democracy, but the leader had a certain responsibility to his constituents, and the responsibility was this: He couldn't afford to be wrong. Like the Old Gray Wolf who protected Mowgli, he had to defend his actions against attack; if he failed to defend, the pack would pull him down.

And Innison thought they needed Tropile-not in spite of the taint of the Citizen that he bore, but because of it.

Haendl bawled: "Tropile! Tropile, where are you?" There was only the wind and the *thrum* of the diesel. It was enormously irritating. Haendl had other things to do than to chase after Glenn Tropile. And where was he? There was the diesel, idling wastefully; there the end of the patterned furrows Tropile had plowed. There a small fire, burning —

And there was Tropile.

Haendl stopped, frozen, his mouth opened, about to yell Tropile's name.

It was Tropile, all right, staring with concentrated, oyster-eyed gaze at the fire and the little pot of water it boiled. Staring. Meditating. And over his head, like flawed glass in a pane, was the thing Haendl feared most of all things on Earth. It was an Eye.

Tropile was on the very verge of being Translated ... whatever that was.

Time, maybe, to find out *what* that was! Haendl ducked back into the shelter of the high grass, knelt, plucked his radio communicator from his pocket, urgently called.

"Innison! Innison, will somebody, for God's sake, put Innison on!"

Seconds passed. Voices answered. Then there was Innison.

"Innison, listen! You wanted to catch Tropile in the act of Meditation? All right, you've got him. The old wheat field, south end, under the elms around the creek. Get here fast, Innison-there's an Eye forming above him!"

Luck! Lucky that they were ready for this, and only by luck, because it was the helicopter that Innison had patiently assembled for the attack on Everest that was ready now, loaded with instruments, planned to weigh and measure the aura around the Pyramid-now at hand when they needed it.

That was luck, but there was driving hurry involved, too; it was only a matter of minutes before Haendl heard the wobbling drone of the copter, saw the vanes fluttering low over the hedges, dropping to earth behind the elms.

Haendl raised himself cautiously and peered. Yes, Tropile was still there, and the Eye still above him! But the noise of the helicopter had frayed the spell. Tropile stirred. The Eye wavered and shook —

But did not vanish.

Thanking what passed for his God, Haendl scuttled circuitously around the elms and joined Innison at the copter. Innison was furiously closing switches and pointing lenses.

They saw Tropile sitting there, the Eye growing larger and closer over his head. They had time-plenty of time; oh, nearly a minute of time. They brought to bear on the silent and unknowing form of Glenn Tropile every instrument that the copter carried. They were waiting for Tropile to disappear —

He did.

* * * * *

Innison and Haendl hunched at the thunderclap as air rushed in to replace him.

"We've got what you wanted," Haendl said harshly. "Let's read some instruments."

Throughout the Translation, high-tensile magnetic tape on a madly spinning drum had been hurtling under twenty-four recording heads at a hundred feet a second. Output to the recording heads had been from every kind of measuring device they had been able to conceive and build, all loaded on the helicopter for use on Mount Everest-all now pointed directly at Glenn Tropile.

They had, for the instant of Translation, readings from one microsecond to the next on the varying electric, gravitational, magnetic, radiant and molecular-state conditions in his vicinity.

They got back to Innison's workshop, and the laboratory inside it, in less than a minute; but it took hours of playing back the magnetic pulses into machines that turned them into scribed curves on coordinate paper before Innison had anything resembling an answer.

He said: "No mystery. I mean no mystery except the speed. Want to know what happened to Tropile?"

"I do," said Haendl.

"A pencil of electrostatic force maintained by a pinch effect bounced down the approximate azimuth of Everest-God knows how they handled the elevation-and charged him and the area positive. A *big* charge, clear off the scale. They parted company. He was bounced straight up. A meter off the ground, a correcting vector was applied. When last seen, he was headed fast in the direction of the Pyramids' binary-fast! So fast that I would guess he'll get there alive. It takes an appreciable time, a good part of a second, for his protein to coagulate enough to make him sick and then kill him. If the Pyramids strip the charges off him immediately on arrival, as I should think they will, he'll live."

"Friction —"

"Be damned to friction," Innison said calmly. "He carried a packet of air with him and there *was* no friction. How? I don't know. How are they going to keep him alive in space, without the charges that hold air? I don't know. If they don't maintain the charges, can they beat the speed of light? I don't know. I can tell you *what* happened. I can't tell you *how*."

Haendl stood up thoughtfully. "It's something," he said grudgingly.

"It's more than we've ever had —a complete reading at the instant of Translation!"

"We'll get more," Haendl promised. "Innison, now that you know what to look for, go on looking for it. Keep every possible detection device monitored twenty-four hours a day. Turn on everything you've got that'll find a sign of imposed modulation. At any sign-or at anybody's hunch that there *might* be a sign —I'm to be called. If I'm eating. If I'm sleeping. If I'm enjoying with a woman. Call me, you hear? Maybe you were right about Tropile; maybe he did have some use. He might give the Pyramids a bellyache."

Innison, flipping the magnetic tape drum to rewind, said thoughtfully: "It's too bad they've got him. We could have used some more readings."

"Too bad?" Haendl laughed sharply. "This time they've got themselves a Wolf."

* * * * *

The Pyramids did have a Wolf—a fact which did not matter in the least to them.

It is not possible to know what "mattered" to a Pyramid except by inference. But it is possible to know that they had no way of telling Wolf from Citizen.

The planet which was their home-Earth's old Moon-was small, dark, atmosphereless and waterless. It was completely built over, much of it with its propulsion devices.

In the old days, when technology had followed war, luxury, government and leisure, the Pyramids' sun had run out of steam; and at about the same time, they had run out of the Components they imported from a neighboring planet. They used the last of their Components to implement their stolid metaphysic of hauling and pushing. They pushed their planet.

They knew where to push it.

Each Pyramid as it stood was a radio-astronomy observatory, powerful and accurate beyond the wildest dreams of Earthly radio-astronomers. From this start, they built instruments to aid their naked senses. They went into a kind of hibernation, reducing their activity to a bare trickle except for a small "crew" and headed for Earth. They had every reason to believe they would find more Components there, and they did.

Tropile was one of them. The only thing which set him apart from the others was that he was the most recent to be stockpiled.

The religion, or vice, or philosophy he practiced made it possible for him to be a Component. Meditation derived from Zen Buddhism was a windfall for the Pyramids, though, of course, they had no idea at all of what lay behind it and did not "care." They knew only that, at certain times, certain potential Components became Components which were no longer merely potential-which were, in fact, ripe for harvesting.

It was useful to them that the minds they cropped were utterly blank. It saved the trouble of blanking them.

Tropile had been harvested at the moment his inhibiting conscious mind had been cleared, for the Pyramids were not interested in him as an entity capable of will and conception. They used only the raw capacity of the human brain and its perceptors.

They used Rashevsky's Number, the gigantic, far more than astronomical expression that denoted the number of switching operations performable within the human brain. They used "subception," the phenomenon by which the reasoning mind, uninhibited by consciousness, reacts directly to stimuli-shortcutting the cerebral censor, avoiding the weighing of shall-I-or-shan't-I that precedes every conscious act.

The harvested minds were-Components.

It is not desirable that your bedroom wall switch have a mind of its own; if you turn the lights on, you want them *on*. So it was with the Pyramids.

A Component was needed in the industrial complex which transformed catabolism products into anabolism products.

* * * * *

With long experience gained since their planetfall, Pyramids received the *tabula rasa* that was Glenn Tropile. He arrived in one piece, wearing a blanket of air. Quick-frozen mentally at the moment of inert blankness his Meditation had granted him-the psychic drunkard's coma-he was cushioned on repellent charges as he plummeted down, and instantly stripped of surplus electrostatic charge.

At this point, he was still human; only asleep.

He remained "asleep." Annular fields they used for lifting and lowering seized him and moved him into a snug tank of nutrient fluid. There were many such tanks, ready and waiting.

The tanks themselves could be moved, and the one containing Glenn Tropile did move, to a metabolism complex where there were many other tanks, all occupied. This was a warm room-the Pyramids had wasted no energy on such foppish comforts in the first "room." In this room, Glenn Tropile gradually resumed the appearance of life. His heart once again began to beat. Faint stirrings were visible in his chest as his habit-numbed lungs attempted to breathe. Gradually the stirrings slowed and stopped. There was no need for that foppish comfort, either; the nutrient fluid supplied all.

Tropile was "wired into circuit."

The only literal wiring, at first, was a temporary one —a fine electrode aseptically introduced into the great nerve that leads to the rhinencephalon-the "small brain," the area of the brain which contains the pleasure centers that motivate human behavior.

More than a thousand Components had been spoiled and discarded before the Pyramids had located the pleasure centers so exactly.

While the Component, Tropile, was being "programmed," the wire rewarded him with minute pulses that made his body glow with animal satisfaction when he functioned correctly. That was all there was to it. After a time, the wire was withdrawn, but by then Tropile had "learned" his entire task. Conditioned reflexes had been established. They could be counted on for the long and useful life of the Component.

That life might be very long indeed; in the nutrient tank beside Tropile's, as it happened, lay a Component with eight legs and a chitinous fringe around its eyes. It had lain in such a tank for more than a hundred and twenty-five thousand Terrestrial years.

* * * * *

The Component was placed in operation. It opened its eyes and saw things. The sensory nerves of its limbs felt things. The muscles of its hands and toes operated things.

Where was Glenn Tropile?

He was there, all of him, but a zombie-Tropile. Bereft of will, emptied of memories. He was a machine and part of a huger machine. His sex was the sex of a photoelectric cell; his politics were those of a transistor; his ambition that of a mercury switch. He didn't know anything about sex, or fear, or hope. He only knew two things: Input and Output.

Input to him was a display of small lights on a board before his vacant face; and also the modulation of a loudspeaker's liquid-borne hum in each ear.

Output from him was the dancing manipulation of certain buttons and keys, prompted by changes in Input and by nothing else.

Between Input and Output, he lay in the tank, a human Black Box which was capable of Rashevsky's Number of switchings, and of nothing else.

He had been programmed to accomplish a specific task-to shepherd a chemical called 3, 7, 12-trihydroxycholanic acid, present in the catabolic product of the Pyramids, through a succession of more than five hundred separate operations until it emerged as the chemical, which the Pyramids were able to metabolize, called Protoporphin IX.

He was not the only Component operating in this task; there were several, each with its own program.

The acid accumulated in great tanks a mile from him. He knew its concentration, heat and pressure; he knew of all the impurities which would affect subsequent reactions. His fingers tapped, giving binary-coded signals to sluice gates to open for so many seconds and then to close; for such an amount of solvent at such a temperature to flow in; for the agitators to agitate for just so long at just such a force. And if a trouble signal disturbed any one of the 517 major and minor operations, he-it? —was set to decide among alternatives:

—scrap the batch in view of flow conditions along the line?

—isolate and bypass the batch through a standby loop?

—immediate action to correct the malfunction?

Without inhibiting intelligence, without the trammels of humanity on him, the intricate display board and the complex modulations of the two sound signals could be instantly taken in, evaluated and given their share in the decision.

Was it-he? —still alive?

The question has no meaning. It was working. It was an excellent machine, in fact, and the Pyramids cared for it well. Its only consciousness, apart from the reflexive responses that were its program, was-well, call it "the sound of one hand alone." Which is to say zero, mindlessness, Samadhi, stupor.

It continued to function for some time-until the required supply of Protoporphin IX had been exceeded by a sufficient factor of safety to make further processing unnecessary-that is, for some minutes or months. During that time, it was Happy. (It had been programmed to be Happy when there were no uncorrected malfunctions of the process.) At the end of that time, it shut itself off, sent out a signal that the task was completed, then it was laid aside in the analogue of a deep-freeze, to be reprogrammed when another Component was needed.

It was totally immaterial to the Pyramids that this particular Component had not been stamped from Citizen but from Wolf.

CHAPTER IX.

Roget Germyn, of Wheeling a Citizen, contemplated his wife with growing concern.

Possibly the events of the past few days had unhinged her reason, but he was nearly sure that she had eaten a portion of the evening meal secretly, in the serving room, before calling him to the table.

He felt positive that it was only a temporary aberration; she was, after all, a Citizeness, with all that that implied. A —a creature-like that Gala Tropile, for example-someone like that might steal extra portions with craft and guile. You couldn't live with a Wolf for years and not have some of it rub off on you. But not Citizeness Germyn.

There was a light, thrice-repeated tap on the door.

Speak of the devil, thought Roget Germyn most appropriately; for it was that same Gala Tropile. She entered, her head downcast, looking worn and-well, pretty.

He began formally: "I give you greeting, Citi —"

"They're here!" she interrupted in desperate haste. Germyn blinked. "Please," she begged, "can't you do something? They're *Wolves!*"

Citizeness Germyn emitted a muted shriek.

"You may leave, Citizeness," Germyn told her shortly, already forming in his mind the words of gentle reproof he would later use. "Now what is all this talk of Wolves?"

Gala Tropile distractedly sat in the chair her hostess had vacated. "We were running away," she babbled. "Glenn-he was Wolf, you see, and he made me leave with him, after the House of the Five Regulations. We were a day's long march from Wheeling and we stopped to rest. And there was an aircraft, Citizen!"

"An aircraft!" Citizen Germyn allowed himself a frown. "Citizeness, it is not well to invent things which are not so."

"I saw it, Citizen! There were men in it. One of them is here again! He came looking for me with another man and I barely escaped him. I'm afraid!"

"There is no cause for fear, only an opportunity to appreciate," Citizen Germyn said mechanically-it was what one told one's children.

But within himself, he was finding it very hard to remain calm. That word Wolf-it was a destroyer of calm, an incitement to panic and hatred! He remembered Tropile well, and there was Wolf, to be sure. The mere fact that Citizen Germyn had doubted his Wolfishness at first was powerful cause to be doubly convinced of it now; he had postponed the day of reckoning for an enemy of all the world, and there was enough secret guilt in his recollection to set his own heart thumping.

"Tell me exactly what happened," said Citizen Germyn, in words that the stress of emotion had already made far less than graceful.

Obediently, Gala Tropile said: "I was returning to my home after the evening meal and Citizeness Puffin-she took me in after Citizen Tropile-after my husband was —"

"I understand. You made your home with her."

"Yes. She told me that two men had come to see me. They spoke badly, she said, and I was alarmed. I peered through a window of my home and they were there. One had been in the aircraft I saw! And they flew away with my husband."

"It is a matter of seriousness," Citizen Germyn admitted doubtfully. "So then you came here to me?"

"Yes, but they saw me, Citizen! And I think they followed. You must protect me —I have no one else!"

"If they be Wolf," Germyn said calmly, "we will raise hue and cry against them. Now will the Citizeness remain here? I go forth to see these men."

There was a graceless hammering on the door.

"Too late!" cried Gala Tropile in panic. "They are here!"

* * * * *

Citizen Germyn went through the ritual of greeting, of deprecating the ugliness and poverty of his home, of offering everything he owned to his visitors; it was the way to greet a stranger.

The two men lacked both courtesy and wit, but they did make an attempt to comply with the minimal formal customs of introduction. He had to give them credit for that; and yet it was almost more alarming than if they had blustered and yelled.

For he knew one of these men.

He dredged the name out of his memory. It was Haendl. The same man had appeared in Wheeling the day Glenn Tropile had been scheduled to make the Donation of the Spinal Tap-and had broken free and escaped. He had inquired about Tropile of a good many people, Citizen Germyn included, and even at that time, in the excitement of an Amok, a Wolf-finding and a Translation in a single day, Germyn had wondered at Haendl's lack of breeding and airs.

Now he wondered no longer.

But the man made no overt act and Citizen Germyn postponed the raising of the hue and cry. It was not a thing to be done lightly.

"Gala Tropile is in this house," the man with Haendl said bluntly.

Citizen Germyn managed a Quirked Smile.

"We want to see her, Germyn. It's about her husband. He-uh-he was with us for a while and something happened."

"Ah, yes. The Wolf."

The man flushed and looked at Haendl. Haendl said loudly: "The Wolf. Sure he's a Wolf. But he's gone now, so you don't have to worry about that."

"Gone?"

"Not just him, but four or five of us. There was a man named Innison and he's gone, too. We need help, Germyn. Something about Tropile-God knows how it is, but he started something. We want to talk to his wife and find out what we can about him. So will you get her out of the back room where she's hiding and bring her here, please?"

Citizen Germyn quivered. He bent over the ID bracelet that once had belonged to the one PFC Joe Hartman, fingering it to hide his thoughts.

He said at last: "Perhaps you are right. Perhaps the Citizeness is with my wife. If this be so, would it not be possible that she is fearful of those who once were with her husband?"

* * * * *

Haendl laughed sourly. "She isn't any more fearful than we are, Germyn. I told you about this man Innison who disappeared. He was a Son of the Wolf, you understand me? For that matter —" He glanced at his companion, licked his lips and changed his mind about what he had been going to say next. "He was a Wolf. Do you ever remember hearing of a Wolf being Translated before?"

"Translated?" Germyn dropped the ID bracelet. "But that's impossible!" he cried, forgetting his manners completely. "Oh, no! Translation comes only to those who attain the moment of supreme detachment, you can be sure of that. I *know*! I've seen it with my own eyes. No Wolf could *possibly* —"

"At least five Wolves did," Haendl said grimly. "Now you see what the trouble is? Tropile was Translated —I saw that with *my* own eyes. The next day, Innison. Within a week, two or three others. So we came down here, Germyn, not because we like you people, not because we enjoy it, but because we're *scared*.

"What we want is to talk to Tropile's wife-you, too, I guess; we want to talk to anybody who ever knew him. We want to find out everything there is to find out about Tropile and see if we can make any sense of the answers. Because maybe Translation is the supreme objective of life to you people, Germyn, but to us it's just one more way of dying. And we don't want to die."

Citizen Germyn bent to pick up his cherished identification bracelet and dropped it absently on a table. There was very much on his mind.

He said at last: "That is strange. Shall I tell you another strange thing?"

Haendl, looking angry and baffled, nodded.

Germyn said: "There has been no Translation here since the day the Wolf, Tropile, escaped. But there have been Eyes. I have seen them myself. It —" He hesitated, shrugged. "It has been disturbing. Some of our finest Citizens have ceased to Meditate; they have been worrying. So many Eyes and nobody taken! It is outside of all of our experience, and our customs have suffered. Politeness is dwindling among us. Even in my own household —"

He coughed and went on: "No matter. But these Eyes have come into every home; they have peered about, peered about, and no one has been taken. Why? Is it something to do with the Translation of Wolves?" He stared hopelessly at his visitors. "All I know is that it is very strange and therefore I am worried."

"Then take us to Gala Tropile," said Haendl. "Let's see what we can find out!"

Citizen Germyn bowed. He cleared his throat and raised his voice just sufficiently to carry from one room to another. "Citizeness!" he called.

There was a pause and then his wife appeared in the doorway, looking ruffled and ill at ease with her guest.

"Will you ask if Citizeness Tropile will join us here?" he requested.

His wife nodded. "She is resting. I will call her."

They called her and questioned her for some time.

She told them nothing.

She had nothing to tell.

CHAPTER X.

On Earth's binary, Glenn Tropile had been reprogrammed for a new task.

The problem was navigation. Earth had been a disappointment to the Pyramids; it was necessary to move rapidly to a more rewarding planet.

The Pyramids had taken Earth out past Pluto's orbit with a simple shove, slow and massive. It had been enough merely to approximate the direction in which they would want to go. There would be plenty of time for refinements of course later.

But now the time for refinements had come, earlier than they might have expected. They had now time to travel, they knew where to —a star cluster reasonably sure to be rich in Componentiferous planets. It was inherent in the nature of Component mines that eventually they always played out.

There were always more mines, though. If that had not been so, it would have been necessary, perhaps, to stock-breed Components against future needs. But it was easier to work the vein out and move on.

Now the course had to be computed. There were such variables to be considered as: motion of the star cluster; acceleration of the binary-planet system; *gravitational influence of every astronomical object in the island universe, without exception.*

Precise computation on this basis was obviously not practical. That was not an answer to the problem, since the time required would approach eternity as one of its parameters.

It was possible to simplify the problem. Only the astronomical bodies which were relatively nearby need be treated as individuals. Farther away, the Pyramids began to group them in small bunches, still farther in large bunches, on to the point where the farthest-and the most numerous-bodies were lumped together as a vague gravitational "noise" whose average intensity alone it was required to know and to enter as a datum.

And still no single Component could handle even its own share of the problem, were the "computer" they formed to be kept within the range of permissible size.

It was for this that the Component which had once been Tropile was taken out of storage.

This was all old stuff to the Pyramids; they knew how to handle it. They broke the problem down to its essentials, separated even those into many parts. There was, for example, the subsection of one certain aspect of the logistical problem which involved locating and procuring additional Components to handle the load.

Even that tiny specialization was too much for a single Component, but fortunately the Pyramids had resources to bring to bear. The procedure in such cases was to hitch several Components together.

This was done.

When the Pyramids finished their neuro-surgery, there floated in an oversized nutrient tank a thing like a great sea-anemone. It was composed of eight Components-all human, as it happened-arranged in a circle, facing inward, joined temple to temple, brain to brain.

At their feet, where sixteen eyes could see it, was the display board to feed them their Input. Sixteen hands each grasped a molded switch to handle their binary-coded Output. There would be no storage of the Output outside of the eight-Component complex itself; it went as control signals to the electrostatic generators, funneled through the single Pyramid on Mount Everest, which handled the task of Component-procurement.

That is, of Translation.

The programming was slow and thorough. Perhaps the Pyramid which finally activated the octuple unit and went away was pleased with itself, not knowing that one of its Components was Glenn Tropile.

* * * * *

Nirvana. (It pervaded all; there was nothing outside of it.)

Nirvana. (Glenn Tropile floated in it as in the amniotic fluid around him.)

Nirvana. (The sound of one hand.... Floating oneness.)

There was an intrusion.

Perfection is completed; by adding to it, it is destroyed. *Duality struck like a thunderbolt. Oneness shattered.*

For Glenn Tropile, it seemed as though his wife were screaming at him to wake up. He tried to.

It was curiously difficult and painful. Timeless poignant sadness, five years of sorrow over a lost love compressed into a microsecond. It was always so, Tropile thought drowsily, awakening. It never lasts. What's the use of worrying over what always happens....

Sudden shock and horror rocked him.

This was no ordinary awakening-no ordinary thing at all —*nothing* was as it ever had been before!

Tropile opened his mouth and screamed-or thought he did. But there was only a hoarse, faint flutter in his eardrums.

It was a moment when sanity might have gone. But there was one curious, mundane fact that saved him. He was holding something in his hands. He found that he could look at it, and it was a switch. A molded switch, mounted on a board, and he was holding one in each hand.

It was little to cling to, but it at least was real. If his hands could be holding something, then there must be some reality somewhere.

Tropile closed his eyes and managed to open them again. Yes, there was reality, too. He closed his eyes and light stopped. He opened them and light returned.

Then perhaps he was not dead, as he had thought.

Carefully, stumbling-his mind his only usable tool-he tried to make an estimate of his surroundings.

He could hardly believe what he found.

Item: he could scarcely move. Somehow he was bound by his feet and his head. How? He couldn't tell.

Item: he was bent over and he couldn't straighten. Why? Again he couldn't tell, but it was a fact. The great erecting muscles of his back answered his command, but his body would not move.

Item: his eyes saw, but only in a small area.

He couldn't move his head, either. Still, he could see a few things. The switch in his hand, his feet, a sort of display of lights on a strangely circular board.

The lights flickered and changed their pattern.

* * * * *

Without thinking, he moved a switch. Why? Because it was *right* to move that switch. When a certain light flared green, a certain switch had to be thrown. Why? Well, when a certain light flared green, a certain switch —

He abandoned that problem. Never mind why; what the devil was going *on*?

Glenn Tropile squinted about him like a mollusc peering out of its shell. There was another fact, the oddness of the seeing. What makes it look so queer, he asked himself.

He found an answer, but it required some time to take it in. He was seeing in a strange perspective. One looks out of two eyes. Close one eye and the world is flat. Open it again and there is a stereoscopic double; the saliencies of the picture leap forward, the background retreats.

So with the lights on the board-no, not exactly; but something *like* that, he thought. It was as though-he squinted and strained-well, as though he had never really *seen* before. As though for all his life he had had only one eye, and now he had strangely been given two.

His visual perception of the board was *total*. He could see all of it at once. It had no "front" or "back." It was in the round. The natural thinking of it was without orientation. He engulfed and comprehended it as a unit. It had no secrets of shadow or silhouette.

I think, Tropile mouthed slowly to himself, that I'm going crazy.

But that was no explanation, either. Mere insanity didn't account for what he saw.

Then, he asked himself, was he in a state that was *beyond* Nirvana? He remembered, with an odd flash of guilt, that he had been Meditating, watching the stages of boiling water. All right, perhaps he had been Translated. But what was this, then? Were the Meditators wrong in teaching that Nirvana was the end-and yet righter than the Wolves, who dismissed Meditation as a phenomenon wholly inside the skull and refused to discuss Translation at all?

That was a question for which he could find nothing approaching an answer. He turned away from it and looked at his hands.

He could see them, too, in the round, he noted. He could see every wrinkle and pore in all sixteen of them....

Sixteen hands!

* * * * *

That was the other moment when sanity might have gone. He closed his eyes. (Sixteen eyes! No wonder the total perception!) And, after a while, he opened them again.

The hands were there. All sixteen of them.

Cautiously, Tropile selected a finger that seemed familiar in his memory. After a moment's thought, he flexed it. It bent. He selected another. Another-on a different hand this time.

He could use any or all of the sixteen hands. They were all his, all sixteen of them.

I appear, thought Tropile crazily, to be a sort of eight-branched snowflake. Each of my branches is a human body.

He stirred, and added another datum: I appear also to be in a tank of fluid and yet I do not drown.

There were certain deductions to be made from that. Either someone-the Pyramids? —had done something to his lungs, or else the fluid was as good an oxygenating medium as air. Or both.

Suddenly a burst of data-lights twinkled on the board below him. Instantly and involuntarily, his sixteen hands began working the switches, transmitting complex directions in a lightninglike stream of on-off clicks.

Tropile relaxed and let it happen. He had no choice; the power that made it *right* to respond to the board made it impossible for his brain to concentrate while the response was going on. Perhaps, he thought drowsily, he would never have awakened at all if it had not been for the long period with no lights....

But he was awake. And his consciousness began to explore as the task ended.

He had had an opportunity to understand something of what was happening. He understood that he was now a part of something larger than himself, beyond doubt something which served and belonged to the Pyramids. His single brain not being large enough for the job, seven others had been hooked in with it.

But where were their personalities?

Gone, he supposed; presumably they had been Citizens. Sons of the Wolf did not Meditate and therefore were not Translated-except for himself, he corrected wryly, remembering the Meditation on Rainclouds that had led him to —

No, wait!

Not Rainclouds but Water!

* * * * *

Tropile caught hold of himself and forced his mind to retrace that thought. He *remembered* the Raincloud Meditation. It had been prompted by a particularly noble cumulus of the Ancient Ship type.

And this was odd. Tropile had never been deeply interested in Rainclouds, had never known even the secondary classifications of Raincloud types. And he *knew* that the Ancient Ship was of the fourth order of categories.

It was a false memory.

It was not his.

Therefore, logically, it was someone else's memory; and being available to his own mind, as the fourteen other hands and eyes were available, it must belong to another branch of the snowflake.

He turned his eyes down and tried to see which of the branches was his old body. He found it quickly, with growing excitement. There was the left great toe of his body. He had injured it in boyhood and there was no mistaking the way it was bent. Good! It was reassuring.

He tried to feel the one particular body that led to that familiar toe.

He succeeded, though not easily. After a time, he became more aware of *that* body—somewhat as a neurotic may become "stomach conscious" or "heart conscious." But this was no neurosis; it was an intentional exploration.

Since that worked, with some uneasiness he transferred his attention to another pair of feet and "thought" his way up from them.

It was embarrassing.

For the first time in his life, he knew what it felt like to have breasts. For the first time in his life, he knew what it was like to have one's internal organs quite differently shaped and arranged, buttressed and stressed by different muscles. The very faint background feel of man's internal arrangements, never questioned unless something goes wrong with them and they start to hurt, was not at all like the faint background feel that a woman has inside her.

And when he concentrated on that feel, it was no faint background to him. It was surprising and upsetting.

He withdrew his attention—hoping that he would be able to. Gratefully, he became conscious of his own body again. He was still *himself* if he chose to be.

Were the other seven still themselves?

He reached into his mind—all of it, all eight separate intelligences that were combined within him.

"Is anybody there?" he demanded.

No answer—or nothing he could recognize as an answer. He drove harder and there still was none. It was annoying. He resented it as bitterly, he remembered, as in the old days when he had first been learning the subtleties of Ruin Appreciation. There had been a Ruin Master, his name forgotten, who had been sometimes less than courteous, had driven hard—

Another false memory!

He withdrew and weighed it. Perhaps, he thought, that was a part of the answer. These people, these other seven, would not be driven. The attempt to call them back to consciousness would have to be delicate. When he drove hard, it was painful—he remembered the instant violent agony of his own awakening—and they reacted with anguish.

* * * * *

More gently, alert for vagrant "memories," he combed the depths of the eightfold mind within him, reaching into the sleeping portions, touching, handling, sifting and associating, sorting. This memory of an old knife wound from an Amok—that was not the Raincloud woman; it was a man, very aged. This faint recollection of a childhood fear of drowning—was that she? It was; it fitted with this other recollection, the long detour on the road south toward the sun, around a river.

The Raincloud woman was the first to round out in his mind, and the first he communicated with. He was not surprised to find that, early in her life, she had feared that she might be Wolf.

He reached out for her. It was almost magic—knowing the "secret name" of a person, so that then he was yours to command. But the "secret name" was more than that. It was the gestalt of the person. It was the sum of all data and experience, never available to another person—until now.

With her memories arranged at last in his own mind, he thought persuasively: "Citizeness Alla Narova, will you awaken and speak with me?"

No answer-only a vague, troubled stirring.

Gently he persisted: "I know you well, Alla Narova. You sometimes thought you might be a Daughter of the Wolf, but never really believed it because you knew you loved your husband-and thought Wolves did not love. You loved Rainclouds, too. It was when you stood at Beachy Head and saw a great cumulus that you went into Meditation —"

And on and on, many times, coaxingly. Even so, it was not easy; but at last he began to reach her. Slowly she began to surface. Thoughts faintly sounded in his mind, like echoes at first, his own thoughts bouncing back at him, a sort of mental nod of agreement: "Yes, that is so." Then-terror. With a shaking fear, a hysterical rush, Citizeness Alla Narova came violently up to full consciousness and to panic.

She was soundlessly screaming. The whole eight-branched figure quivered and twisted in its nutrient bath.

The terrible storm raged in Tropile's own mind as fully as in hers-but he had the advantage of knowing what it was. He helped her. He fought it for the two of them ... soothing, explaining, calming.

At last her branch of the snowflake-body retreated, sobbing for a spell. The storm was over.

He talked to her in his mind and she "listened." She was incredulous, but there was no choice for her; she *had* to believe.

Exhausted and passive, she asked finally: "What can we do? I wish I were dead!"

He told her: "You were never a coward before. Remember, Alla Narova, I *know* you as nobody has ever known another human being before. That's the way you will know me. As for what we can do-we must begin by waking the others, if we can."

"If not?"

"If not," Tropile replied grimly, "then we will think of something else."

She was of tough stuff, he thought admiringly. When she had rested and absorbed things, her spirit was almost that of a Wolf; she had very nearly been right about herself.

Together they explored their twinned members. They found through them exactly what task was theirs to do. They found how the electrostatic harvesting scythe of the Pyramids was controlled, by and through them. They found what limitations there were and what freedoms they owned. They reached into the other petals of the snowflake, reached past the linked Components into the whole complex of electrostatic field generators and propulsion machinery, reached even past that into —

Into the great single function of the Pyramids that lay beyond.

CHAPTER XI.

Haendl was on the ragged edge of breakdown, which was something new in his life.

It was full hot summer and the hidden colony of Wolves in Princeton should have been full of energy and life. The crops were growing on all the fields nearby; the drained storehouses were being replenished.

The aircraft that had been so painfully rebuilt and fitted for the assault on Mount Everest were standing by, ready to be manned and to take off.

And nothing, absolutely nothing, was going right.

It looked as though there would *be* no expedition to Everest. Four times now, Haendl had gathered his forces and been all ready. Four times, a key man of the expedition had-vanished.

Wolves didn't vanish!

And yet more than a score of them had. First Tropile-then Innison-then two dozen more, by ones and twos. No one was immune. Take Innison, for example. There was a man who was Wolf through and through. He was a doer, not a thinker; his skills were the skills of an artisan, a tinkerer, a jackleg mechanic. How could a man like that succumb to the pallid lure of Meditation?

But undeniably he had.

It had reached a point where Haendl himself was red-eyed and jumpy. He had set curious alarms for himself-had enlisted the help of others of the colony to avert the danger of Translation from himself.

When he went to bed at night, a lieutenant sat next to his bed, watchfully alert lest Haendl, in that moment of reverie before sleep, fell into Meditation and himself be Translated. There was no hour of the day when Haendl permitted himself to be alone; and his companions, or guards, were ordered to shake him awake, as violently as need be, at the first hint of an abstracted look in the eyes or a reflective cast of the features.

As time went on, Haendl's self-imposed regime of constant alertness began to cost him heavily in lost rest and sleep. And the consequences of that were-more and more occasions when the bodyguards shook him awake; less and less rest.

He was very close to breakdown indeed.

On a hot, wet morning a few days after his useless expedition to see Citizen Germyn in Wheeling, Haendl ate a tasteless breakfast and, reeling with fatigue, set out on a tour of inspection of Princeton. Warm rain dripped from low clouds, but that was merely one more annoyance to Haendl. He hardly noticed it.

There were upward of a thousand Wolves in the Community and there were signs of worry on the face of every one of them. Haendl was not the only man in Princeton who had begun laying traps for himself as a result of the unprecedented disappearances; he was not the only one who was short of sleep. When one member in forty disappears, the morale of the whole community receives a shattering blow.

To Haendl, it was clear, looking into the faces of his compatriots, that not only was it going to be nearly impossible to mount the planned assault on the Pyramid on Everest this year, it was going to be unbearably difficult merely to keep the community going.

The whole Wolf pack was on the verge of panic.

* * * * *

There was a confused shouting behind Haendl. Groggily he turned and looked; half a dozen Wolves were yelling and pointing at something in the wet, muggy air.

It was an Eye, hanging silent and featureless over the center of the street.

Haendl took a deep breath and mustered command of himself. "Frampton!" he ordered one of his lieutenants. "Get the helicopter with the instruments here. We'll take some more readings."

Frampton opened his mouth, then looked more closely at Haendl and, instead, began to talk on his pocket radio. Haendl knew what was in the man's mind-it was in his own, too.

What was the use of more readings? From the time of Tropile's Translation on, they had had a superfluity of instrument readings on the forces and auras that surrounded the Eyes-yes, and on Translations themselves, too. Before Tropile, there had never been an Eye seen in Princeton, much less an actual Translation. But things were different now. Everything was different. Eyes roamed restlessly around day and night.

Some of the men nearest the Eye were picking up rocks and throwing them at the bobbing vortex in the air. Haendl started to yell at them to stop, then changed his mind. The Eye didn't seem to be affected-as he watched, one of the men scored a direct hit with a cobblestone. The stone went right through the Eye, without sound or effect; why not let them work off some of their fears in direct action?

There was a fluttering of vanes and the copter with the instruments mounted on it came down in the middle of the street, between Haendl and the Eye.

It was all very rapid from then on.

The Eye swooped toward Haendl. He couldn't help it; he ducked. That was useless, but it was also unnecessary, for he saw in a second that it was only partly the motion of the Eye toward him that made it loom larger; it was also that the Eye itself was growing.

An Eye was perhaps the size of a football, as near as anyone could judge. This one got bigger, bigger. It was the size of a roc's egg, the size of a whale's blunt head. It stopped and hovered over the helicopter, while the man inside frantically pointed lenses and meters —

Thundercrash.

Not a man this time-Translation had gone beyond men. The whole helicopter vanished, man, instruments, spinning vanes and all.

Haendl picked himself up, sweating, shocked beyond sleepiness.

The young man named Frampton said fearfully: "Haendl, what do we do now?"

"Do?" Haendl stared at him absently. "Why, kill ourselves, I guess."

He nodded soberly, as though he had at last attained the solution of a difficult problem. Then he sighed.

"Well, one thing before that," he said. "I'm going to Wheeling. We Wolves are licked; maybe the Citizens can help us now."

* * * * *

Roget Germyn, of Wheeling, a Citizen, received the message in the chambers that served him as a place of business. He had a visitor waiting for him at home.

Germyn was still Citizen and he could not quickly break off the pleasant and interminable discussion he was having with a prospective client over a potential business arrangement. He apologized for the interruption caused by the message the conventional five times, listened while his guest explained once more the plan he had come to propose in full, then turned his cupped hands toward himself in the gesture of Denial of Adequacy. It was the closest he could come to saying no.

On the other side of the desk, the Citizen who had come to propose an investment scheme immediately changed the subject by inviting Germyn and his Citizeness to a Sirius Viewing, the invitation in the form of rhymed couplets. He had wanted to transact his business very much, but he couldn't *insist*.

Germyn got out of the invitation by a Conditional Acceptance in proper form, and the man left, delayed only slightly by the Four Urgings to Stay. Almost immediately, Germyn dismissed his clerk and closed his office for the day by tying a triple knot in a length of red cord across the open door.

When he got to his home, he found, as he had suspected, that the visitor was Haendl.

There was much doubt in Citizen Germyn's mind about Haendl. The man had nearly admitted to being Wolf, and how could a citizen overlook that? But in the excitement of Gala

Tropile's Translation, there had been no hue and cry. Germyn had permitted the man to leave. And now?

He reserved judgment. He found Haendl distastefully sipping tea in the living room and attempting to keep up a formal conversation with Citizeness Germyn. He rescued him, took him aside, closed a door—and waited.

He was astonished at the change in the man. Before, Haendl had been bouncy, aggressive, quick-moving—the very qualities least desired in a Citizen, the mark of the Son of the Wolf. Now he was none of these things, but he looked no more like a Citizen for all that; he was haggard, tense.

He said, with an absolute minimum of protocol: "Germyn, the last time I saw you, there was a Translation. Gala Tropile, remember?"

"I remember," Citizen Germyn said. Remember! It had hardly left his thoughts.

"And you told me there had been others. Are they still going on?"

* * * * *

Germyn said: "There have been others." He was trying to speak directly, to match this man Haendl's speed and forcefulness. It was hardly good manners, but it had occurred to Citizen Germyn that there were times when manners, after all, were not the most important thing in the world. "There were two in the past few days. One was a woman-Citizeness Baird; her husband's a teacher. She was Viewing Through Glass with four or five other women at the time. She just-disappeared. She was looking through a green prism at the time, if that helps."

"I don't know if it helps or not. Who was the other one?"

Germyn shrugged. "A man named Harmane. No one saw it. But they heard the thunderclap, or something like a thunderclap, and he was missing." He thought for a moment. "It is a little unusual, I suppose. Two in a week—"

Haendl said roughly: "Listen, Germyn. It isn't just two. In the past thirty days, within the area around here and in *one other place*, there have been at least fifty. In *two* places, do you understand? Here and in Princeton. The rest of the world-nothing much; a few Translations here and there. But just in these two communities, fifty. Does that make sense?"

Citizen Germyn thought. " —No."

"No. And I'll tell you something else. Three of the-well, victims have been children under the age of five. One was too young to walk. And the most recent Translation wasn't a person at all. It was a helicopter. Now figure that out, Germyn. What's the explanation for Translations?"

Germyn was gaping. "Why-you Meditate, you know. On Connectivity. The idea is that once you've grasped the Essential Connectivity of All Things, you become One with the Cosmic Whole. But I don't see how a baby or a machine —"

"No, of course you don't. Remember Glenn Tropile?"

"Naturally."

"He's the link," Haendl said grimly. "When he got Translated, we thought it was a big help, because he had the consideration to do it right under our eyes. We got enough readings to give us a clue as to what, physically speaking, Translation is all about. That was the first real clue and we thought he'd done us a favor. Now I'm not so sure."

He leaned forward. "Every person I know of who was Translated was someone Tropile knew. The three kids were in his class at the nursery school-we put him there for a while to keep him busy, when he first came to us. Two of the men he bunked with are gone; the mess boy who served him is gone; his wife is gone. Meditation? No, Germyn. I know most of those people. Not a damned one of them would have spent a moment Meditating on Connectivity to save his life. And what do you make of that?"

* * * * *

Swallowing hard, Germyn said: "I just remembered. That man Harmane —"

"What about him?"

"The one who was Translated last week. He also knew Tropile. He was the Keeper of the House of the Five Regulations when Tropile was there."

"You see? And I'll bet the woman knew Tropile, too." Haendl got up fretfully, pacing around. "Here's the thing, Germyn. I'm licked. You know what I am, don't you?"

Germyn said levelly: "I believe you to be Wolf."

"You believe right. That doesn't matter any more. You don't like Wolves. Well, I don't like you. But this thing is too big for me to care about that any more. Tropile has started something happening, and what the end of it is going to be, I can't tell. But I know this: We're not safe, either of us. Maybe you still think Translation is a fulfillment. I don't; it scares me. *But it's going to happen to me* —and to you. It's going to happen to everybody who ever had anything to do with Glenn Tropile, unless we can somehow stop it-and I don't know how. Will you help me?"

Germyn, trying not to tremble when all his buried fears screamed *Wolf!*, said honestly: "I'll have to sleep on it."

Haendl looked at him for a moment. Then he shrugged. Almost to himself, he said: "Maybe it doesn't matter. Maybe we can't do anything about it anyhow. All right. I'll come back in the morning, and if you've made up your mind to help, we'll start trying to make plans. And if you've made up your mind the other way-well, I guess I'll have to fight off a few Citizens. Not that I mind that."

Germyn stood up and bowed. He began the ritual Four Urgings.

"Spare me that," Haendl growled. "Meanwhile, Germyn, if I were you, I wouldn't make any long-range plans. You may not be here to carry them out."

Germyn asked thoughtfully: "And if you were *you?*"

"I'm not making any," Haendl said grimly.

* * * * *

Citizen Germyn, feeling utterly tainted with the scent of the Wolf in his home, tossed in his bed, sleepless. His eyes were wide open, staring at the dark ceiling. He could hear his wife's decorous breathing from the foot of the bed-soft and regular, it should have been lulling him to sleep.

It was not. Sleep was very far away.

Germyn was a brave enough man, as courage is measured among Citizens. That is to say, he had never been afraid, though it was true that there had been very little occasion. But he was afraid now. He didn't want to be Translated.

The Wolf, Haendl, had put his finger on it: *Perhaps you still think Translation is a fulfillment.* Translation-the reward of Meditation, the gift bestowed on only a handful of gloriously transfigured persons. That was one thing. But the sort of Translation that was now involved was nothing like that-not if it happened to children; not if it happened to Gala Tropile; not if it happened to a machine.

And Glenn Tropile was involved in it.

Germyn turned restlessly.

If people who knew Glenn Tropile were likely to be Translated, and people who Meditated on Connectivity were likely to be Translated, then people who knew Glenn Tropile and didn't want to be Translated had better not Meditate on Connectivity.

It was very difficult to *not* think of Connectivity.

Endlessly he calculated sums in arithmetic in his mind, recited the Five Regulations, composed Greeting Poems and Verses on Viewing. And endlessly he kept coming back to Tropile, to Translation, to Connectivity. He didn't *want* to be Translated. But still the thought had a certain lure. What was it like? Did it hurt?

Well, probably not, he speculated. It was very fast, according to Haendl's report-if you could believe what an admitted Son of the Wolf reported. But Germyn had to.

Well, if it was fast-at that kind of speed, he thought, perhaps you would die instantly. Maybe Tropile was dead. Was that possible? No, it didn't seem so; after all, there was the fact of the connection between Tropile and so many of the recently Translated. What was the connection there? Or, generalizing, what connections were involved in —

He rescued himself from the dread word and summoned up the first image that came to mind. It happened to be Tropile's wife-Gala Tropile, who had disappeared herself, in this very room.

Gala Tropile. He stuck close to the thought of her, a little pleased with himself. That was the trick of *not* thinking of Connectivity-to think so hard and fully of something else as to leave no room in the mind for the unwanted thought. He pictured every line of her face, every wave of her stringy hair....

It was very easy that way. He was pleased.

CHAPTER XII.

On Mount Everest, the sullen stream of off-and-on responses that was "mind" to the Pyramid had taken note of a new input signal.

It was not a critical mind. Its only curiosity was a restless urge to shove-and-haul, and there was no shove-and-haul about what to it was perhaps the analogue of a man's hunger pang. The input signal said: *Do thus.* It obeyed.

Call it craving for a new flavor. Where once it had patiently waited for the state that Citizens knew as Meditation on Connectivity, and the Pyramid itself perhaps knew as a stage of ripeness in the fruits of its wristwatch mine, now it wanted a different taste. Unripe? Overripe? At any rate, different.

Accordingly, the high-frequency wheep, wheep changed in tempo and in key, and the bouncing echoes changed and ...there was a ripe one to be plucked. (Its name was Innison.) And there another. (Gala Tropile.) And another, another-oh, many others —a babe from Tropile's nursery school and the Wheeling jailer and a woman Tropile once had coveted on the street.

Once the ruddy starch-to-sugar mark of ripeness had been what human beings called Meditation on Connectivity and the Pyramids knew as a convenient blankness. Now the sign was a sort of empathy with the Component named Tropile. It didn't matter to the Pyramid on Mount Everest. It swung its electrostatic scythe and the-call them Tropiletropes-were harvested.

It did not occur to the Pyramid on Mount Everest that a Component might be directing its actions. How could it?

Perhaps the Pyramid on Mount Everest wondered, if it knew how to wonder, when it noticed that different criteria were involved in selecting components these days. If it knew how to "notice." Surely even a Pyramid might wonder when, without warning or explanation, its orders were changed-not merely to harvest a different sort of Component, but to drag along with the flesh-and-blood needful parts a clanking assortment of machinery and metal, as began to happen. Machines? Why would the Pyramids need to Translate machines?

But why, on the other hand, would a Pyramid bother to question a directive, even if it were able to?

In any case, it didn't. It swung its scythe and gathered in what it was caused to gather in.

Men sometimes eat green fruit and come to regret it. Was it the same with Pyramids?

* * * * *

And Citizen Germyn fell into the unsuspected trap. Avoiding Connectivity, he thought of Glenn Tropile-and the unfelt h-f pulses found him out.

He didn't see the Eye that formed above him. He didn't feel the gathering of forces that formed his trap. He didn't know that he was seized, charged, catapulted through space, caught, halted and drained. It happened too fast.

One moment he was in his bed; the next moment he was-elsewhere. There wasn't anything in between.

It had happened to hundreds of thousands of Components before him, but, for Citizen Germyn, what happened was in some ways different. He was not embalmed in nutrient fluid, formed and programmed to take his part in the Pyramid-structure, for he had not been selected by the Pyramid but by that single wild Component, Tropile. He arrived conscious, awake and able to move.

He stood up in a red-lit chamber. Vast thundering crashes of metal buffeted his ears. Heat sprang little founts of perspiration on his skin.

It was too much, too much to take in at once. Oily-skinned madmen, naked, were capering and shouting at him. It took him a moment to realize that they were not devils; this was not Hell; he was not dead.

"This way!" they were bawling at him. "Come on, hurry it up!"

He reeled, following their directions, across an unpleasantly warm floor, staggering and falling-the binary planet was a quarter denser than Earth-until he got his balance.

The capering madmen led him through a door-or sphincter or trap; it was not like anything he had ever seen. But it was a portal of a sort, and on the other side of it was something closer to sanity. It was another room, and though the light was still red, it was a paler, calmer red and the thundering ironmongery was a wall away. The madmen were naked, yes, but they were not mad. The oil on their skins was only the sheen of sweat.

"Where-where am I?" he gasped.

Two voices, perhaps three or four, were all talking at once. He could make no sense of it. Citizen Germyn looked about him. He was in a sort of chamber that formed a part of a machine that existed for the unknown purposes of the Pyramids on the binary planet. And he was alive-and not even alone.

He had crossed more than a million miles of space without feeling a thing. But when what the naked men were saying began to penetrate, the walls lurched around him.

It was true; he had been Translated.

He looked dazedly down at his own bare body, and around at the room, and then he realized they were still talking: " —when you get your bearings. Feel all right now? Come on, Citizen, snap out of it!"

Germyn blinked.

Another voice said peevishly: "Tropile's got to find some other place to bring them in. That foundry isn't meant for human beings. Look at the shape this one is in! Some time somebody's going to come in and we won't spot him in time and-pfut!"

The first voice said: "Can't be helped. Hey! Are you all right?"

Citizen Germyn looked at the naked man in front of him and took a deep breath of hot, sour air. "Of course I'm all right," he said.

The naked man was Haendl.

* * * * *

The Tropile-petal "said" to the Alla Narova-petal: "Got another one! It's Citizen Germyn!" The petal fluttered feebly in soundless laughter.

The Alla Narova-petal "said": "Glenn, come back! The whole propulsion-pneuma just went out of circuit!"

Tropile pulled his attention away from his human acquisitions in the chamber off the foundry and allowed himself to fuse with the woman-personality. Together they reached out and explored along the pathways they had laboriously traced. The propulsion-pneuma was the complex of navigation-computers, drive generators, course-vectoring units that their own unit had been originally part of-until Glenn Tropile, by waking its Components, had managed to divert it for purposes of his own. The two of them reached out into it —

Dead end.

It was out of circuit, as Alla Narova had said. One whole limb of their body-their new, jointly tenanted body, that spanned a whole planet and reached across space to Earth-had been lopped off. Quick, quick, they separated, traced separate paths. They came together again: Still dead end.

The dyad that was Tropile and the woman reached out to touch the others in the snowflake and communicated-not in words, not in anything as slow and as opaque as words: *The Pyramids have lopped off another circuit.* The compound personality of the snowflake considered its course of action, reached its decision, acted. Quick, quick, three of the other members of the snowflake darted out of the collective unit and went about isolating and tracing the exact area that had been affected.

Tropile: "We expected this. They couldn't help noticing sooner or later that something was going wrong."

Alla Narova: "But, Glenn, suppose they cut *us* out of circuit? We're stuck here. We can't move. We can't get out of the tanks. If they know that we are the source of their trouble —"

Tropile: "Let them know! That's what we've got the others here for!" He was cocky now, self-assured, fighting. For the first time in his life, he was free to fight-to let his Wolf blood strive to the utmost-and he knew what he was fighting for. This wasn't a matter of Haendl's pitiful tanks and carbines against the invulnerable Pyramids; this was the invulnerability of the whole Pyramid system turned against the Pyramids!

It was a warning, the fact that the Pyramids had become alert to danger, had begun cutting sections of their planetary communications system out of the main circuit. But as a warning, it didn't frighten Tropile; it only spurred him to action.

Quick, quick, he and the woman-personality dissolved, sped away. Figuratively they sought out the most restive Components they could find, shook them by the shoulder, tried to wake them. Actually-well, what is "actually?" The physical fact was surely that they didn't move at all, for they were bound to their tank and to the surgical joinings, each to each, at their temples. No crawling child in a playpen was more helplessly confined than Tropile and Alla Narova and the others.

And yet no human being had ever been more free.

* * * * *

Regard that imbecile servant of Everyman, the thermostat.

He runs the furnace in Everyman's house, he measures the doneness of Everyman's breakfast toast, he valves the cooling fluid through the radiator of Everyman's car. If Everyman's house stays too hot or too cold, the man swears at the lackwit switch and maybe buys a new one to plug in. But he never, never thinks that his thermostat might be plotting against him.

Thermostat : Man = Man : Pyramid. Only that and nothing more. It was not in the nature of a Pyramid to think that its Components, once installed, could reprogram themselves. No Component ever had. (But before Glenn Tropile, no Component had been Wolf.)

When Tropile found himself, he found others. They were men and women, real persons with gonads and dreams. They had been caught at the moment of blankness-yes; and frozen into that shape, true. But they were palimpsest personalities on which the Pyramids had programmed their duties. Underneath the Pyramids' cabalistic scrawl, the men and women still remained. They had only to be reached.

Tropile and Alla Narova reached them-one at a time, then by scores. The Pyramids made that possible. The network of communication that they had created for their own purposes encompassed every cell of the race and all its works. Tropile reached out from his floating snowflake and went where he wished-anywhere within the binary planet; to the brooding Pyramid on Earth; through the Eyes, wherever he chose on Earth's surface.

Physically, he was scarcely able to move a muscle. But, oh, the soaring range of his mind and vision!

* * * * *

Citizen Germyn was past shock, but just the same it was uncomfortable to be in a room with several dozen other persons, all of them naked. Uncomfortable. Once it would have been brain-shattering. For a Citizen to see his own Citizeness unclothed was gross lechery. To be part of a mixed and bare-skinned group was unthinkable. Or had been. Now it only made him uneasy.

He said numbly to Haendl: "Citizen, I pray you tell me what sort of place this is."

"Later," said Haendl gruffly, and led him out of the way. "Stay put," he advised. "We're busy."

And that was true. Something was going on, but Citizen Germyn couldn't make out exactly what it was. The naked people were worrying out a distribution of some sort of supplies. There were tools and there were also what looked to Citizen Germyn's unsophisticated eyes very much like guns. Guns? It was foolishness to think they were guns, Citizen Germyn told himself strongly. *Nobody* had guns. He touched the floor with an exploratory hand. It was warm and it shook with a nameless distant vibration. He shuddered.

Haendl came back; yes, they were guns. Haendl was carrying one.

"Ours!" he crowed. "That Tropile must've looted our armory at Princeton. By the looks of what's here, I doubt if he left a single round of ammunition. What the hell, they're more use here!"

"But what are we going to do with *guns?*"

Haendl looked at him with savage amusement. "Shoot."

Citizen Germyn said: "Please, Citizen. Tell me what this is all about."

Haendl sat down next to him on the warm, quivering floor and began fitting cartridges into a clip.

"We're fighting," he explained gleefully. "Tropile did it all. You've been shanghaied and so have all the rest of us. Tropile's alive! He's part of the Pyramid communications network-don't ask me how. But he's there and he has been hauling men and weapons and God knows what all up from Earth-you're on the binary planet now, you know-and we're going to bust things up so the Pyramids will *never* be able to put them back together again. Understand? Well, it doesn't matter if you don't. All you have to understand is that when I tell you to shoot this gun, you shoot."

Numbly, Citizen Germyn took the unfamiliar stock and barrel into his hands. Muscles he had forgotten he owned straightened the limp curve of his back, squared his shoulders and thrust out his chest.

It had been many generations since any of Citizen Germyn's people had known the feeling of being an Armed Man.

A naked woman with wild hair and a full, soft figure came toward them, jiggling in a way that agonized Citizen Germyn. He dropped his eyes to his gun and kept them there.

She cried: "Orders from Tropile! We've got to form a party and blow something up."

Haendl demanded: "Such as what?"

"I don't know what. I only know where. We've got a guide. And Tropile particularly asked for you, Haendl. He said you'd enjoy it."

And enjoy it Haendl did-anticipation was all over his face.

* * * * *

They formed a party of a dozen. They armed themselves with the guns Tropile had levitated from the bulging warehouse at Princeton. They supplied themselves with gray metal cans of

157

something that Haendl said were explosives, and with fuses and detonators to match, and they set off-with their guide.

A guide! It was a shambling, fearsome monster!

When Citizen Germyn saw it, he had to fight an almost irresistible temptation to be ill. Even the bare skins about him no longer mattered; this new horror canceled them out.

"What-What —" he strangled, pointing.

Haendl laughed raucously. "That's Joey."

"What's Joey?"

"He works for us," said Haendl, grinning.

Joey was neither human nor beast; it was not Pyramid; it was nothing Citizen Germyn had ever seen or imagined before. It crouched on many-jointed limbs, and even so was twice the height of a man. Its ropy arms and legs were covered with fine chitinous spines, laid on as close as hairs in a pelt, and sharp as thorns. There was a layer of chitin around its reddish eyes. What was more horrible than all, it spoke.

It said squeakily: "You all ready? Come on, snap it up! The Pyramids have got something big building up and we've got to squash it."

Citizen Germyn whispered feverishly to Haendl: "That voice! It sounds odd, yes-but isn't it Tropile's voice?"

"Sure it is! That's what old Joey is good for," said Haendl. "Tropile says he's telepathic, whatever that is. Makes it handy for us."

And it did. Telepathy was the alien's very special use to Glenn Tropile, for what Joey was in fact was another Component, from a previous wristwatch mine. Joey's planet had once circled a star never visible from Earth; his home air was thin and his home sunlight was weak, and in consequence his race had developed a species of telepathy for communicating at long range. This was handy for the Pyramids, because it simplified the wiring. And it was equally handy for Glenn Tropile, once he managed to wake the creature-with its permission, he could use its body as a sort of walkie-talkie in directing the tactics of his shanghaied army.

That permission was very readily given. Joey remembered what the Pyramids had done to its own planet.

"Come on!" ordered Joey in Tropile's filtered voice, and they hastened through a straight and achingly cramped tunnel in single file, toward what Tropile had said was their target.

They had nearly reached it when, abruptly, there was a thundering of explosions ahead.

The party stopped, looked at each other, and got ready to move on more slowly.

At last it had started. The Pyramids were beginning to fight back.

CHAPTER XIII.

Citizeness Roget Germyn, widow, woke from sleep like a well-mannered cat on the narrow lower third of the bed that her training had taught her to occupy, though it had been some days since her husband's Translation had emptied the Citizen's two-thirds permanently.

Someone had tapped gently on her door.

"I am awake," she called, in a voice just sufficient to carry.

A quiet voice said: "Citizeness, there is exceptional opportunity to Appreciate this morning. Come see, if you will. And I ask forgiveness for waking you."

She recognized the voice; it was the wife of one of her neighbors. The Citizeness made the appropriate reply, combining forgiveness and gratitude.

She dressed rapidly, but with appropriate pauses for reflection and calm, and stepped out into the street.

It was not yet daylight. Overhead, great sheets of soundless lightnings flared.

Inside Citizeness Germyn long-unfelt emotions stirred. There was something that was very like terror, and something that was akin to love. This was a generation that had never seen the aurora, for the ricocheting electron beams that cause it could not span the increasing distance between the orphaned Earth and its primary, Old Sol, and the small rekindled suns the Pyramids made were far too puny.

Under the sleeting aurora, small knots of Citizens stood about the streets, their faces turned up to the sky and illuminated by the distant light. It was truly an exceptional opportunity to Appreciate and they were all making the most of it.

Conscientiously, Citizeness Germyn sought out another viewer with whom to exchange comments on the spectacle above. "It is more bright than meteors," she said judiciously, "and lovelier than the freshly kindled Sun."

"Sure," said the woman. Citizeness Germyn, jolted, looked more closely. It was the Tropile woman-Gala? Was that her name? And what sort of name was *that*? But it fitted her well; she was the one who had been wife to Wolf and, more likely than not, part Wolf herself.

Still, the case was not proved. Citizeness Germyn said honestly: "I have never seen a sight to compare with this in all my life."

Gala Tropile said indifferently: "Yeah. Funny things are happening all the time these days, have you noticed? Ever since Glenn turned out to be —" She stopped.

Citizeness Germyn rapidly diagnosed her embarrassment and acted to cover it up. "That is so. I have seen Eyes a hundred times and yet has there been a Translation with the Eyes? No. But there have been Translations. It is queer."

"I suppose so," Gala Tropile said, looking upward at the display. She sighed.

Over their heads, a formed Eye was drifting slowly about, but neither of the women noticed it. The shifting lights in the sky obscured it.

"I wonder what causes that stuff," Gala Tropile said idly.

Citizeness Germyn made no attempt to answer. It was not the sort of question that would normally have occurred to her and therefore not a sort to which she could reply.

Moreover, it was not the question closest to Gala Tropile's heart at that moment-nor, for that matter, the question closest to Citizeness Germyn's. The question that underlay the thoughts of both was: *I wonder what happened to my husband.*

It was strange, but true, that the answers to all their questions were very nearly the same.

* * * * *

The Alla-Narova mind said sharply: "Glenn, come back!"

Tropile withdrew from scanning the distant dark street. He laughed soundlessly. "I was watching my wife. God, we're giving them fits down there! The Pyramids must be churning things up, too-the sky is full of auroral displays. Looks like there's plenty of h-f bouncing around the atmosphere."

"Pay attention!" the Alla-Narova mind commanded.

"All right." Obediently, Tropile returned to the war he was waging.

It was a strange conflict, strangely fought. Tropile's mind searched the abysses and tunnels of the Pyramid planet, and what he sensed or saw was immediately communicated to all of the awakened Components who were his allies.

It was a godlike position. Was he sane? There was no knowing. Sanity no longer meant anything to Tropile. He was beyond such human affairs as lunacy or its reverse. An insane man is one who is out of joint with his environment. Tropile was himself his environment. His mind encompassed two planets and the space between. He saw with a thousand eyes. He worked with a thousand hands.

And he struck mighty blows.

The weakness of a network that reaches everywhere is that it is everywhere vulnerable. If a teletype repeater in Omaha garbles a single digit, printing units in Atlanta and Bangor will type out errors. Tropile, by striking at the Pyramids' net at a thousand points, garbled their communications and made them nearly useless. More, he took the Pyramid network for his own. The Tropile-pulse sped through the neurone guides of the Pyramid net, and what it encountered it mastered, and what it mastered it changed.

The Pyramids discovered that they had been attacked.

Frantically (if they felt frenzy), the Pyramids replaced Components; the Tropile-pulse woke the new ones. Unbelievingly (did they know how to "believe"?), the Pyramids isolated contaminated circuits; the Tropile-pulse bypassed them.

Desperately (or joyously or uffishly-one term fits exactly as well as another), the Pyramids returned to shove-and-haul, and there was much destruction, and some Components died.

But by then, the Components had reprogrammed themselves.

* * * * *

The first job had been the matter of finding hands for the Tropile-brain to work with. Bring hands in, then! Tropile commanded the Pyramids' network and obediently it was done. The Translation mechanism, the electrostatic scythe that had harvested so many crops from the wristwatch mines, suffered a change and went to work not for the pickers but for the fruit.

The essential change in the operation of that particular pneuma had been simple; first, to "harvest" or "Translate" the men and women Tropile wanted as fighters instead of the meditative Citizen kind. Second, to divert the new arrivals to where they would not go straight to deepfreeze. It happened that the only alternate space Tropile could find was a sort of foundry that was nearly Hell, but that was only a detail. The important thing was that new helpers were arriving, with minds of their own and the capacity to move and act.

Then Tropile needed to communicate with them. He found the alien, ropy-limbed Component whose name vaguely approached "Joey." Joey's limited sense of telepathy was needed and so, with enormous difficulty, Tropile and Alla Narova, combined, managed to reach and wake it.

And so he had an army, captured humans for troops, an awakened Joey for liaison.

Tropile was lord of two worlds. Not only the Pyramids were under his thumb, but his own fellow humans whom he had drafted into his service. They ate when a captured circuit he controlled fed synthetic mush into troughs for them. They breathed because a captured circuit he directed created air. They would return to Earth when-and only when —a captured circuit he operated sent them home.

Sane?

By what standards?

And what difference did it make?

CHAPTER XIV.

With a series of grinding shocks, like an enormous earthquake-fault relieving a strain, the Pyramids began to fight back.

"Tropile!" the Alla-Narova mind called urgently.

Tropile flashed to the trouble spot. Through eyes that were not his own, Tropile scanned the honeycombed world of the Pyramids. There was an area where huge and ancient vehicles lay covered with the slow dust of centuries, and the vehicles were beginning to move.

Caterpillar-treaded hauling machines were loading themselves with what Tropile judged were quickly synthesized explosives. Almost forgotten wheeled vehicles were creeping mindlessly out of nearly abandoned storage sections and lumbering painfully along the tunnels of the planet.

"Coming toward us," Tropile diagnosed dispassionately.

Alla Narova queried: "They mean to fight?"

"Of course. You see if you can penetrate the circuit that controls them. I —" already he was flashing away —"I'll get to the boys through Joey."

It was queer, looking through the eyes of the alien they called Joey; colors were all wrong, perspective was flat. But he could see, though cloudily. He saw Haendl joyously fitting a bayonet —*a bayonet!* —to a rifle; he saw Citizen Germyn, naked but square-shouldered, puffing valiantly along in the rear.

Tropile said through the strange vocal cords that belonged to the alien: "You'll have to hurry." (Strange to speak in words again!) "The Pyramids are heading toward the chambers where the Components are kept. I think they mean to kill us."

He flashed away, located the area, flashed back. "You'll have to go without me —I mean without Joey-me. The only way I see to get there is through a narrow little ventilation tunnel —I guess ventilation is what it was for."

Quickly (but against the familiar race of thought, it seemed agonizingly slow) he laid out the route for them and left; it was up to them. Watching from a dozen viewpoints at once, he saw the slow creep of the Pyramids' machines and the slower intersecting march of his little army. He studied the alternate cross routes and contrived to block some of them by interfering with the control-circuits of the emergency doors and portals.

But there were some circuits he could not control. The Pyramids had withdrawn whole sections of their net and areas of the planet were now hidden from him entirely. Sections of the vast maintenance-propulsion-manufacturing complex were no longer subject to his interference or control.

* * * * *

It would be, Tropile thought dispassionately, a rather close thing. The chances were perhaps six out of ten that his hastily assembled task force would be able to intercept the convoy of automatic machines before it could reach the racks of nutrient tanks.

And if they were not in time?

Tropile almost laughed out loud, if that had been possible. Why, then, his body would be destroyed! How trivial a thing to worry about! He began to forget he owned a body; surely it was someone else's bone and tissue that lay floating in the eight-branched snowflake. He knew that this was not so. He knew that if his body were killed, he would die. And yet there was no sense of fear, no personal involvement. It was an interesting problem in scheduling and nothing more.

Would the human fighters get there in time?

Perhaps the automatic machines had senses, for as the first of the humans burst into the tunnel they were using, a few hundred yards ahead of the lead load-carrier, the machines shuddered to a stop. Pause for a second; then, laboriously, they began to back toward the nearest of the side passages that Tropile had been unable to block. He scanned it hurriedly. Good, good!

The circuits surrounding the passage proper were out of his reach, but it led to another passage, an abandoned pipeline of sorts, it seemed to be. And *that* he could reach....

Patiently (how slowly the machines crept along!) he waited until one of the Pyramids' machines bearing explosives passed through an enormous valve in the line-and then the valve was thrown.

The explosion triggered every vehicle in the line. The damage was complete.

Scratch one threat from the Pyramids—
And almost at once, there was another urgent call from Alia Narova: "Tropile, quickly!"

* * * * *

The Pyramids were the mightiest race of warriors the Universe had ever known. They were invulnerable and unconquerable, except from within. Like Alexander the Great, they had met every enemy and whipped them all. And, like dying Alexander, they writhed and raged against the tiny, unseen bacillus within themselves.

Blindly, almost suicidally, the Pyramids returned to their ancient principle of shove-and-haul.

The geography of the binary planet was like a hive of bees, nearly featureless on the surface, but internally a congeries of tunnels, chambers, warrens, rooms, tubes and amphitheaters. Machinery and metal Components were everywhere thick under the planet's crust. The more delicate and more useful Components of flesh and blood were, to a degree, concentrated in a few areas....

And one of those areas had disappeared.

Tropile, battering futilely with his mind at the periphery of the vanished area, cried sharply to Alla Narova and the others: "It looks as though they've broken a piece right out of the planet! Everything stops here-there's a physical gap which I can't cross. Hurry, one of you-what was this section for?"

"Propulsion."

"I see." Tropile hesitated, confused for the first time since his awakening. "Wait."

He retreated to the snowflake and communed with the other eight-branched members, now become something that resembled his general staff. He told them-most of them already knew, but the telling took so little time that it was simpler to go through it from beginning to end:

"The Pyramids attempted to cut the propulsion-pneuma out of circuit some seconds or days ago and were unsuccessful; we awakened additional Components and were able to maintain contact with it. They have now apparently cut it loose from the planet itself. I do not think it is far, but there is a physical space between."

"The importance of the propulsion-pneuma is this: It controls the master generators of electrostatic force, which are used both to move this planet and ours, and to perform the act of Translation. If the Pyramids control it, they may be able to take us out of circuit, perhaps back to Earth, perhaps throwing us into space, where we will die. The question for decision: How can we counteract this move?"

* * * * *

A rush of voices all spoke at once; it was no trick for Tropile and the others to sort them out and follow the arguments of each, but it cannot be reproduced.

At last, one said: "There is a way. I will do it."

It was Alla Narova.

"What is the way?" Tropile demanded, curiously alarmed.

"I shall go with them, trace the areas the Pyramids are attempting to isolate, place my entire self—" by this she meant her "concentration," her "psyche," that part of all of them which flashed along the neurone guides unhampered by flesh or distance —"in the most likely point they will next cut loose. And then I shall cause the propulsion units on the severed sections to force them back into circuit."

Tropile objected: "But you don't know what will happen! We have never been cut off from our physical bodies, Alla Narova. It may be death. It may not be possible at all. You don't know!"

Alla Narova thought a smile and a farewell. She said: "No, I do not." And then, "Good-by, Tropile."

She had gone.

Furiously, Tropile hurled himself after her, but she was quick as he, too quick to catch; she was gone. *Foolishness, foolishness!* he shouted silently. How could she do an insane, chancy thing like this?

And yet what else was there to do? They were all ignorant babes, temporarily successful because there had been no defense against them, for who expects babes to rise up in rebellion? They didn't *know*. For all they could guess or imagine, the Pyramids had an effective counter for any move they might make. Temporary success meant nothing. It was the final decision that counted, when either the Pyramids were vanquished or the men, and what steps were needed to make that decision favor the men were anyone's guess-Alla Narova's was as good as his.

Tropile could only watch and wait.

Through a great many viewpoints and observers, he was able to see roughly what happened.

* * * * *

There was a section of the planet next the severed chunk where the mind and senses of Alla Narova lay coiled for a moment-and were gone. For what it had accomplished, her purpose succeeded. She had been taken. She was out of circuit.

The overwhelming consciousness of loss that flooded through Glenn Tropile was something outside of all his experience.

Next to him in the snowflake, the body which he had learned to think of as the body of Alla Narova twisted sharply as though waking from a dream-and lay flaccid, floating in the fluid.

"Alla Narova! *Alla Narova!*"

There was no answer.

163

A voice came piercingly: "Tropile! Here now, quickly!"

Good-by, Alla Narova! He flashed away to see what the other voice had found. Great mindless boulders were chipping away from the crust of the binary planet and whirling like midges in the void around it.

"What is it?" cried one of the others.

Tropile had no answer. It was the Pyramids, clearly. Were they attempting to demolish their own planet? Were they digging away at the crust to uncover the maggot's-nest of awakened Components beneath?

"The air!" cried Tropile sharply, and knew it was true. What the Pyramids were up to was a simple delousing operation. If you could destroy their own machinery for maintaining air and pressure and temperature, they would destroy all living things within-including Haendl and Citizen Germyn and thus, in the final analysis, including the bodies of Tropile and his awakened fellows. For without the mobile troops to defend their helpless cocoons against the machines of the Pyramids, the limp bodies could be destroyed as easily as a larva under a farmer's heel.

So Alla Narova had failed.

Alone against the Pyramids, she had been unable to bring the recaptured sections back into the circuit that Tropile's Components now dominated. It was the end of hope; but it was not the fear of defeat and damnation for the Earth that paralyzed Tropile. It was Alla Narova, gone from him forever.

The Pyramids were too strong.

And yet, he thought, quickening, they had been too strong before and still a weak spot had been found!

"Think," he ordered himself desperately.

And then again: "Think!" Components stirred restlessly around him, questioning. "Think!" he cried mightily. "All of you, think! Think of your lives and hopes!

"Think!

"Hope!

"Worry!

"Dream!"

The Components were reaching toward him now, wonderingly. He commanded them violently: "Do it-concentrate, wish, think! Let your minds run free and think of Earth, pleasant grass and warm sun! Think of loving and sweat and heartbreak! Think of death and birth! *Think*, for the love of heaven, *think*!"

And the answer was not in sound, but it was deafening.

* * * * *

In the cut-off sections, Alla Narova's soaring mind lay trapped. It had not been enough; she could not force her will against the dull inflexibility of the Pyramids....

Until that inflexible will began to waver.

There was a leakage of thought.

It maddened and baffled the Pyramids. The whole neuronic network was resounding to a babble of thoughts and emotions that, to a Pyramid, were utterly demented! The rousing Component minds throbbed with urge and emotion that were new to Pyramid experience. What could a Pyramid make of a human's sex drive? Or of the ropy-armed aliens' passionate deification of the Egg? What of hunger and thirst and the blazing Wolf-need for odds and advantage that streamed out of such as Tropile?

They wavered, unsure. Their reactions were slow and very confused.

For Alla Narova succeeded in her purpose. She was able to reach out across the space and barrier to Tropile and the propulsion-pneuma was back in circuit. The section that controlled the master generators of the electronic scythe lay under his hands.

"Now!" he cried, and all of the Components reached out to grasp and move.

"Now!" And the central control was theirs; the full flood of power from the generators was at their command.

"Now! Now! Now!" And they reached out, with a fat pencil of electrostatic force and caught the sluggish, brooding Pyramid on Mount Everest.

It had squatted there without motion for more than two centuries. Now it quivered and seemed to draw back, but the probing pencil caught it, and whirled it, and hurled it up and out of Earth, into the tiny artificial sun.

It struck with a flare of blue-white light.

"One gone!" gloated Tropile. "Alla Narova, are you there?"

"Still here," she called from a great distance. "Again?"

"Again!"

They reached for the Pyramids and found them, wherever they were. Some lay close to the surface of the binary planet, and some were hundreds of miles within, and a few, more desperate than the others or merely assigned to the task, they discovered at the very portal of the single spaceship of the Pyramids.

But wherever they were and whatever they chose to do, each one of them was found and seized. They came wriggling and shaking, like trout on an angler's line. They came bursting through layer on layer of impenetrable metal that, nevertheless, they penetrated. They came by the dozens and scores, and at last by the thousands; but they came.

There were more and more flares of blue-white light on the tiny sun-so many that Tropile found himself scouring the planet in a desperate search for one surviving Pyramid-not to destroy as an enemy, but to keep for a specimen.

But he searched in vain.

The Pyramids were destroyed, gone. There was not one left. The Earth lay open and free under its tiny sun for the first time in centuries.

It had been a strange war, but a short one.

And it was over.

CHAPTER XV.

Tropile swam up out of hammering blackness into daylight and pain.

It *hurt*. He was being born again-coming back to life-and it had all the agonies of parturition, except that they were visited upon the creature being born, himself. There were crushing blows at his temples that pounded and pained like no other ache he had ever felt. He moaned raspingly.

Someone moved blurrily over his shut eyes. He felt something sting sharply at the base of his brain. Then it tingled, warming his scalp, comforting it, numbing it. Pain went slowly away.

He opened his eyes.

Four masked torturers were leaning over him. He stared, not understanding; but the eyes were not torturers' eyes, and in a moment the masks came off. Surgical masks-and the faces beneath the masks were human faces.

Surgeons and nurses.

He blinked at them and said groggily: "Where am we?" And then he remembered.

He was back on Earth; he was merely human again.

Someone came bustling into the room and he knew without looking that it was Haendl.

"We beat them, Tropile!" Haendl cried. "No, cancel that. *You* beat them. We've destroyed every Pyramid there was, and a nice hot fire they're making up there on the sun, eh? Beautiful work, Tropile. Beautiful! You're a credit to the name of Wolf!"

The surgeons stirred uneasily, but apparently, Tropile thought, there had been changes, for they did no more than that.

Tropile touched his temples fretfully and his fingers rested on gauze bandages. It was true: he was out of circuit. The long reach of his awareness was cut short at his skull; there was no more of the infinite sweep and grasp he had known as part of the snowflake in the nutrient fluid.

"Too bad," he whispered hopelessly.

"What?" Haendl frowned. The nurse next to him whispered something and he nodded. "Oh, I see. You're still a little groggy, right? Well, that's not hard to understand-they tell me it was a tricky job of surgery, separating you from that gunk the Pyramids had wired into your head."

"Yes," said Tropile, and closed his ears, though Haendl went on talking. After a while, Tropile pushed himself up and swung his legs over the side of the operating table. He was naked. Once that would have bothered him enormously, but now it didn't seem to matter.

"Find me some clothes, will you?" he asked. "I'm back. I might as well start getting used to it."

* * * * *

Glenn Tropile found that he was a returning hero, attracting a curious sort of hero-worship wherever he went. It was not, he thought after careful analysis, *exactly* what he might have expected. For instance, a man who went out and killed a dragon in the old days was received with great gratitude and rejoicing, and if there was a prince's daughter around, he married her. Fair enough, after all. And Tropile had slain a foe more potent than any number of dragons.

But he tested the attention he received and found no gratitude in it. It was odd.

What it was like most of all, he thought, was the sort of attention a reigning baseball champion might get-in a country where cricket was the national game. He had done something which, everybody agreed, was an astonishing feat, but about which nobody seemed to care. Indeed, there was an area of accusation in some of the attention he got.

Item: nearly ninety thousand erstwhile Components had now been brought back to ambient life, most of them with their families long dead, all of them a certain drain on the limited resources of the planet. And what was Glenn Tropile going to do about it?

Item: the old distinctions between Citizen and Wolf no longer made much sense now that so many Componentized Citizens had fought shoulder to shoulder with Componentized Sons of the Wolf. But didn't Glenn Tropile think he had gone a little too far *there*?

And item-looking pretty far ahead, of course, but still-well, just what *was* Glenn Tropile going to do about providing a new sun for Earth, when the old one wore out and there would be no Pyramids to tend the fire?

He sought refuge with someone who would understand him. That, he was pleased to realize, was easy. He had come to know several persons extremely well. Loneliness, the tortured loneliness of his youth, was permanently behind him, *definitely*.

For example, he could seek out Haendl, who would understand everything very well.

Haendl said: "It is a bit of a letdown, I suppose. Well, hell with it; that's life." He laughed grimly. "Now that we've got rid of the Pyramids, there's plenty of other work to be done. Man, we can breathe now! We can plan ahead! This planet has maundered along in its stupid, rutted, bogged-down course too many years already, eh? It's time we took over! And we'll be doing it, I promise you. You know, Tropile —" he sniggered —"I only regret one thing."

"What's that?" Tropile asked cautiously.

"All those weapons, out of reach! Oh, I'm not *blaming* you. But you can see what a lot of trouble it's going to be now, stocking up all over again-and there isn't much we can do about bringing order to this tired old world, is there, until we've got the guns to do it with again?"

Tropile left him much sooner than he had planned.

* * * * *

Citizen Germyn, then? The man had fought well, if nothing else. Tropile went to find him and, for a moment at least, it was very good. Germyn said: "I've been doing a lot of thinking, Tropile. I'm glad you're here." He sent his wife for refreshments, and decorously she brought them in, waited for exactly one minute, and then absented herself.

Tropile burst into speech as soon as she left. "I'm beginning to realize what has happened to the human race, Germyn. I don't mean just now, when we licked the Pyramids and so on. No, I mean hundreds of years ago, what happened when the Pyramids arrived, and what has been happening since. Did you ever hear of Indians, Germyn?"

Germyn frowned minutely and shrugged.

"They were, oh, hundreds *and* hundreds of years ago. They were a different color and not very civilized-of course, nobody was then. But the Indians were nomads, herdsmen, hunters-like that. And the white people came from Europe and wanted this country for themselves. So they took it. And do you know something? I don't think the Indians ever knew what hit them."

"*They* didn't know about land grants and claiming territory for the crown and church missions and expanding populations. They didn't have those things. It's true that they learned pretty well, by and by-at least they learned things like guns and horses and firewater; they didn't have those things, either, but they could see some sense to them, you know. But I really don't think the Indians ever knew exactly what the Europeans were up to, until it was too late to matter.

"And it was the same with us and the Pyramids, only more so. What the devil *did* they want? I mean, yes, we found out what they did with the Translated people. But what were they *up* to? What did they *think*? *Did* they think? You know, I've got a kind of a crazy idea-maybe it's not crazy, maybe it's the truth. Anyway, I've been thinking. Suppose even the *Pyramids* weren't the Pyramids? We never talked to one of them. We never gave it a Rorschach or tested its knee jerks. We licked them, but we don't know anything about them. We don't even know if they were the guys that started the whole bloody thing, or if they were just sort of super-sized Components themselves. Do we?

"And meanwhile, here's the human race, up against something that it not only can't understand, same as the Indians couldn't the whites, but that it can't begin to make a *guess* about. At least the Indians had a clue now and then, you know —I mean they'd see the sailors off the great white devil ship making a beeline for the Indian women and so on, and they'd begin to understand there was *something* in common. But we didn't have that much.

"So what did we do? Why, we did like the reservation Indians. We turned inward. We got loaded on firewater-Meditation-and we closed our minds to the possibility of ever expanding again. And there we were, all tied up in our own knots. Most of the race rebelled against action, because it had proven useless-Citizens. A few of the race rebelled against *that*, because it was not only useless but *deliberately* useless-Wolves. But they're the same kind of people. You've seen that for yourself, right? And —"

Tropile stopped, suddenly aware that Citizen Germyn was looking tepidly pained.

"What's the matter?" Tropile demanded harshly.

Citizen Germyn gave him the faint deprecatory Quirked Smile. "I know you thought you were a Wolf, but —I told you I've been thinking a lot, and that's what I was thinking about. *Truly*, Citizen, you do yourself no good by pretending that you really thought you were Wolf. Clearly you were not; the rest of us might have been fooled, but certainly you couldn't fool yourself.

"Now here's what I think you ought to do. When I found you were coming, I asked several rather well-known Citizens to come here later this evening. There won't be any embarrassment. I only want you to talk to them and set the record straight, so that this terrible blemish will no longer be held against you. Times change and perhaps a certain latitude is advisable now, but certainly you don't want —"

Tropile also left Citizen Germyn sooner than he had expected to.

* * * * *

There remained Alla Narova, but, queerly, she was not to be found.

Instantly it became clear to Tropile that it was she above all whom he needed to talk to. He remembered the shared beauty of their plunging drive through the neurone-guides of the Pyramids, the linked and inextricable flow of their thoughts and of their most hidden feelings.

She could not be very far, he thought numbly, cursing the blindness of his human eyes, the narrowness of his human senses. Time was when two worlds could not have hidden her from him; but that time was gone. He walked from place to place with the angry resentful tread of one used to riding-no, to flying, or faster than flying. He asked after her. He searched.

And at last he found-not her. A note. At one of the stations where the re-awakened Components were funneled back into human affairs, there was a letter waiting for him:

> *I'm sure you will look for me. Please don't. You thought that there were no secrets between us, but there was one.*
>
> *When I was Translated, I was sixty-one years old. Two years before that, I was caught in a collapsing building; my legs are useless, and I had grown quite fat. I do not want you to see me fat and old.*
>
> *Alla Narova.*

And that was that, and at last Glenn Tropile turned to the last person of all those on his list who had known him well. Her name was Gala Tropile.

* * * * *

She had got thinner, he observed. They sat together quietly and there was considerable awkwardness, but then he noticed that she was weeping. Comforting her ended the awkwardness and he found that he was talking:

"It was like being a god, Gala! I swear, there's no feeling like it. I mean it's like-well, maybe if you'd just had a baby, and invented fire, and moved a mountain, and transmuted lead into gold-maybe if you'd done all of those things, then you might have some idea. But I was everywhere at once, Gala, and I could do anything! I fought a whole world of Pyramids, do you realize that? Me! And now I come back to —"

He stopped her in time; it seemed she was about to weep again.

He went on: "No, Gala, don't misunderstand, I don't hold anything against you. You were right to leave me in the field. What did I have to offer you? Or myself, for that matter? And I don't know that I have anything now, but —"

He slammed his fist against the table. "They talk about putting the Earth back in its orbit! Why? And how? My God, Gala, we don't know *where* we are. Maybe we could tinker up the gadgets the Pyramids used and turn our course backward-but do you know what Old Sol looks like? I don't. I never saw it.

"And neither did you or anyone else alive.

"It was like being a god —

"And they talk about going back to things as they were —

"I'm sick of that kind of thinking! Wolves or Citizens, they're dead on their feet and don't know it. I suppose they'll snap out of it in time, but I can't wait. I won't live that long.

"Unless —"

He paused and looked at her, confused.

Gala Tropile met her husband's eyes.

"Unless what, Glenn?"

He shrugged and turned away.

"Unless you go back, you mean." He stared at her; she nodded. "You want to go back," she said, without stress. "You don't want to stay here with me, do you? You want to go back into that tub of soup again and float like a baby. You don't want to *have* babies-you want to *be* one."

"Gala, you don't understand. We can own the Universe. I mean mankind can. And I can do it. Why not? There's nothing for me —"

"That's right, Glenn. There's nothing for you here. Not any more."

He opened his mouth to speak, looked at her, spread his hands helplessly. He didn't look back as he walked out the door, but he knew that his back was turned not only on the woman who happened to be his wife, but on mankind and all of the flesh.

* * * * *

It was night outside, and warm. Tropile stood in the old street surrounded by the low, battered houses-and he could make them new and grand! He looked up at the stars that swung in constellations too new and changeable to have names. *There* was the Universe.

Words were no good; there was no explaining things in words. Naturally he couldn't make Gala or anyone else understand, for flesh couldn't grasp the realities of mind and spirit that were liberated from flesh. Babies! A home! And the whole grubby animal business of eating and drinking and sleeping! How could anyone ask to stay in the mire when the stars challenged overhead?

He walked slowly down the street, alone in the night, an apprentice godling renouncing mortality. There was nothing here for him, so why this sense of loss?

Duty said (or was it Pride?): "Someone must give up the flesh to control Earth's orbit and weather-why not you?"

Flesh said (or was it his soul-whatever that was?): "But you will be *alone*."

He stopped, and for a moment he was poised between destiny and the dust....

Until he became aware of footsteps behind him, running, and Gala's voice: "Wait! Wait, Glenn! I want to go with you!"

And he turned and waited, but only until she caught up, and then he went on.

But not-forever and always again-not alone.